THE LITTLE TRAGEDY

Jeff Haws

The Little Tragedy

Copyright © 2018 Jeff Haws

All rights reserved. This book or any portion thereof may not be reproduced or used in any manner whatsoever without the express written permission of the publisher, except for the use of brief quotations in a book review. This is a work of fiction. Names, characters, places, and incidents either are the products of the author's imagination or are used fictitiously. Any resemblance to actual persons, living or dead, businesses, companies, events, or locales is entirely coincidental.

Printed in the United States of America

First Printing, 2018

ISBN: 978-1-945768-06-4

Publisher: Shifty Squid, LLC

P.O. Box 170392

Atlanta, GA 30317

Visit the author's website and blog at www.jeffhaws.com

1

"Wake up! Wake up, damn it!" Laura screamed, standing over her oldest son's bed.

She fell to her knees and turned his face toward hers.

"Kevin...Look at me! Open your eyes!" she slapped him across the cheek, her body beginning to shake. Her younger son, Ryan, stood just outside the room in the hall, clutching a stuffed rabbit he got for Christmas. "It's not time. No! It can't be. It *fucking* can't be!"

Stephen noticed Ryan looking on and walked over to him, then knelt to meet him eye to eye.

"Hey, kiddo, just go to your room. Mommy and daddy will take care of this, okay?"

"Is...Is Kevin gonna be all right?"

Stephen swallowed hard, his throat seeming to contract to the width of a straw, saliva forced down like a bundle of razor wire. Tears threatened to come, but he tried to hold them back.

"Just go to your room. Okay?" Behind him, he heard Laura pounding the bed, the springs creaking beneath her fists. They both turned to look for a second, then Stephen turned back to Ryan. "Please. We'll come talk to you in a few minutes."

Ryan reached out and hugged Stephen, who pulled him in tight and kissed his cheek. The tears he had held back streamed down, leaving wet spots on the back of Ryan's Spider-Man pajamas.

"I don't want him to go," Ryan begged quietly.

Stephen squeezed his son a little tighter and sniffed loudly, trying to maintain some control of himself.

"Me either, son. Me either."

He put down Ryan, who shuffled down the hall to his bedroom. As he went through the door, he peeked back at Stephen, who was still crouched in the same spot. Stephen forced a smile and waved, then motioned for Ryan to keep going inside. When he did, Stephen stood and closed the door. He looked back at Laura, her head buried in the crook of her arm.

He walked over and knelt beside her.

"I'm sorry, honey. I wish there was something we could do."

She raised her head and looked at him, her eyes swollen with spindles of red dancing through them.

"We have to wake him up, Stephen. We…we *have* to. This isn't over. It's *not*!"

Stephen sighed and closed his eyes. He reached out to wrap his arms around her, but she pushed him away.

"God damn it, no! No! It's *too fucking soon*, Stephen! This wasn't supposed to happen. Not now. Not to us. Not to *him*! I'm not…I'm not…*ready*."

Stephen was verging on tears again. He opened his mouth, but nothing came out. He wanted to comfort her, to tell her everything would be fine. That *they'd* be fine. But would they? He didn't know. They wouldn't be the first couple that couldn't deal with this.

What came next was the hardest part—one son in an endless coma, and another a ticking time bomb for that same fate. They'd known this day was coming. But nothing can prepare you for the moment your ten-year-old son won't wake up, and you have every reason to think he never will.

Laura turned to Kevin and pressed her face close to his, stroking his hair gently. She kissed him on the forehead and then laid her head on the pillow beside him, her chin against his hairline. Stephen moved closer to her and leaned against the bed, his hand resting on the small of her back.

After several minutes, she looked up at Stephen.

"I'm not ready."

She fell into his arms, and they both cried. He thought they might never stand again.

2

"I'm done for the day, Mister Fraser," said Brent Harris, Kevin's nurse who came by once a week to give a full check of Kevin's vitals and be sure Laura and Stephen were doing everything well to care for him while he was in a coma. "Everything looks normal. I'll see you guys next week."

"Thanks, Brent," said Stephen. He had moved his physical therapy practice into their house's enclosed garage after Kevin went into a coma, so he could be at home with him full time. "Appreciate the help. Have a good one."

The previous year had been difficult. When Kevin wouldn't wake up, it wasn't a shock, but no matter how inevitable it had become, it was never easy. Since 1999, every child in the world had fallen into a coma on the night of their tenth birthday. That's twenty years of parents weeping at the bedsides of their children. Twenty years of kids who never even made it to puberty.

There was no scientific consensus on why this was happening, even as money from around the world poured into research. One popular theory was that it was a form of the Swedish Uppgivenhetssyndrom—Resignation Syndrome—a phenomenon where children fall into a catatonic state when they appear to have no hope for the future. For many years, it only happened to the children of refugee families in Sweden, when told they were being deported back to the country they'd fled. It was thought by many that their young minds couldn't process their dismal fate, and simply stopped responding to the world around them, and even their own bodies. Despite having no evident physical problems, they seemed to have lost the will to live.

Then, seemingly overnight, the phenomenon was everywhere. One child after another, in communities from Switzerland to Canada, Argentina to Thailand, just stopped waking up. No pain. No physical trauma. Just a ten-year-old Snow White, in a persistent sleep.

The world responded first with disbelief, then with terror for parents and their children who were also approaching their tenth birthday. That terror never ended, and neither did the parents' hopes that theirs would be the miracle child, the one who would break this curse. The one who would give hope to the world that the human race was going to beat this.

But they never were.

Twenty years in, society had changed immensely. There were no functioning humans between ten and thirty years old. Few public schools still stood, though private schools for young children could still be found in most affluent communities. Marriage was becoming more rare every year, as many adults in their thirties and forties didn't see much point in getting married if they weren't going to have children. The birth rate had plummeted, with fewer marriages and fewer people wanting to take on the burden of giving birth to, raising, and loving a child only to see that child turn to stone in a mere decade.

For couples who did take the plunge into having kids, it was hard to ignore the dark cloud looming over them as the child got older. Many justified it by saying science might find a cure any day now, or that ten years of life was better than none. But nothing could prepare them for that moment when their child just lay still, with little else but a pulse. And then there was the aftermath—not just potentially reassuring the siblings and gathering their own emotions, but the gut-wrenching practical decisions: Keep him alive, or give him up? If they kept him alive, could they afford to care for him?

The hospitals quickly ran out of space, funding, and

manpower to accommodate all these comatose children, so there was little option but to care for them at home. For the wealthy, that simply meant designating a room in their house, purchasing the necessary equipment—hospital bed, monitor screen, pressure relief mattresses, ventriculostomy tubes, ventilator, lots of catheters—and hiring a full-time nurse to look after the child for as long as was needed. For the vast majority of people, though, this was far too expensive.

There were small medical facilities that would take in the children of less fortunate families and care for them as best as they could, but their resources and space were limited. A year after each child's tenth birthday, euthanasia was the only viable option in these facilities, to free up a bed for a child who had suffered less atrophy, and had more time to hang on in the hopes that something might change.

For Stephen and Laura, the decision to have kids had been a hard one, just like with all parents. They had spent so many late nights lying in bed, discussing the pros and cons, weighing whether or not it was the right decision, and even if it should be their decision to make. Ultimately, they'd vowed to have one kid, and give him the best ten years they could. Holding Kevin in her arms for the first time, Laura felt the most intense combination of love and sadness. Lying in a hospital bed with her hair matted to her forehead, clutching her first-born son against her breast, she knew she'd do anything for him—but she also knew there was nothing she could do. They'd invested everything in a little tragedy, and it would come in due time.

Just six months later, Laura was pregnant again; she screamed and smashed a vase against the wall when she found out. "Stupid!" she'd yelled, at herself as much as at Stephen, knowing one night of drunken flirting and her sliding the condom off him and tossing it across the room meant they were bringing a second child into this hopeless world. She was adamant for the first few days that she was going to get an abortion, and Stephen said he'd support whatever she decided. But one day turned into two, and she hadn't scheduled the appointment. Soon enough, it'd been a week, then a month.

"I just couldn't bring myself to do it," she said to him. "I know it's not my head talking, but I'm telling my head to shut up for once. I'm having this kid. Can we do this?"

"We can, baby. We'll make it work," Stephen said. "We're gonna spoil the hell out of both of 'em."

All the spoiling in the world didn't do anything to stop Kevin from meeting the fate of all the world's children. Now he lay frozen, right where his mom had tucked him in fourteen months earlier, a lightly beeping machine next to his bed the only obvious sign his heart was still beating. And, as the spring of 2019 approached, there was no avoiding the truth that rested heavy on them each day—Ryan was next.

3

Sitting on his bed, Ryan wrapped his arms around his legs and pulled his knees to his chest, jammed underneath his chin. His teeth clenched together, he rocked slowly, Spider-Man pajamas stretching against his shoulders. It wasn't yet five in the morning, but he couldn't sleep. It was exactly one week before his tenth birthday. If he ever needed a reminder of what was coming for him, he needed only take a few steps to the closed door down the hall. His parents didn't like him visiting Kevin by himself, but he knew if he pressed his ear hard enough to the closed door, he could hear the faint beeps that assured him his brother was at least still alive. And that was hope. Not just for Kevin, but for Ryan as well. Kevin's battle was Ryan's battle. Kevin's hope was Ryan's hope.

He didn't feel anything, though. Just seven days away, he didn't have any sense of anything changing. No feeling that his brain was about to turn on him, to send him into a state of sleep from which he would never stir. Was he old enough to even notice subtle changes that might be gradually leading him to that point? Or was it just as sudden as death—alive and thinking about what to have for lunch one moment, lights out the next?

It was hard for Ryan not to think about. The worries crept into his mind in quiet moments, when the lights were out and no one was around. Even when he couldn't hear the beeping down the hall, he lived with the knowledge it was there. His parents could keep the door closed all they wanted, but they were fooling themselves if they thought they were truly hiding anything. He saw them slip in quickly to check on Kevin's vitals, maybe change a catheter or a set of sheets.

Kevin was lifeless in his bed, but he came to Ryan in his dreams. Sometimes, he was his old self, cracking jokes and teasing girls, his mop of dark brown hair an unkempt mess. Other times, though, Ryan saw a different Kevin, one who was decaying and beckoning him to death, a Reaper who reflected the unavoidable fate that awaited him, just a few days away. That version of Kevin seemed possessed, with eyes that glowed orange and a stilted walk that belied the real Kevin's athleticism. He urged Ryan to follow him, to walk into the darkness.

"It's a world of kids our age," Kevin would say, a lopsided smile curling across his pockmarked lips. "There are no parents. No one to tell you what to do. No one gets older. It's heaven. Come play with us, Ryan."

And there was a certain temptation to it. Ryan wondered if his brother could be right. Were all the ten-year-olds abandoning this world and finding their own, one free of the political divisions, wars, and strife of the world they were born into? Could they be living in paradise?

There was no way to know. But, to Ryan's not-quite-ten-year-old mind, it seemed as likely as any of the other theories he'd heard adults spout on the internet. His parents tried to shield him from people talking about it when some doctor or scientist would give the latest update on the search for a cure, or at least a cause. Again, though, like trying to keep kids from hearing any curse words, there was no way to fully protect them from learning about The Sleep, and knowing that, even after twenty years, no one really had answers. It was a constant reminder that adults didn't know everything, that the world was often an unfair, uncaring place, and parents were ultimately powerless to even keep you awake for more than ten years.

What if there *were* another world, though? What if The Sleep wasn't a death, but an exit? What if the world Kevin was calling

Ryan to in his dreams wasn't an end, but a beginning? Should he be terrified of his turning ten, or celebrating it?

No one seemed to be coming back to tell him. Once a kid crossed into The Sleep, not a single one had returned to provide any answers. There was no why, only guesses. You could stare at sleeping children for days and learn nothing, pull their eyelids apart and try to look into their souls. Like billions of parents around the world, Ryan's held out hope that if they kept his brother alive one more day, maybe that'd be the day something changed. Maybe a cure would finally be found. Maybe he'd wake up. Maybe there'd be an end to all of this. One more day. That was all it might take.

Imagine being the parents who let their child die, and then found out the next day that scientists were close to a cure. If the cure ever came, such parents would exist. There'd likely be hundreds of them. Thousands, even. Dreading that regret was what kept many of them going, pumping all their time, money, and love into keeping a vegetable alive while their family died around them.

Ryan's parents said many of the right things, but there was no way around him feeling like a burden in their lives since The Sleep took Kevin. It took so much of them to care for his brother that there was little energy left to put into Ryan, or each other. They tried, and in some ways he even felt *more* visible to them, but he also required more attention than they had to give. Even if some miracle brought Kevin back to them, Ryan often wondered what would be left. Would it just be a husk of the family they once knew? Could they learn to be happy again? How to spend time with each other without this black cloud hanging over them?

These were thoughts no nine-year-old should endure, but Ryan's brain circled them, doubling back and starting over again as he rocked in his bed. No sleep was coming tonight. But even if it did, Kevin would be in his dreams waiting for him. There was no

escape.
One week. He shivered.

4

This was her escape. From everything. From the eleven-year-old son who had been lying in a coma in his bed for more than a year. From the nine-year-old son fast approaching the same fate. From the stress of holding her family together amid it all, of trying to maintain a marriage, a household, a business, and her own sanity.

This was where Laura could always come to let go of it all—her brewery. In these final days before The Sleep would come for Ryan, she was trying to spend as much time as she could at home, but she still found she needed whatever respites she could find at her second home.

She opened Palmyra Brewing in 2010, leasing a small space in an otherwise empty strip mall in Knoxville's Fourth and Gill neighborhood, two years after the last of her students moved on from her high school chemistry class. It was an idea that'd been in the back of her mind for some time, as she saw the craft beer industry taking off. Holding a Masters in Chemistry from the University of Tennessee, the science part of brewing appealed to her. She also appreciated the community-focused mindset of so many breweries, approaching their business from a hyperlocal point of view, concentrating not on serving the people of their country or their region or their state, but zeroing in on their city, their town, their neighborhood.

Laura grew up in Knoxville, and she loved it there. Her brewery reflected that, named Palmyra after a city that 18th-century politician William Blount dreamed of building adjacent to Knoxville. It was supposed to be his grand vision for East

Tennessee. It never came to fruition, but Laura enjoyed telling the story to people who sat at the bar and asked about the name. She adorned the walls of the brewery with old pictures of downtown Knoxville, showing long-lost landmarks like the Staub Opera House, Farragut Hotel, and the old Market House on Market Square. Her beers got names significant to Knoxville history. The Brownlow Brown Ale was named after Parson Brownlow, who started an early newspaper in the city and later became Governor of the state. The Crozier Kolsch was a tribute to Lizzie Crozier French, one of the most prominent leaders of Tennessee's women's rights and suffragist movement of the early 1900s. And there was the Old Gray Ghost Porter, a nod to the Old Gray Cemetery—which sat just blocks from the brewery—where the majority of Knoxville's most prominent citizens had been buried since it was founded in 1850.

Walking through the doors of this place—*her* place—around seven-thirty most every morning felt like a release. It'd be a few hours before the lunchtime crowd started arriving, and she could get some work done. There was always cleaning to do—so very much cleaning of tanks and kegs. It was one of the tedious and less glamorous parts of her job that rarely occurred to patrons as they sipped on the latest release. She'd spend some time with her brewmaster checking the gravities and temperatures of specific beers, or deciding what needed to be racked so it'd be ready to condition and carbonate in order to go on tap. And, as owner, she also had to keep an eye on the financials, checking over the previous day's and week's take to gauge the health of the business.

Laura's days were long, but there was nothing she'd rather be doing with her life. Knoxville had fallen on difficult times, with the university closing in 2011, taking with it the twenty-five thousand beer-swilling twenty-somethings who used to prowl the downtown area. Several breweries had opened and closed since she started Palmyra, but the ones that were standing up against the test—among them, Knox Partners nearby and Angry Squid Brewing on the south side across the river—had formed a camaraderie that belied any competition they had for the ever-shrinking drinking-age population.

Knoxville had always relied on the university for a continuous influx of young, educated people, along with thousands of jobs, so it was a big blow to all the local businesses when the university shut down. When there are no conscious people between ten and thirty years old, there's no way for a massive university to keep its doors open. By 2019, the city's population had dropped from 176,000 in 2000 to 110,000.

But one thing Laura knew was always going to be needed—a place to drink. And not just any place, but someplace that would welcome all, and provide people that same escape she felt when she walked through the doors. People needed that, and she was going to give it to them.

When Laura opened the doors to Palmyra at noon, employees were gathered behind the bar and in the back near the brite tanks to help get the day going. She walked back behind the bar herself to double-check the spelling on all of the beer names on the chalkboard she hung on the bar's back wall.

A few minutes later, as she scrubbed out an S with the back of her hand so she could insert a missing T for one of the beer names, a familiar face strolled through the door and settled into a stool behind her.

"Just can't let a typo go, can you?" he said as he sat down.

She stopped and spun her head around. "It's not a typo if you write it in chalk, doc."

"What did they call those before typewriters?"

"Fuck-ups, I'm pretty sure." She laid the chalk down, and it rolled toward him. He caught it as it fell off the front of the bar. He held the piece of chalk up and smiled.

"Nice catch, man," she said. "You just saved me at least ten cents."

"Enough for a free beer?"

She set an elbow on the bar and leaned toward him. "You'll need to catch a whole box of chalk for that."

"Guess I need you to get a little clumsier, then."

Laura laughed. "Not possible. What'll it be, doctor?"

"Let's go with a full pour of Crozier," he said. "And you know it's Nathan to you, Laura."

Nathan Marshall was a child psychologist, a job that had come into high demand over the previous couple of decades, seeing an influx of applicants to the better university programs in the final years before schools across the country were forced to close their doors. Even with the swelling of doctorates in the field, it was difficult to meet the demand as children saw siblings fall into a coma, and crept closer to the ten-year-old mark themselves, gaining more awareness of their own future fate. Most child psychologists felt it was important to keep kids in therapy for most of their ten years in order to help them cope with that looming reality.

Child psychologists were also essential for understanding more about why The Sleep was happening, interviewing children at different stages throughout their first ten years to try to identify patterns of thought that might help scientists learn what was causing all children to fall into irreversible comas.

Similar to many of his colleagues, Nathan had a group of twelve children he had been talking to monthly since they were four years old, two of them being Ryan and Kevin Fraser. He hadn't found any real answers yet for Laura and Stephen, but he had become a friend of the family, often staying for dinner or taking Ryan to the park when his parents needed a break.

One night, six months earlier, Laura asked Nathan if he

wanted to stay for a drink while she put Ryan to bed. She got out a bottle of whiskey and set it on the kitchen island, then clinked two glasses beside it. Stephen had gone to New Orleans for a physical therapists' conference, and Laura didn't want to drink alone.

"Ah, that's the bottle I gave to you for your birthday," Nathan said. "Haven't opened it yet?"

"I've been tempted, but I wanted to save it for the right occasion."

"*This* is the right occasion?"

"Well, Stephen's not much of a whiskey drinker. And sometimes, the right occasion never comes," she said. "So, fuck it. I'm making it happen now. You got a problem with that?"

"No. I'm honored. Let's do it. You're gonna love this."

"Pour me *that* much," she said to Nathan, her index finger and thumb an inch apart. "I'll be back in five."

He picked up the bottle, and she turned around to leave the kitchen. Then she stopped and spun on her heel.

"Make it *this* much," she opened her fingers another inch and raised an eyebrow. "And it'll be less than five."

He laughed and began pouring as she went upstairs.

Three minutes later, he was sipping the whiskey when she came back into the kitchen, half-jogging.

"Told ya," she said.

"You're a wonder. How'd you get him to sleep so fast?"

"Tranquilizer dart in the ass."

He nodded. "Effective."

"Glad you approve, doc."

She picked up her glass and raised it to her lips, letting the warmth coat her tongue and throat.

"Oh, shit, that's good," she said. "Why didn't you tell me this stuff was amazing?"

"Didn't want to ruin the surprise."

"Nice job, then."

He downed another sip. "It really is terrific."

"Orgasmic."

"Let's not go crazy now."

"True. This is *way* better than that."

He was about to take another sip but paused, laughing. "Been awhile, huh?"

She rolled her eyes. "*Jesus.* You have *no* idea."

"Rough times in the Fraser household?" he finished his first glass and poured another few fingers.

"This is, like, attorney-client privilege, right?"

"I'm a doctor, not an attorney."

She took another swig.

"You know what I mean. HIPPA or some shit."

He laughed. "Sure, Laura. Whatever you tell me doesn't leave this room."

"There ya go," she said, grabbing the bottle and splashing more whiskey into the glass. She took a drink. "So, not to sound morbid or anything, but there's nothing that's less of an aphrodisiac than a comatose ten-year-old in the next room."

"Damn, Laura."

She put her index finger up to his lips. "HIPPA, remember?"

He paused until she pulled her hand back, then shook his head. "Yeah, I know. But that's your *son*."

"I know exactly who it is, *Nate*. Nobody loves that kid more than I do, or wants him to wake back up and be his crazy self again. He was so full of *life*. Ya know? Even *knowing* what was going to happen to him, it was impossible to fully believe it. You know what I mean?"

He nodded and drank.

"My brain knew The Sleep was going to get him, just like it did every other kid, but a part of me thought maybe he was different. Maybe we could give him enough love, or enough…I don't know…*something* to keep him with us. To let him stay awake, at least for a while longer. I mean, how could a kid that seemingly happy and funny and silly just shut down out of nowhere? My heart breaks every second he doesn't wake up."

Nathan looked down at the streaked-marble surface in front of them. She threw back the rest of her whiskey and slammed the glass down.

"But none of that changes the fact that I need a good fuck from time to time."

A smile slowly lit up her face as she pulled herself up on the island and crawled across it toward him. His eyes grew large, and he was frozen in place. She reached out and put her hands on both sides of his face, pulling him closer and pressing her lips to his. His lips didn't move, as hers opened slightly, trying to tempt him further.

She swung her legs around and straddled him, kicking her shoes to the floor as they dangled to either side of him. Her tongue penetrated his lips, dancing against his teeth, coaxing him to open his mouth and turn his head. Nathan put his hand behind her neck and pulled her closer, yanking at her hair just a bit. She felt his tongue against hers, twisting and circling playfully.

Then suddenly, Laura put her hands on his chest and pushed back, bolting upright.

"Oh, shit. I'm…sorry," she said, running her hand through her hair and looking at the ceiling. "That was—God, I shouldn't have done that."

He rubbed his mouth, working his jaw open and shut.

"No, it's okay. It was just the whiskey talking. I understand."

"It's *not* okay." She pulled her legs back up and jumped off the island on the opposite side from Nathan. "The alcohol's no excuse. I shouldn't have done it, but I *did* do it. Okay? That was me. But it's not gonna happen again. It was a momentary lapse of judgment, that's all. No excuses, but it's over. Done and done."

Nathan nodded. "Agreed. And I should probably be going."

"That's a good idea. You okay to drive?"

He smiled. "I'm pretty sure you sobered me up."

She walked him to the door and opened it, letting him onto the porch. He turned to face her.

"Sorry again for what happened," she said. "I don't know what that was about."

"It's forgotten." He shook his head.

"HIPPA?"

He chuckled. "HIPPA."

Nathan sipped on the Crozier Kolsch that Laura had poured him as she took an order from another customer three stools down from him, the bar beginning to fill up with the lunchtime crowd. He was nearing the end of his glass.

"Want another, doc?" she said, as she pulled the tap handle for the Brownlow Brown.

"I think I'm good. Got some errands to knock out this afternoon."

"Look at you, getting stuff done. Ready to settle up, then?"

"Keep the change," he said, slapping down a ten-dollar bill.

She turned around and saw him laying the money on the bar.

"That's too—" She was interrupted by her bartender Erin tapping her on the shoulder. She was holding Laura's phone.

"When Stephen called your phone three times in five minutes, I figured somebody should pick up."

A rock filled her stomach, and the air sucked out of her lungs. She grabbed the phone out of Erin's hand.

"What happened?"

"It's about Ryan. Can't talk about it on the phone. Can you come home right now?"

"Headed to the car."

She hung up and looked at Nathan. "It's Ryan. You're gonna

want to come with me."

5

Flipping a grilled cheese sandwich over in a pan, Stephen glanced back at Ryan sitting at the kitchen island playing on his phone. Ryan may have looked like his mom, but he could bury his head in a book or a game just like his dad. Stephen felt like they understood each other in a way that Laura couldn't quite get, but Kevin had been her kid all the way, the first one to crack a joke in front of his friends, and the first kid everybody wanted on their team when they played baseball. It was almost like they'd both had little versions of themselves around to entertain them.

Of course, that didn't last—not any more than it had for any other families for the previous couple of decades, anyway. Stephen thought often about what it must have been like prior to The Sleep to watch your child die a slow death at the hands of cancer or leukemia or some other awful disease. Was that worse? Or better? Losing a child was always tragic, but was there a certain level of preparedness you'd gain from watching your child slowly wither away, changing into a different person day by day, week by week, month by month until he was, perhaps, someone you didn't really recognize, someone you could let go?

The challenge of The Sleep was the sheer abruptness of it. They knew it was coming—intellectually, at least. But there was no gradual transition from life to death. There was just a light switch flipping off. One day, Kevin was Ryan's big brother, a goofy kid cracking jokes and pulling Ryan's shirt up over his head. The next, he was nothing more than a heart beating inside a body, a burden they carried as long as they could afford to do so.

Stephen couldn't help but feel sad for the future. Not only was

Ryan just a week from his tenth birthday, but his pending coma was going to stretch Stephen and Laura's resources to their limits. Could they realistically care for *two* comatose boys alive in twenty-four-seven care? That was a psychological question as much as it was a financial one. Even if they could figure out the money, could they handle this? Kevin was taking enough of a toll on their family and their marriage, but at least they still had Ryan to enjoy, and pour themselves into. Once he was gone, the pall that was going to settle over the house might suffocate them both. They wouldn't be the first couple to see their marriage quickly dissolve in these situations, nor would they be the first to get into a yelling match in court over the decision of whether their children should live or die. In most circumstances, the government would grant a euthanasia request from a comatose child's parents, given the limited resources available to care for them. But making that request was a heart-wrenching decision. And they also wouldn't be the first parents to choose their own death over having to make it.

Stephen had no idea what was going to happen in the coming week-plus, but that didn't mean he couldn't enjoy making lunch for his son in the meantime.

"Want extra butter on your bread, big guy?" he said cheerfully.

"Yes!" Ryan looked up from the phone and clapped his hands together. "Super buttery!"

Stephen turned from the stove and looked at Ryan. "Is that how you ask for something?"

"No." He gave an exaggerated frown. "Please, can I have lots and lots of butter, daddy?"

"Now you're talkin'."

After lunch, Ryan had gone back upstairs while Stephen did the dishes and got ready for his afternoon therapy patient. He was scrubbing charred cheese off the pan when he heard a loud thump on the floor of Ryan's room. He stopped scrubbing and stood still for a moment, his eyes turned toward the ceiling.

He listened for several seconds, but only heard the light clicking of the clock on the wall. His patient was scheduled to be there in fifteen minutes. That meant he couldn't stall much longer; he needed to make sure the room was ready.

It was probably nothing. He may be messing around with toys, or he kicked the floor, or he dropped something. He'd be crying if he'd hurt himself, and you'd hear it. Don't let yourself get paranoid about your kid up in his own room. He's fine.

He knew that was almost certainly right, but he couldn't shake the nagging feeling that something could be wrong. Why, though? Ryan seemed happy earlier in the morning. How could he not be happy after eating his favorite sandwich?

Stephen waited another couple of beats longer, then started scrubbing again.

As soon as he did, there was another noise. This time, it wasn't on the floor. He couldn't pinpoint what it was. It wasn't especially loud, but it wasn't a sound he was used to hearing.

Could it be a window opening? But it's still winter…why would he be—

Stephen dropped the plate and sprinted for the stairs, screaming Ryan's name as he climbed. There was no response. When he got to the upstairs hallway, he saw Ryan's door was closed. His door was never closed. They wouldn't allow it.

"Ryan! Ryan! Open this door, *now!*" Stephen grabbed the doorknob with one hand and pounded hard on the door with the other. When he tried to push it open, it wouldn't budge. He rattled it on his hinges. These doors didn't have locks on them. Why wouldn't it open? "I'm serious, Ryan! Open…this…door!"

Stephen stepped back and looked at the door. It wasn't particularly thick or strong. It was stamped hardboard, even though it was formed to look like it was natural wood grain. He wasn't sure what it was filled with, but he was hoping the answer was "not much."

He lifted his leg and drove all his weight forward into the door. His foot went through the front, and his shoe got caught up in the jagged hardboard on the other side. He scraped his calf while yanking his leg back out. Blood poured down his leg onto his sock as he backed up and braced himself in a crouch, one foot well behind the other, and took off, launching himself into the door again.

He felt it bend, then break under his weight, as little shards of wood poked into his sides and cut his shirt. Lying on the collapsed door, Stephen rolled over and banged his shin into an overturned chair lying next to him, sending a wave of pain up his leg. Pushing the pain down, he looked up, scrambling to find Ryan. His bed was empty, and the room was quiet. As Stephen stumbled to his feet, his leg still stinging, he felt a chilly breeze and saw the curtains swaying in the corner of the room. Then he saw Ryan, and his heart nearly stopped.

6

Ryan walked into his room and flopped down on his bed, his belly full. He sat up cross-legged and stuck a pillow in his lap to prop his arms up as he held his phone in front of him. Since The Sleep took Kevin, Ryan had become gradually more withdrawn, with less to prove to everyone around him. He'd become obsessed with various tower defense games, where the computer would send gradually larger and fiercer sets of hordes at him, and he'd have to allocate his resources efficiently to build up his defenses in order to hold them off. What would protect him from the coming onslaught? Should he spend his currency on bigger, stronger walls, or more ammo to take out the intruders? There was no stopping the invasion. It would come for him turn after turn after turn. The only question was how long he could hold it off.

There were numerous versions of this game, and he'd downloaded many of them. He'd fire up one and play for hours, until he'd figured out the best combination of defense and offense to beat even the biggest, most ruthless horde of bad guys. It also didn't hurt that he'd found his dad's credit card number, and would use it to buy extra coins every now and then. What were they going to do? Ground him for the last few days before The Sleep took him? He had a hunch he'd be safe.

This was how Ryan spent a lot of his time since The Sleep took Kevin. There was no school. His parents would coax him out of his room for lessons on reading or math from time to time, but they weren't great about it. Sometimes, they'd send him outside with Doctor Nathan for a couple hours, but it was rarely Ryan's idea.

Kevin had always wanted to go outside and play, or he'd run off with his friends. Sometimes, Ryan tried to join them, and his parents would encourage it, but it usually ended with him sitting in the dirt, watching Kevin hit home runs, make a diving catch, or fire up three-pointers from the corner. By comparison, Ryan was clumsy, both physically and socially, and being more than a year younger—and almost a foot shorter—didn't help.

So, Ryan often gravitated to his room to play video games or practice reading, neither of which made him feel like a bumbling little twerp. He had idolized his brother, and wanted to be like him, but he knew he wasn't. In a way, The Sleep taking Kevin had been good for Ryan, taking away that older brother who seemed like he was better at everything, to compare himself to. It allowed him to be a bit more comfortable in his own skin. When Kevin would be at the park striking some kid out, Ryan would often sulk, torn between walking down there to be with his brother only to embarrass himself, or sitting in his room feeling like a loser without any friends.

With Kevin lying motionless in bed, though, there was less anxiety, fewer reasons for Ryan to feel bad about just doing whatever felt right to him. And, most of the time, he found that what felt right was immersing himself in video games that gave him a level playing field. It didn't matter if the guy he was facing up against was six feet tall and three hundred pounds, or if the program threw a thousand massive thugs at his tower. He might be less than four-and-a-half feet tall and not even seventy pounds. But if he could outthink them, out-maneuver them, he could come away the winner. And nobody would know he couldn't hit a ball, or make a basket.

As Ryan used some of his coins to build a turret into one of his castle's towers, he heard a noise and looked up. It was a voice, but nobody was there. Still holding the phone in his lap, the voice called again. It was coming from the other side of the window in the corner of the room, and he quickly recognized it.

"Kevin?" he said. "Is that you?"

He couldn't make out the words, but he was sure it was Kevin's voice. He couldn't see anyone, though. He crawled off the bed, onto the floor, stumbling and banging his knee. He winced, then climbed to his feet, rubbing his leg.

"Close the door, Ryan," he heard the voice say. "We should chat."

Ryan stopped and stood straight up. He understood the words. It was definitely his brother, though it didn't sound exactly the same as he remembered. It was like Kevin talking into a desk fan, sounding wobbly and vaguely robotic.

"I...I can't. I'll get in trouble."

"Like you'll get in trouble with the credit card? Close it, Ryan. Just do it."

Ryan turned and felt another twinge in his knee, stumbling for a second before pushing forward and quietly shutting the door, then mindlessly wedging a chair under the doorknob and angling it against the floor to make the door virtually impossible to push open from the outside. It was like he was acting on autopilot, his brain being controlled remotely by a force he didn't understand. He walked back to the window.

"Okay. The door's closed," he said, looking around. "Where are you, Kevin?"

"I'm outside your window. Open it, and you'll see me."

"What? How..."

"Just trust me, little bro."

Ryan nodded and stepped forward to put his hands underneath the window. His fingers felt for the latch and pulled on it, using all his strength. It probably hadn't been opened in years, and it didn't slide easily. He thought for a second it might only crack open an inch or two. He crouched down and turned his palms up to get all his bodyweight underneath the window, then stretched up with his legs. The window creaked upward at first, then slid faster, slamming to the top of the frame with a bone-rattling jolt. Ryan cringed, afraid the glass would shatter, but it held firm.

"That's better, isn't it?" the voice warbled.

Ryan wrapped his arms across his chest and shivered. "It's cold."

"Never mind that. Just look out the window. Try not to even blink. You trust me?"

"Of...course. Sure."

Ryan straightened his back and dropped his arms to his sides, then looked out at the morning sun peeking above the horizon, tossing a front-yard tree into a ragged late-winter silhouette as rain began to fall, lightly at first, then steadily becoming a deluge. Then, all at once, the world seemed to drop around him. The sun disappeared, and so did the front yard, followed by the house underneath his feet. The world was black. Nothing. He felt panic wanting to rise in his chest, but something was holding it down, countering it with a feeling of peace and tranquility. His eyes darted around, but he saw nothing. He couldn't move. Or, maybe he *was* moving, but there was nothing he could measure his movement against, so he couldn't *tell* he was moving. He felt paralyzed, but not fearful.

Then he saw Kevin. Or, at least, a reasonable approximation of the Kevin he knew—gaunt, his cheeks hollow, and his words seeming to tumble from a mouth moving in slow motion.

"Welcome t-to The In Between," Kevin spoke strangely, in a voice that echoed against itself, vibrating with the air around it. He walked toward Ryan on an invisible floor.

"What is this?"

"This is the t-transition phase between y-y-your world and the one we've created. I kn-know it's not much, but it's a good p-p-place for us to meet up for now."

"Am I going to sleep now?"

"Not y-yet, buddy." His words came slow, with noticeable effort. "Not quite y-yet. But you're close. I can feel it. Can't w-wait to hang out again."

"I'm...scared, Kevin. Can you show me this new place?"

Kevin's mouth strained into a mangled frown, and he shook his head. "I w-wish I could. Just know you don't need to be scared. It's a g-g-great place. You trust me, right?"

Ryan nodded, and a tear dribbled down his cheek.

"Then stop worrying, a-and listen to the w-w-water fall." Kevin tried to smile, but it looked like a scowl, yellowing teeth peeking out between his lips. "Do you hear the w-water, Ryan? Pattering below. The w-water is washing this all away. Nothing will be left."

Ryan could hear water pattering below. He nodded, and realized he could move again. He bent his elbows and flexed his knee, which didn't hurt anymore. He lifted his arms and took a step forward, lunging for Kevin, wanting just to touch him briefly to assure himself his brother was really there and not just a trick of his imagination.

Kevin stepped back an inch or so beyond the tips of Ryan's fingers, just as Ryan was yanked backward, and the world was restored around him again. He was lying on the floor of his room, looking up at the ceiling.

"Ryan!" cried Stephen, cradling Ryan's head in the crook of his arm. "What were you *thinking*? You could have really hurt yourself if you fell out that window. You know that?"

Ryan shook his head, adjusting back to being on solid ground. He looked around before realizing it was his dad who was talking to him.

"Where am I?" Ryan said, dreamily.

"Where *are* you? You're in your room, Ryan. Are you okay?"

Ryan blinked and stretched his eyelids open, as if they'd shut forever if he didn't get them as wide as possible. He felt woozy, like he'd been spun around several times before crumpling to the ground. The solid world felt less steady than the empty one. Everything was both in place and out of place at the same time. Then his dad's voice broke through the fog.

"Did you hear me? Ryan?"

Wide-eyed, he looked up at his dad.

"Why were you climbing out your window?" Stephen asked, his arms shaking.

Ryan turned his head right, then it wobbled a bit. He brought it around and unsteadily rested it back onto his dad's arm, making eye contact with him. For a few moments, there was silence, only the curtain flapping beside him in the cool winter breeze. The sun was casting daggers of light onto the wall, filtered through the dormant, jagged limbs of the birch outside the window.

Ryan took a deep breath, then exhaled.

"To get to Kevin," he said, as his eyes closed and his head fell meekly into his dad's arms.

Stephen fumbled in his pocket for his phone, and began to dial.

7

"He's awake! He's awake!" Laura rose halfway from her knees by Ryan's bed, shouting toward the hall behind her. "Stephen! Nathan! Come up!"

She turned back around and leaned forward to kiss Ryan's forehead. She began rubbing his head, letting her fingers get lost in his dirty blonde hair.

"Oh god, Ryan. My *baby*. You gave us a scare," she said, fighting tears as she looked into his sleepy eyes. Her red eyes and damp cheeks gave away that she'd been crying. "We're so glad you're awake."

A timid smile seemed to be trying to cross his face as he looked up at her.

"I'm sorry, mom," he said, his voice cracking. "I didn't mean to scare anyone."

"No, no. Everything's fine, honey." She put her finger to his lips and wrapped her arms around his head, pressing him to her chest. "It's fine. Don't worry about it. Everybody's here, and we're just happy you're still with us."

Stephen and Nathan walked into the room, and Stephen smiled at Ryan.

"Hey, big guy! How ya feelin'?" Stephen got down on his knees next to Laura, leaning against the bed, and grabbed Ryan's left hand.

"Okay, I guess." Ryan shrugged.

"Well, that's great! Glad to see you awake again. You want anything to eat or drink? I could bring you something up."

He looked down at his chest, then took a breath. "Water?"

"You got it. Be right back, kiddo."

Stephen ruffled Ryan's hair, then went downstairs. As he walked out of the room, Ryan turned to his mom. "Doctor Nathan's here?" he asked.

She glanced at Nathan, then back to Ryan. "Um, yeah. Doctor Nathan has been here the whole time. He refused to go until we made sure you were okay. Wasn't that nice of him?"

Ryan's brow wrinkled, and his eyebrows curled. "How...long have I been asleep?"

"It's..." She looked at Nathan and tilted her head uncertainly. "...not important. What matters is you're feeling better. Right?"

Ryan lay still, looking into his mother's eyes.

"Right?" she repeated.

"Right," he said, his lips barely parting.

Behind Laura, Stephen came back in with a glass of water. He set it down on the table beside Ryan's bed.

"I even put a bendy straw in there. The ones you like," Stephen said. "That'll make it easier to drink while you're lying down."

Ryan nodded and smiled uncomfortably. "Thanks, dad."

The adults looked at each other, and Stephen cocked his head to motion into the hallway.

"We're gonna have a quick chat in the hall, okay?" Laura stroked Ryan's forehead. "Then Doctor Nathan is gonna come back in, and you guys are going to talk for a little bit. Just tell him whatever comes into your head, like usual. You got it?"

Ryan nodded and reached for his glass of water. Laura picked it up and handed it to him, then followed Stephen and Nathan out of the room. They walked several steps down the hall, and kept their voices low since there was no door left to close to Ryan's room.

"Okay, I think we're out of the woods now," Nathan said. "But that was nearly twenty-four hours. If he'd have been out another hour or two, we'd have been going to the hospital."

"Thanks for staying so long," Stephen said. "If you want to go and come back tomorrow, we'll understand. He looks stable to me."

"No, really. I'm here. It's best to see what I can get out of him as soon as possible. His memory of what happened isn't gonna get sharper with time."

"Do you feel like you know everything that happened?" Laura said.

"I know as much as I *can* know. Stephen's gone over it with me a few times, so I should know everything he does. His exact words were 'To get to Kevin'?"

Stephen nodded. "That's what he said. What do you make of it?"

"It's really tough to say." Nathan grimaced. "It's not that uncommon for younger siblings to have separation anxiety when their older brothers and sisters fall into The Sleep. Nightmares. Some go into a shell. But actual *hallucinations* are pretty rare, if that's what's going on here. If so, it's not necessarily *harmful*, though we obviously can't have him trying to leap out of windows.

"The key is going to be talking to him, understanding where his head is at. Then I can figure out where we go from here. The hope is to manage whatever his symptoms are for now. As we all know, he only has a few days left. I know that's hard to hear, but it's true. And what's also true is, while specific hallucinations have been rare, nine-year-olds becoming suicidal has become far too common. Especially in the final weeks before The Sleep. I'm not saying that's what's happening here. I just want to prepare you for that possibility. Okay? And if I think that's where we are, I'll have a plan for it. Are we on the same page?"

Stephen and Laura looked at each other, then back at Nathan.

"Yeah, we've got it," she said.

"Mind if I come in?" Nathan said as he peeked his head into Ryan's door-less room, rapping his knuckles a few times against the wall by the entryway.

Ryan tapped the pause button on the game on his phone and laid it beside him on the bed.

"Sure. Come on in."

"Thanks." Nathan stepped inside, skirting the splintered door lying on the floor as he walked to the other side of the bed. He pulled a chair from Ryan's desk and slid it next to the bed. Ryan sat up and crossed his legs, sleep creases still lining his left cheek.

"So, how ya feelin'?" Nathan asked.

Ryan shrugged. "Okay, I guess. A little tired."

"Yeah, I bet. You were out for a long time. Did you know that?"

"Well, that's what dad said." He looked down at the bed and began absent-mindedly tracing figure eights with his index finger across the sheets. "How long was I asleep?"

"Pretty much a full day."

"Wow." Ryan looked up, his eyebrows arched, then his head bobbed lightly up and down for a few seconds. His eyes drifted left, away from Nathan, looking at the window where he'd seen Kevin. There were new keyed locks installed on both sides of it. He scanned right and saw the same ones on the other window.

"What do you remember about yesterday, Ryan?" Nathan reached out and touched Ryan on the knee, causing him to flinch, his shoulders shuddering violently. He stared at Nathan for several seconds before answering.

"I...I don't know," he spoke in just above a whisper. Nathan scooted his chair closer in order to hear. "It's just...I didn't know I was going to cause any problems, Doctor Nathan. I was just..."

"It's okay, Ryan. It's *okay*. Nobody's angry with you. It's just...what?"

Ryan's chin dug into his shoulder and he frowned, shaking his head back and forth, knotting the bed sheet between his legs.

"It's just...It's just...Have you ever had a dream that you didn't know if it was real?"

"Of course, Ryan. That's totally normal. Everybody's had that."

"Well...I have too. But you eventually *know*, right? You eventually figure out that it was just a dream. That it wasn't really happening. That it was all in your head. Right?"

Nathan nodded. "Usually, yes. You do."

"Yeah, that's what I thought." Then: "And what if you don't?"

"What if you don't what, Ryan?" Nathan cocked his head left, furrowing his brow.

"What if you don't figure out it was a dream? What if you don't think that something that *has* to be a dream really *is* a dream? Does that mean it's real?"

"What was your dream, Ryan? You said something to your dad about Kevin."

Ryan looked down at the bed, twisting the bedsheet with both hands until it looked like a rope wrapped up in his fists.

"Ryan, tell me what your dream was about. I won't tell your mom and dad if you don't want me to. You trust me, right?"

Ryan's head snapped up, and he sat up straight. "That's what he kept saying."

"What's what *who* kept saying?"

"Trust me."

"Someone wants you to trust them?"

"Kevin. He came to get me."

"Hold on, Ryan. You're saying that *your brother, Kevin*, came to you in a dream, to *get* you?"

"It wasn't a dream, Doctor Nathan. You said so yourself. If it were a dream, I'd know."

"No. You would *probably* know—"

"But I *don't* know it was a dream. I know it was *real*. Kevin was right there, outside my window!" Ryan said, his voice raising an octave as he pointed at the window in the corner of the room. "He wanted me to come. He told me about the other world, where he's living now!"

Ryan turned to look at Nathan, who was stiff in his chair.

"He's coming for me. They're coming for us all."

8

The temperature was touching sixty-seven degrees as Laura walked by the old bandstand in downtown Knoxville's Market Square, her youngest son clutching her hand while they enjoyed the mid-afternoon sun. It was one of those late-March days that remind you why you live in the South, where you can get a kiss of springtime even in the depths of winter, and where you can sometimes even feel the sun touch your cheek before April.

Market Square was the cultural, if not the physical, center of downtown, a thirteen-acre parcel of concrete more than 150 years old, rung by restaurants, bars, shops, and apartments. When it was built in the mid-nineteenth century, it was a market place for regional farmers, with a large market house sitting in the center. As with many historic buildings in Knoxville and elsewhere in the country, the market house was torn down in the mid-twentieth century. Fortunately for the city, the land wasn't turned into a parking lot, but preserved as a pedestrian mall, and it became a major cog in the revitalization of the downtown area in the early 2000s, just as The Sleep was first becoming known.

This part of downtown was hit hard by the university's closure and the general population decline. Many of the businesses that once lined Market Square had closed. Just two remained—Tomato Stand, a pizza place that had outlasted nearly everything on the square, and Patty Melt, a burger spot that opened a few years earlier on the opposite corner. When Laura opened the door to Tomato Stand, the tables inside were empty.

"Sit anywhere ya like," a female voice came from the back.

Laura looked down at Ryan. "How's that table by the

window? We can look outside while we eat."

Ryan ran over to the table and sat down. If there was anything that could make sitting at the brewery all day with his mom bearable, Laura knew it was the promise of Tomato Stand pizza for lunch.

"What are you gonna get on your pizza?" Laura asked, sitting down across from him.

"Ham!" he blurted out, his mouth open wide, skin flush. "And pineapple!"

"Oh, Hawaiian, huh?"

"Yeah. It feels like Hawaii today."

Laura laughed. "Well, I don't know about that. But it is nice for March. I'll give you that much."

The waitress stopped at their table, and laid down two menus. "I'm Gillian, and I'll be taking care of you guys," she said, smiling widely. With no college kids or twenty-somethings for cheap labor, restaurants had been having a hard time finding staff in recent years. Places like Tomato Stand that remained open often did so by having their owners take on the job of waiting tables and cooking. "Can I get you two something to drink?"

"I'm okay with water," Laura said.

Ryan rubbed his chin thoughtfully. "Strawberry lemonade?"

Gillian glanced at Laura and smiled. Then she turned back to Ryan. "I think we can whip something up." She winked and walked away.

Ryan picked up his menu and scanned it absent-mindedly. Laura looked out the window at the square, and saw a lone man in a suit walking away from them, possibly to the bank just down the street.

"Am I being punished, mom?"

Laura's head rattled, and she looked at Ryan, who had laid his menu back down and was frowning.

"If I'm punishing you with pizza, I'm pretty terrible at

punishments."

"No, not the pizza. Me being with you at work today."

Laura bit her lip and swallowed hard. "No, baby. Why would you think that?"

"After the…*thing* with the window and Kevin." Ryan paused, looking into his lap, speaking so low Laura could barely hear him. "I just feel like nobody's letting me out of their sight. And I've never come to work with you all day before. It felt like I was being grounded."

After Nathan told them about his talk with Ryan, they'd all agreed they needed to keep him within sight as often as possible in order to monitor him. Normally, it worked well for Stephen to stay home with him, but he couldn't keep an eye on Ryan and give therapy sessions to his patients at the same time. So they decided to have Laura take him to the brewery, where there'd always be someone who could keep at least one eye on him during the day. Stephen didn't have any weekend patients, so he'd be able to watch Ryan the next couple of days, but this was what they could come up with to get through Friday.

It wasn't the most elegant solution to their problem, but they figured it'd do in a pinch, as opposed to risking whatever Ryan might get into when left to himself at home. The Sleep was a funny thing, straining families to hold themselves together even when they knew they were about to be pulled apart. Laura felt like they were clinging to the side of a mountain, about to plunge to their deaths. It was inevitable. But everybody hangs on as long as they can, until their fingernails are bent and screaming, until their shoulders are full of battery acid and their arms feel like they're going to tear apart in a mangled string of tendons and muscles. Everybody hangs on. Laura sure as hell was, too.

"It's just temporary, kiddo. Don't worry about it. Everything's gonna be fine."

Ryan curled his lips and glanced at Gillian, who was walking up to the table.

"You guys know what you wanna get?" she asked.

Laura cocked her head. "What'll it be, Ry?"

He didn't answer, and Laura was worried his enthusiasm for pizza had faded. She wanted to do something to make him happy; she knew he was dealing with a lot that he wasn't equipped to understand. There was nothing more in the world she wanted than to see him smile, and scarf down a big helping of pizza. She also knew—and this likely wasn't lost on him either—that this could be the last pizza he'd ever have. She wondered if that had dawned on the waitress too. She could probably guess Ryan was eight or nine, and might not have many more lunches in his future. Laura definitely had such thoughts as she walked around town, or saw people bring their kids into the brewery, often hanging on tightly to them as if they'd float away if they let go. She'd wonder how old the kid was. *How close are they? Do they have another year, or just another month? Or a week, even?* She couldn't bear the thought, but it was there all the same.

Laura put her hand to the side of her mouth, like she was telling Gillian a secret. "How's your Hawaiian pizza?"

Gillian leaned down, her mouth close to Laura's ear. "We'll make the best one he's ever had. How's that?"

Laura mouthed, "Thank you," and Gillian headed to the back.

"What's wrong, sweetie?" she said, tilting her head to try to make eye contact with Ryan's drooping head.

He sighed deeply. "I don't want to disappoint you guys."

"We could never be disappointed in you, Ryan. We love you."

"But I'm gonna end up like Kevin. I'm gonna leave you guys alone, and there's no way you can take care of us both. I'm gonna mess up everything."

Laura got out of her side of the booth and came around to sit next to Ryan. Trying to fight back tears, she wrapped her arms around him and pulled him to her chest.

"Oh, baby. It's not your fault. None of it is your fault. We're not disappointed in you. We couldn't be more proud of the little man you're turning into. We love you more than anything. You know that, right?"

"Yeah," his head was buried in her shirt, soaking it. "I know. I wish you could come with me."

"Come with you?"

He sniffled hard, blowing his nose on her collar. "You and dad. I wish you could come with me when I leave. Then we could all be together. But adults aren't allowed there."

She lifted his head up. "What do you mean, they're 'not allowed'?"

"That's what Kevin told me."

9

The sun tossed streaks through the window above the kitchen sink, sparkling in the black coffee sitting in front of Laura on the island, as she sipped slowly, coming awake on Saturday morning. For the past year or so, as the brewery's revenue finally started to pick up to a more consistent level, she'd taken on the habit of coming in a little later on these weekend mornings. With the late-night hours that were often required of just about any business owner—but particularly of a brewery owner—these early mornings, when Stephen rarely had any patients, gave her a little more time to spend with the family, and enjoy a cup of coffee.

It was almost nine. Within another hour, the house would be buzzing with the sounds of small feet tapping across the floor. That'd been her reality for close to eleven years, and she knew it was coming to an end. The impending change was so palpable that it almost felt like a physical force, shifting the sands beneath their feet. She could feel it deep within her bones; it was a veritable presence. There was something coming for her family, and nothing was going to be the same as it had been.

Sitting there in the quiet of the house, she kept replaying her lunch conversation with Ryan in her head. Did he actually think Kevin had been talking to him? And what did he mean by "adults aren't allowed there"? Was this all just stress building up as he got closer to his birthday? Part of her thought she shouldn't spend too much time dwelling on the fantasies of a frazzled, not-quite-ten-year-old kid, but another part of her thought there was something more there. Especially when combined with his episode with the window, and what he'd told Stephen and Nathan.

She lifted the mug to her lips and took another hesitant nip; it burned across her tongue into her throat, warming her on an unusually cold late-March morning. Behind her, she heard footsteps.

"Morning," Stephen said, leaning in for a quick kiss. He was wearing what he called his "swaddling clothes," which meant some baggy pajama pants and an orange Tennessee Vols hoodie. The school's orange lived on in Knoxville as a point of pride, a reminder of what once was and what might be again if they could solve the riddle of The Sleep.

"G'morning, handsome. How'd you sleep?"

"Just fine, thank you. You taste like coffee."

"Big surprise there. You taste like you just woke up."

"Sounds sexy."

Stephen opened the fridge and pulled out a bottle of orange juice, then poured a glass and sat down across the island from Laura.

"He's still asleep," Stephen said.

"He does tend to sleep in on weekends unless I make cinnamon rolls."

"Gonna make 'em this morning?"

"Probably. Got a can in the fridge. Think I'll let him sleep a little longer, though."

"I *do* enjoy some cinnamon rolls."

"Who said you were getting any?" She smiled.

"Who's gonna stop me?" he said, his eyes playful. "I'm a year younger than you, and I'm spry."

"Ouch. Low blow," she said. "Well, Ryan's only nine, and he'll melt us both into a puddle when he says 'Please.'"

Stephen laughed, then nodded and took a sip of juice. The two said nothing for a few moments before he broke the silence.

"Should I say it?"

"Say what?"

Stephen's head bobbed toward the ceiling. "Ryan. Four days."

"You think I don't know that?"

"We both *know* it. It's one thing to know it, and quite another to have a plan for it. We still don't know what we're doing, do we?"

"What do you want me to say?" Laura said under her breath. "I've got one son who's basically dead, and another who's about to be. It's not the easiest thing to plan for."

"Look, I know. And it's clearly on *both* of us. But there are plenty of resources to help with this. Nathan isn't gonna lean on us too hard, but he's told us a number of times he'll point us in the right direction whenever we're ready."

She started to pick up her coffee, but her hand was shaking and she had to put it back down.

"Shit." She sighed and rattled her head back and forth, pulling her hair out from in front of her face. "*Are* we ready? You and I both know the money isn't there to take care of them both. We've been saving what we can, but Kevin's eating up a lot of that. We've got *what* in savings? *Maybe* a thousand bucks? There's no way."

Stephen looked away, silent for several seconds.

"I mean, there are subsidies that can help."

Laura blinked and wrinkled her mouth, staring at him.

"Yeah, I know," he said. "It's not enough."

"Not *nearly* enough."

He took off his glasses and rubbed his eyes. "No, it's not."

"So, you know the conversation we have to have. If we can't afford to care for two children in a coma in our home, what are our options?"

"We've talked about this before. We just haven't made a decision. And the clock's ticking."

"Let's go over it again, all right? What, there's the state—"

"Right. We can turn one over to the state."

"But we both know what that means."

"Ryan would have a better shot. He's younger. They might keep him alive for…I don't know. Six months? A year?"

"Then what?"

He sighed. "You *know* what."

"Right. And they'd probably kill Kevin in the van once they pulled out of our driveway."

Stephen said nothing.

"So, what else?"

"Nathan said there are some non-profit 'farms' set up, where they'll take kids," said Stephen, staring into his glass of juice. "They have big barns full of beds, with nurses who come by in shifts. Some of them seem to do a pretty good job."

"Yeah, but didn't he say we needed to get on a waiting list for the good ones? That they only have so much space, and they fill up fast?"

"We probably would have had to initiate that sooner, yeah. Otherwise—"

"Otherwise, the kid dies anyway."

Stephen took in a deep breath, then raised his head. "That's right."

"What else, then?"

"The only other thing."

"That's it? I could have sworn we had more choices."

"The government has a program." Stephen swallowed hard. "They'll take care of everything. It's…painless."

Laura ran her hand through her hair, yanking at strands, feeling the gentle tug against her scalp.

"You're talking about…" she looked around, then leaned forward, her hair a tangled nest atop her head. She whispered, "…having one of our sons killed."

"I'm talking about being practical."

"You're talking about state-sanctioned *murder*."

His mouth opened, then closed. He rubbed the back of his neck and twisted his head.

"I'm not saying I like it. I'm not saying it's easy, or anything short of heart-wrenching."

"What *are* you saying?"

"I'm saying…who are we hanging onto them for? Them, or us?"

"*Them*. What if something changes? What if doctors figure out a cure?"

"Is there any reason to think that's gonna happen?"

She shook her head, tears wanting to come. "They've made some advances."

"Have they?"

"And we don't *know* everything, Stephen!" She listened for sounds of Ryan moving around upstairs, but she didn't hear anything. Then, in a quieter voice: "How do we know what advances they've made? Maybe they're closer than we think."

Stephen shook his head, then shrugged. "It's wishful thinking. I get it. I want to think it's true too. But what if it isn't? And it *probably* isn't. What kind of life are they living? Kevin's been in that bed for over a year, without moving a muscle, barely kept alive by machines. Is that the best thing for him?"

"It is if they find a cure tomorrow."

"There are twenty years of yesterdays when they haven't found one that tell us it's almost certainly not coming tomorrow either. We're their parents, and we have to do what's best for them."

"And you're saying death is what's best for them?"

"I'm saying *this* life might not be."

Stephen got off his stool, turning to rinse the glass out before laying it in the sink. He looked out the window, and thought he might see the first spring buds of green on a nearby tree. He paused for a moment, then turned back to Laura, who was sitting silently.

"All I'm saying is—"

A piercing scream came from upstairs, and a deep chill enveloped Laura, every hair on her body stiffening as if sounding an alarm. The scream lasted for three seconds that seemed much longer, then abruptly stopped. Laura's stool tumbled to the ground underneath her as she scrambled to her feet, and Stephen was fast behind her to the stairs.

10

Ryan used to sleep soundly most nights. But, in the previous several months, especially since Kevin started showing up more often in his dreams, his sleep had gotten more fitful, with him waking every half hour or so, rolling over, taking awhile to get back to sleep, then going through that cycle again and again throughout the night. Sometimes, his mind would be so full of swirling thoughts that shutting it down was like trying to stop a raging river by catching the water in hand-held buckets. No matter how much water filled each bucket, there was still far more coming than you had any chance to catch, and it would eventually overwhelm you.

He didn't want to be awake at nine on a Sunday morning. He wanted to be tucked tightly under his covers, his head buried in one pillow and his arms clutching another one. But here he was, lying flat on his back, his eyes open, staring blankly at the ceiling.

He could hear his parents below him, talking and moving around in the kitchen. He couldn't clearly make out what they were saying—he thought it sounded like they were talking more softly than usual—but he was picking up words here and there. It sounded like idle chit-chat, until he heard what he thought was "still asleep."

That's gotta be me, he thought. *And that means they're probably talking about me. I want to hear what they're saying.*

Ryan knew they were directly below him, and they'd hear him get out of bed if he wasn't careful. Slowly, he bent his legs and pulled them toward the rest of his body, sliding out from under the covers and rolling to his left side. He scooted across the bed to the side closest to his door, avoiding the creak he'd make by bouncing on the bedsprings. He let his legs swing off the edge and placed his feet on the floor. He crawled out to the hall, where the sound would carry better up the stairs; that's when he heard it: "Ryan. Four days."

There was no question what his dad was referring to. It was four days until Ryan's tenth birthday. That was the dread hovering over all of their lives, and it centered around him. There was no escaping it. Two years earlier, it felt like that tenth birthday would never come. But then it came for Kevin. The Sleep came for him. Just like it would come for Ryan. And now he knew it.

He slid a little further down the hall so he could hear more clearly, keeping contact to the floor with all four limbs to minimize any noise he might make. He stopped again and heard his mom talking: "I've got one son who's basically dead, and another who's about to be. It's not the easiest thing to plan for."

Ryan's breath caught in his throat, and he stopped. She wasn't wrong, but he'd never heard her put it in such blunt terms before—Kevin was dead, and Ryan was next. Or, at least, dead to *this world*. If the Kevin from his dreams was right, these ten years were a sort of penance paid in order to enter this new world, where kids could stay kids, and be together with no wars, no strife, no adults mortgaging their future in order to settle their minor squabbles. Once you were there, you didn't have to worry anymore. Was that true, though? To his parents, it wasn't. Couldn't be. To him, though, maybe it was the only hope to cling to.

His dad's voice carried up into the hall: "Ryan would have a better shot. He's younger. They might keep him alive for...I don't know. Six months? A year?"

Ryan didn't know who "they" were. Were they going to give him and Kevin away once The Sleep took him? Just throw them out like trash? He was old enough to know, though, that it had to cost money to do everything they had to in order to keep Kevin's physical body alive. He had no idea how much, but it probably wasn't cheap. And now he heard his parents talking about not having the resources to keep it up for *two* kids instead of just one. That made Ryan a burden. In less than a week, Ryan knew he was going to put his parents in an impossible position—which one of your sons do you want to kill? Would the body dying take a kid away from this new, amazing world? If so, where would they go? Kevin seemed happy where he was. Ryan wasn't going to let them take that away from him. He could only think of one option. He'd stashed what he needed in Kevin's room, so he didn't have far to go.

    He glanced to his left, and the door of his brother's room was closed, as usual. He scooted over to it and stretched his arm above his head, trying to keep his balance without making noise. If they heard this door open, they'd come running immediately. He was only allowed in to see Kevin while they were there. They always said it was for the best that he didn't spend time alone with Kevin, and Doctor Nathan had always agreed.

    Carefully, Ryan turned the doorknob as slowly as he could, sure the latch clicking open was as loud to his parents downstairs as it was rattling in his head like the blast of a shotgun. He paused, cringing and waiting to hear footsteps pounding up the stairs. But there was nothing but voices wafting through the air. They were still talking.

    He scooted toward the bed, then slowly stood beside it. He stared at Kevin's face, with tubes coming out of his nose and mouth. He'd been in the room before since The Sleep took Kevin, but it had always been for very short periods, and he'd never really taken stock of everything that was there. He didn't know what any of the tubes, liquid bags or machines were for, exactly, but they were everywhere—tubes attached to seemingly everything, from his forehead to his chest, sides and even between his legs. They ran in all different directions, some connecting to monitors, and some to bags partly full of some sort of liquid. There was a machine with an accordion-looking device, expanding and contracting, off to the side of his bed. Behind him was the big monitor that beeped incessantly, squiggly lines hopping across the screen That was how they knew Kevin was breathing, his mom had told him. When it beeped like that, it was a good thing.

Ryan looked around the room and saw a chair a couple of feet away. He grabbed its legs, pulling it closer to Kevin's bed. He climbed onto the chair, first sitting, then standing up. Now he could look down on Kevin. This was the full view of what awaited him. It was an out-of-body experience. Ryan was seeing himself. It was time to put an end to it. No more waiting. He climbed down to get the tool he needed out of its hiding place.

11

Laura took the stairs two at a time, her legs pumping with a force she would have sworn was impossible. Her thighs burned from the effort, but adrenaline chased the pain into the deep recesses of her mind. She was swimming in the deep ocean, all around her water, bobbing up and down, moving in the right direction but feeling like she was making no progress. And the ominous silence above them scared the hell out of her.

She didn't have time to think exactly where the brief scream came from. But she knew. Somewhere, instinctually, she knew—Kevin's room. Ryan wasn't supposed to be in there, and he knew that. That *scream*, though. It wasn't a normal kid's scream. It was a shriek. Shrill and frightened. She couldn't get the sound out of her head. It was still rattling there, echoing, filling her mind with fear, fresh and intense. What could make a nine-year-old scream like that? And, maybe worse yet, what could make him stop so suddenly? She'd have rather been hearing the most ear-piercing scream possible than nothing at this point. Anything but nothing.

When she hit the hall at the top of the stairs, her foot nearly slid out from under her as she veered right toward Kevin's room. Stephen was no more than a couple of steps behind, and she could hear his feet landing behind her hard.

Kevin's door was open, and the light was on. That confirmed her feeling that the scream had come from there. Ryan had snuck in, and she didn't know why. In another circumstance, she'd have been pondering his punishment, but her mind was elsewhere; she couldn't get too far ahead of herself. There was no way getting past the scream. Something happened. And, after what Nathan had told them, part of her worried she knew what it was. That part of her was trying to assert itself, but she was fighting it back.

No, he wouldn't do that. Not to himself. Not to us. Not to his family. He wants to live as long as he can. There's still hope.

She lunged for the doorjamb, wrapping her fingers around it and catching herself as she swung her head around and looked inside. When she did, she thought her heart may stop. Breath wouldn't come. She was straining to suck in air, and to comprehend the scene before her. Ryan was standing in the corner of the room, stiff, his face frozen, hands tucked neatly behind his back. But her eyes went back to the bed.

Bumping her from behind was Stephen, nudging her shoulder as he peered around her to see what was happening. His eyes expanded like balloons filled with helium, ready to burst. He grabbed Laura's shoulder and squeezed, his fingertips digging deep into her flesh.

How could this be? The thought rose up within her. *I can't understand...*

"Kevin!" she finally said, her back and shoulders beginning to ache as stress drained from her body. "Oh my god, Kevin! You're awake."

It isn't possible. It simply isn't possible.

Those thoughts kept reverberating in Stephen's head as he stared, his mouth agape, at Kevin's open eyes. Laura was kneeling at the bed, crying, hugging him deliriously while trying not to get tangled in the wires criss-crossing everywhere. Stephen had to get Ryan down off the bed because he kept trying to prod Kevin into getting up; he didn't understand that people who lie motionless in bed for over a year can't just stand up and sprint down the hall.

Kevin's vocal cords were too weak to function, he was very sluggish and groggy, but he seemed to know who they were. Stephen considered that a victory in itself. No child had ever awaken from The Sleep, and there had been a lot of discussion about what sort of state they'd be in even if the medical community could come up with a way to jolt them out of the coma. Would they have brain damage? Amnesia? A completely different personality? On the last point, it was tough to say so far, but Kevin wasn't immediately showing any signs of cognitive problems. He seemed in good spirits, though his lips were chapped and cracking, and he motioned that he wanted to get rid of all the tubes that were latched onto him. Laura told him they had to talk to a doctor first, so they could make sure he was healthy enough to do that.

Stephen's first call was to Nathan, who said he was running to his car before he even hung up the phone. The second call went to Brent, Kevin's nurse, who dropped his phone when Stephen told him about Kevin. At first, Stephen thought he'd hung up on him. Then, Brent's wife picked up and said, "He just flew out the door. Didn't even come back for his phone. I think he'll be there soon."

While they waited for them to arrive, Stephen marveled at the scene playing out in front of him—all the worrying, all the pain and turmoil. Maybe it was worth it after all. They had their son back. Their outgoing, funny, athletic, playful, miraculous son. As a physical therapist himself, Stephen knew Kevin would have a tough road in front of him, to get back even twenty or thirty percent of the physical abilities he had before the coma. And he might never fully recover. Would he walk again? Would he run, jump, play outside? Those were probably all questions for another day. For the moment, there was just a smile plastered across Stephen's face, and it wouldn't go away.

Then another question came to mind: Was this happening everywhere? The odds seemed astronomical that Kevin would be the first, but they hadn't seen anything online. Of course, they hadn't read the news in the morning, or even jumped on Twitter to catch up on what was going on in the world. Maybe there was an awakening happening. Maybe Kevin wasn't the only one, and there were millions starting to stir. Perhaps whatever awful plague struck the world's children so suddenly and without warning had run its course, and ended itself just as suddenly and just as inexplicably.

He certainly hoped so.

If not, the implications were much more complicated. Why Kevin? Why now? Those were tough questions they'd have to ask themselves, and others would undoubtedly be asking as well. People were going to find out, and there was no telling what the reaction would be. How would he have felt if someone else's kid woke up while his laid there in a coma? Happy for them? Jealous? Angry? Bitter? Some combination of all of those?

Stephen's eyes left Kevin for a moment and turned to Ryan, who was sitting in a chair by the bed. He was smiling, but you could tell he didn't know what to do with a brother who couldn't talk or play.

Then, there was the other question.

Amid the joy over Kevin's recovery, unless the cloud of The Sleep was actually lifting, nothing had necessarily changed about Ryan's fate. He was still just a few days from falling into a coma of his own. And now, there was obviously no question that they'd keep him in the house and continue to pour resources into keeping him alive, while they tried to jump-start Kevin's rehabilitation.

For more than a year, they'd been so afraid of losing their second son just as they'd lost the first. Now, it looked like the two boys might be about to trade places.

Stephen loved seeing Ryan smile for a brief time. He liked that his youngest son could feel joy, even with such darkness still hanging over them. Stephen felt it too. But he wondered what the next weeks and months would bring, and if they were ready to face it together.

12

Brent closed the door to Kevin's room as he walked out, and turned around to see Stephen, Laura, Nathan, and Ryan standing behind him.

"We couldn't wait," Laura said.

"Understandable." Brent smiled, then looked down at his notes. "This…is pretty amazing. I mean, first of all, obviously, he's *awake*. This gives hope to so many families out there. It really is incredible. I didn't think I'd see it happen. And when I tell my colleagues, they're gonna want to see it too. The CDC will be calling as well, and they'll want to have someone examine him. I'm happy to act as a liaison for you guys, if you don't want to deal with the calls. Because, I'll warn you, there's gonna be a lot. Not just medical, but media too."

Laura looked at Stephen, her eyebrows raised, then back at Brent.

"That'd be wonderful if you could handle a lot of that for us," she said. "We're fine with having some experts do a quick examination if it helps figure out how to put an end to The Sleep, but we don't want our house turning into a zoo. We just got our family back, and we don't know how much longer we'll have it."

"I understand. Let's just stay in touch on that. Now, as far as his health is concerned, this is honestly probably about a best-case scenario, considering how long he's been in that bed. He has significant muscle atrophy throughout most of his body. We'll eventually want to get him on a scale, but I'd estimate his weight at forty to forty-five pounds. We gave him what nutrition we could, but it's never enough over that long a period of time. He can lift his hands an inch or so off the bed; same with his feet. His reflexes respond well. He eyes are able to follow light, and his pupils appear normal. I've removed the tracheostomy tube, and I've disconnected the most invasive equipment, as he appears to be breathing on his own. He likely won't be able to talk for at least a week, maybe much more, but I suspect his voice will recover. Of course, I was flipping him regularly to try to avoid bed sores, but he does have some minor sores on his back, buttocks, and feet."

Brent let the notepad fall to his sides.

"As you know well, Stephen, he'll need a tremendous amount of physical rehab to get back to walking on his own. You can handle a lot of that, which helps. But I'll continue our regular medical therapy, too, once he's ready, which won't be for at least a few weeks, maybe a month or more. The general rule of thumb is one month of rehab for every day of unconsciousness. At more than 440 days, you can do the math there. Kevin's cleared one *huge* hurdle, but the honest truth is he's likely to need pretty much full-time care for years, if not the rest of his life. But he's also very young, and that means he *could* recover strength and brain function at a faster rate than we're used to seeing in coma patients. The brain's ability to repair cells is faster in young children than in adults, so my hope is that we'll see his recovery accelerate quickly. But I don't want us to get our hopes up just yet."

"So…are you saying he's okay?" Laura said, her eyes narrowing.

"I think he's as 'okay' as we could possibly have hoped, given the circumstances." He nodded quickly. "Yes."

Laura threw her head back and screamed, then lunged at Brent, throwing her arms around his neck. Stephen looked at Nathan, and they walked over to join the hug.

Ryan watched them embrace each other, but hung back, a wallflower on this morning of jubilation.

While his parents and the doctors were hugging and cheering in the hall, celebrating Kevin's return to their lives in whatever capacity he could muster, Ryan knew this wasn't a dream, and he couldn't help but wonder what this meant for him. Did any of them remember that Ryan still just had a few days left before The Sleep would take him? Would any of them remember that, or would they be so engrossed in helping Kevin that Ryan would go back to being the second-class sibling?

He'd always looked up to Kevin, but there'd been plenty of jealousy there too. Ryan suspected his parents liked Kevin better, and he couldn't really blame them. Hell, *he* liked Kevin better. But now, the playing field should have been more even. All the advantages Kevin had—his quick wit, fun personality, and athleticism—were gone. The doctor even said it: He might need full-time care the rest of his life. But even then, everyone was *still* going to gush all over him. They were standing there crying tears of joy over a subpar Kevin while the full version of Ryan stood behind them alone, arms crossed, staring at them, wondering if he'd just drift off in a few days and no one would notice.

13

"I seriously wouldn't have believed it if I hadn't seen it with my own eyes," said Amanda, a childhood friend of Laura's who lived a few blocks away. "What was it like when you saw he was actually *awake*?"

Laura took a sip of her vodka and tonic, then put it back down on the island. She paused, looking into the glass.

"It's hard to explain. I think we'd fully accepted it was impossible. I mean, as much as you *can* 'accept' that your kid is basically dead even though he's still technically alive, anyway. We were trying to figure out what the hell to do once…"

She stopped speaking and looked around, peeking over to catch a glimpse up the stairs to see if anyone was there. Then she leaned forward, closer to Amanda, and spoke in a soft voice.

"Well…Ryan. We had no idea what to do once The Sleep took him too. It's just four days away."

"Wow. I didn't realize it was that close."

"Yeah." Laura took another swig.

"So…what are you gonna do *now*?"

"This certainly limits our options. No way we don't keep them both now."

"But how? Isn't Kevin gonna need a shit ton of rehab? If Stephen's doing that, doesn't that mean he can't do as much work that actually *pays*? Unless Kev's got cash, of course."

Laura laughed. "Let's just say Kevin's been out of work for awhile."

"So…?"

Laura looked up at the window over the sink. The spruce's

jagged limbs were blowing in a stiff wind, almost scraping against the glass, like they were trying to get inside out of the afternoon cold.

"I guess we still don't know." She shrugged, her eyes still on the window. "We really don't know. I'm not sure if we're ready to figure all that out yet."

"Fair enough. But don't put this off too long, Laura. Be happy your son's back for right now, but you and Stephen have a lot of talking to do."

"I know, I know." Laura's eyes fell back to Amanda. "It's just...hard."

Amanda nodded and took a small sip of a rum and Coke. "So the doctors say Kevin really *is* the first? Like, in the *world?*"

Laura smiled. "Seems that way."

"That's just *crazy*. I wouldn't know how to feel in your shoes."

"Like I need a drink. You want another?" Laura reached for the vodka and poured.

"I'm not done with *this* one. Brewery girl's clearly got me beat on tolerance these days. It's like you're back in college now."

She took a sip. "But, seriously, you get what I mean?"

Amanda nodded. "I do."

They both raised their glasses, light blue tumblers that looked translucent in the sun cutting through the window. They clinked them together.

"Here's to life," Amanda said.

"Here's to life."

Laura's parents didn't take long to arrive, driving up to Knoxville from their house an hour away on Watts Bar Lake as soon as they got the call that their oldest grandson was awake again.

Kevin wasn't much to interact with yet, on his first day in more than a year with his eyes open. Someone was always in his room with him, though, whether it was Stephen reading to him, Laura brushing his hair and trying to catch him up on everything he'd missed, or Laura's parents crying so much it probably embarrassed him.

Her mom, Paula, had been retired from teaching for six years, and her dad, James, sold his plumbing business just a few months before The Sleep took Kevin. James had always loved being outdoors, whether it was camping, hiking, boating, or hunting. When Laura was young, he'd never treated her like some dads treat a girl, letting her play with dollhouses while he did his "man work." He taught her how to change the oil in his car, how to take apart a carburetor or a flush valve, how to pull a stubborn hook out of a fish's mouth, and how to shoot. She grew up around guns, with a healthy respect for their presence, and their potential to kill—always keep them pointed at the ground, treat them as loaded, know what's beyond your target, and never point them at anything you don't intend to shoot. Keep a wide stance. Shoulders up. Eyes down the sightline. Elbows firm but not too firm. She'd gotten pretty good at target shooting, and still went shooting a few times a year with a Smith & Wesson M&P and a CZ-USA 85 Combat handgun she kept locked up in the house. Stephen never wanted to even see them, but Laura always felt more comfortable having them around.

Where James was happiest, though, was on a boat, navigating channels, the wakes lapping against the bow, the camaraderie among other boaters out on the lakes and rivers. So, after retiring, they'd found an affordable home an hour west of the city and lived their dream of waking up to the sun glistening on the lake each morning. There was something about the possibilities of water that he said made each day seem hopeful, like there could always be something new out there in front of you. Especially since retiring, James took advantage of the abundance of time and water as much as he could, taking his dream purchase from the retirement money—the Outer Reef 580 motor yacht—out on the water whenever he could, reliving his younger years when he'd been a deckhand for several summers on fishing vessels along the Gulf of Mexico, developing a love for the water and for the freedom it provided. He'd taken Paula along trips with some old boating friends all the way down the Tennessee River via the Tennessee-Tombigbee to Mobile, Alabama, and the Gulf of Mexico. It took a couple of weeks, but the scenery and the wind in his hair was worth it. They'd dock in small towns and eat at little diners, drop anchor in a wide spot and pull in some river trout. He'd found his heaven.

And since they were still so close, they could get back to see their grandchildren pretty much any time as the kids moved closer to the end. Laura and Stephen sometimes thought they'd been more a part of their lives since retiring than they were when they lived five minutes away, as James and Paula would find an excuse to come up to Knoxville almost every weekend they were in town. And they'd just about always bring Ryan some toys he didn't need and some chocolate he probably shouldn't have. But that was sort of what grandparents were for.

Now Laura was watching her dad putting a too-big blue captain's hat on Kevin's head, and Kevin struggling to turn the weak muscles of his face into a smile, while her mom told him about the house, the boat, and how they couldn't wait to take him for a river trip.

It was all a little surreal. She could only imagine what this felt like for Kevin. Because he couldn't yet talk, and didn't have the strength to write, he couldn't communicate much beyond barely perceptible head nods and simple finger gestures. What was this like for him? How long did he think he'd been asleep? Did it feel like no time at all had passed, or was he conscious of some time falling by the wayside? Did he remember anything from his time in a coma? Was there anything important he forgot? Did he just want to be left alone to rest for a while?

Everybody in the family wanted a piece of him, and it was hard to blame them. She had to stand there and look at him to remind herself this was real, that her son really *had* returned from wherever he'd gone, that she wasn't imagining this. She was dreading the evening, when she was going to have to turn off the lights and let him close those beautiful blue eyes again. The last time she'd watched those eyelids fall, they hadn't lifted again for some fifteen months. Was this a momentary fluke, a brief gift granted to them by whatever force was in charge of this madness? And would this glimpse of happiness be torn away from them as abruptly as it was bestowed?

There was no way to know. No precedent to refer back to. They were in unmarked territory, wandering in a dark forest without a map. One of the curses that came along with this blessing was the knowledge that it could be taken from them at any time. The Sleep had taken Kevin once, and there was every reason to think it could do so again. No one understood the force behind this phenomenon; once Kevin fell asleep again, he *could* never wake up. It could come on the first night or the hundredth. They'd never fully escape that fear.

But if the popular Uppgivenhetssyndrom theory were true, and children were falling into a coma because of an inability to emotionally deal with their lack of hope for the future, was there a reason Kevin was now awake? Was there something special about their family and their home that gave him a surge of hope and brought him back? It was self-gratifying to think that could be true, that they'd figured something out that no one else had.

If that were true, though, Laura couldn't for the life of her figure out what it might be. They weren't the worst family; she felt like they were pretty normal, struggling with stress, fighting against human nature, making the best of what they had. She didn't feel like they had any magic potion. They'd made their share of mistakes. She'd worried on more than one occasion that the marriage might not survive much longer, but they'd both made a daily commitment to each other. She didn't always wake up excited about the relationship, but she did *sometimes*. And that was enough for her. At least for the moment.

Still, she didn't feel special. Not any more so than any of the families she knew whose children laid motionless, nearly lifeless in bed still. Why did her family deserve this? Looking at her parents engaging with her oldest son, it was tempting not to ask herself that question, but it was hard for it not to bubble to the surface. It was akin to Survivor's Guilt after a tragic accident, when the people who lived through a plane crash or a mass shooting could struggle to understand why they were among the few who didn't die. Each member of the Fraser family was a survivor of a tragedy that impacted the entire world. The scale of it all was unimaginable. Why them? It just seemed so random. But it couldn't be. Could it?

She felt a finger tap her shoulder and turned in the doorway to see Stephen standing behind her with his phone held up in front of him.

"You've gotta read this," he said.

"Read what?"

"It's about Kevin. I'm not sure this is gonna be good."

14

"No fucking *way*," Nathan's wife, Denise, pressed the phone against her shoulder with her right cheek as she pulled a glass out of the kitchen cabinet. "You're kidding."

She listened as she poured a shot of whiskey, and threw it back.

"That's unbelievable. Good for Kevin, I guess. But Laura doesn't deserve this. Why *her* kid? We lost Matthew years ago. He's not coming back, ya know? Your Penelope, rest in peace. All these families that have been through so much, why her?"

Denise paced around the living room, scooting across the hardwood floors as her friend talked and a stock ticker ran across the muted TV.

"Oh, I *know*. And that girl tried to get my Nate in bed," she said, her voice rising. "No, really. I swear to God. He's over there all the time, talking to those kids. I've been over to their house and had to play nice, but I could see it in her eyes, the way she looks at him, ya know? Hell, maybe she did bang him at some point. It's not like he'd tell me. But I *know* she tried."

She walked to the back door and unlocked it, stepping out onto their back deck that overlooked a two-acre plot of land. They had moved here a few years before, after turning Matthew over to the state. They had hoped the bigger house and large yard in neighboring Loudon County would help give them each the space they needed to keep their marriage alive, but it had only extinguished what little spark was left. Denise stayed because Nathan made good money and she didn't feel like starting over with someone else, and Nathan stayed because he didn't want to lose the house. He had spent years pushing for them to go to a marriage counselor; professional courtesy even meant they wouldn't have to pay a dime for the services if they went to someone he knew. But he'd given up on that after being stonewalled one too many times. They put on smiling public faces, but they hadn't slept in the same bed in at least eight months. They were more like estranged roommates than spouses at this point.

Denise got out a cigarette and stuck it between her lips. She lit it and puffed in the cool March air.

"Well, look, I'm happy for the boy. And I don't have anything against her husband. But it's bullshit that everybody's gonna think Laura's Mother of the Year now. I don't think I'm gonna be able to stand it."

She took a drag from the cigarette, flicking ashes onto the wood between her feet, then laughed.

"That's hilarious. I hope you do that," she said. "Oh. Yeah, that's fine. Thanks for calling. I seriously can't believe this. Yeah, yeah. Let's grab lunch soon. Sure. Okay, bye."

Denise shoved her phone into her pocket and took another deep drag, sucking the smoke into her lungs and holding it for a second before she exhaled. She wasn't much of a smoker these days, but she always kept a pack handy, hidden behind the coffee mugs in the kitchen cabinet. She knew Nathan would never find it there because he hated coffee with a white-hot passion, and he wouldn't drink it if Jesus himself walked up to him, rubbed his beard, and personally requested it. Nathan also hated when she smoked, but she mostly didn't even care at this point; she just didn't want to hear the shit he'd give her if he found out. The only times she smoked now, though, were when she needed something to calm her down; something about those nicotine sticks brought a sense of Zen to her mind. Between that and the whiskey, she felt like she could stare down a pack of wild dogs with no more than a yawn.

Hearing that Kevin woke up was a punch in the gut for her. That should have been her son. Not Laura, the woman she was convinced had been trying to break up her family for years. She was far too friendly with Nathan, and he spent too much time at their house. How much therapy could those kids actually need? Of course this was hard on them. It was hard on everybody. But it was like they were the biggest priority in Nathan's life. Or, at least, it seemed that way to Denise. She used to think she was paranoid until she started paying close attention to Laura when they went over there for dinner and drinks a few times. Denise knew "Fuck me" eyes when she saw them. Hell, she'd used those eyes plenty herself when she and Nathan were young and full of energy to roll around in bed all night. That seemed like a long time ago, but she wasn't about to let some other woman show her up like that, and play her for a fool.

So yeah, Denise felt like karma owed her a debt, and didn't owe Laura anything. But instead, it was Laura who got the jackpot to end all jackpots, while Denise sat alone in her big, empty house, staring out onto a barren expanse of dormant yellow grass and wondering why the life she planned had eluded her so thoroughly.

She pulled her phone back out of her pocket and tapped to spring it to life. She opened up the app for the "Knoxville Neighbors" message board, where people could post about anything happening in their community.

"Let's see if she likes a little attention," Denise said, taking another drag.

15

Sitting at the island, Laura stared at her laptop with wide eyes, rage boiling inside her. It hadn't taken long for news of Kevin's awakening to get out to the public. Busybodies chatted on message boards, where they could gossip and discuss the crazy and the mundane of their neighborhood with the seriousness of *Meet the Press* and the fact-checking prowess of *The National Enquirer*.

It could be fun rubbernecking when they were lamenting nine-year-olds wearing their pants too low on their waist, or accusing the local flower truck of being a front for some burglary scheme, but this time it was her Kevin they were talking about. And not just Kevin, but their entire family had been put on display, like exotic creatures behind plexiglass for them to ogle, examine, and laugh at. Most felt the need to express happiness for Kevin, but then so many launched into all sorts of stories about "those fucking Frasers." It was horrifying.

According to the comments, Laura was a godless slut and a drunk who brought even more drunks and crime to the town when she started "this stupid beer thing." Stephen was bad at his job, and was just waiting on the second kid to fall out before divorcing Laura. It was also apparently "extremely selfish" for them to have two kids when they knew the consequences, and a couple of people said Ryan was "weird."

It was infuriating to read, but Laura felt like she needed to at least know what was being said. And she needed to not let Ryan or Kevin anywhere near this site.

"This is incredible," she said, looking over her laptop at

Stephen sitting across from her, sipping on a soft drink. "Do we know who any of these people are?"

"You mean like PuffPass2017?"

Laura shrugged. "Well, yeah. Or…TheInBetween? That's who started the whole thread, and called me a bad mother."

"Good luck figuring out who's behind those stupid screen names."

"I *know*. It's just…How did they even find out so soon?"

"I don't know, but we haven't exactly kept the news inside the house. Nathan and Brent know. So does Amanda. Both our parents. Who knows who they told?"

"But they wouldn't. They're our friends…and family."

"We didn't swear them to secrecy, babe. It honestly didn't occur to me that it could get this ugly. Maybe it should have. Especially on an anonymous message board when IAmTheWalrus69 knows he can write whatever he wants without repercussions, but I just didn't see this coming. I thought people would be jealous, sure. But mostly happy, amazed, hopeful."

"Maybe they are. *Hopefully* they are. It's worth remembering this is just a small sliver of the people around here. A very *vocal* sliver. But a small one nonetheless. Let's not let this turn us into hermits or anything. There's a lot more good than bad out there. I believe that."

Stephen blinked.

"You don't?" she said.

He turned and looked at a drawing that was hanging on the wall in the kitchen. Ryan had made it six months earlier. He'd been trying to draw their family together, with Kevin awake. They were all standing in a row, holding hands. Stephen with his stringy black hair streaking in squiggly lines to both sides of his head. Laura beside him, a bit shorter, perky eyelashes pointing toward the sky and a marigold dress that seemed way too short for a family outing. Ryan was next, with a yellow smudge of hair atop his head and a striped shirt not quite drawn within the lines. Then there was Kevin—tall and slender. There was something haunting about him. He was the only one of the four Ryan hadn't colored flesh tone, leaving him white, with crooked stick arms and legs, and a mouth that didn't smile but sat there in a quizzical slant. Behind them, he'd drawn clouds in a dark gray hue. Five, six of them, hovering above like harbingers of doom watching over them. There was no sun.

Ryan had been so excited about his drawing that Stephen and Laura didn't think they had any choice but to tell him they loved it, and display it proudly. But whenever Stephen looked at it, he worried. He worried what Ryan had been thinking when he drew it, and what was creeping into his mind. He worried about what Ryan thought about Kevin. He worried those clouds were real.

He turned back to face Laura.

"Sure. Sure I do. It's just…"

"This is a little jarring?"

"That may be an understatement. I just didn't know everybody hated us so much."

Laura tilted her head. "Everybody doesn't hate us. They're jealous. It should have been them. Right? So many other people lost kids, and we're the only ones who got ours back. I'd be jealous too if it were them."

"But would you *hate* them like this?"

"It's not *hate*. It's…an expression of frustration. A lashing out. They can't fight against Mother Nature. They can't make their kids wake up. They can't make The Sleep go away. It makes them feel helpless, and now we become a target for them to direct all of that. Everybody's looking for someone to blame, but that someone doesn't really exist, so we're the closest thing, at least for the moment. They get to vent."

"You a psychologist now?"

Laura smiled. "Maybe. I *am* a bartender, which is basically the same thing."

"Yeah, well. Why don't you ply these people with some alcohol, and see if they come around?"

"That always works."

The doorbell rang, and they glanced at each other. As Laura rose to go to the door, Stephen's phone rang. Laura walked across the living room and put her hand on the doorknob. Normally, she'd just open it. But then the message board comments rattled through her head in a quick flash. She was sure it was temporary jealousy, aided by anonymity, and maybe a little drunkenness. Face to face, she was sure people would keep all of that in check. But, still, she wasn't willing to take that chance. This was a relatively small town without much crime, but she had a family to protect behind that door.

She stood tall and peered through the peephole.

"Who is it?"

"Laura! Is it true? Is it true about Kevin?" It was Chandra from next door. She had a son whom The Sleep had taken a few months earlier. Laura wouldn't call her a close friend, but they were friendly. They'd wave from their driveways when they were jumping in their cars. She always seemed nice enough. "I've got to know what you did. I'll do anything! Can I come in?"

Laura spun and looked back at Stephen, who was walking in her direction.

"It's the *News Press* on the phone," he whispered in her ear. "They want to come over and interview the family. Clearly, word is out."

He pulled back and spoke in a normal voice. "What's Chandra want?"

Ryan tugged on the tail of his grandfather's shirt.

"Pa-pa! Pa-pa!" he pleaded, hopping excitedly. "Look what I can do."

He got no response, as his grandfather remained fixated on Kevin, grinning madly and laughing as he and grandma talked to him incessantly.

It was like going back in time; suddenly, Ryan was the forgotten child again. Even his doting grandparents couldn't be bothered to acknowledge his presence.

Finally, after several tugs, his grandfather's head swiveled in his direction.

"What *is* it, Ryan?" he said, an annoyed edge to his voice. "We're trying to visit with your brother. We haven't seen him in a long time. You should be excited."

"I...I got a high score in my tower defense game!" Ryan held up his phone, with the high-score screen showing RBF at number one.

"That's great, little man. Why don't you climb up in Pa-Pa's lap, and let's catch up with your brother. You must be dying to tell him about how things are going."

Ryan's eyes narrowed, and the corners of his mouth buried themselves in his cheeks. "But he can't even *talk*."

His grandfather leaned down and grabbed him by both shoulders. His voice was a seething shout-whisper.

"That's *not nice*, Ryan. That's your *brother* in that bed. He's been asleep for a *long* time, and we all missed him very much. He can't help that he can't talk right now. He's doing his best, and you shouldn't be mean to him. He needs all the support we can give him right now. *Especially* from you. If you can't give him that, you probably shouldn't be here."

Ryan frowned and looked at the floor at his feet. He didn't know how to respond. Kevin charmed the pants off everyone when he could talk, and now he was doing the same when he could barely move a muscle. Ryan couldn't figure out if he was more upset because he'd disappointed Pa-Pa, or because he was once again being relegated to second-kid status.

He was glad to see Kevin back awake. He loved his brother. He had very much wanted him back. But part of him had hoped maybe something would have changed. Maybe he wouldn't be pushed aside quite so much this time. And, frankly, he'd gotten used to being the only living kid for a while. There hadn't been the same pressure to try and be like Kevin anymore, when "being like Kevin" meant lying lifeless on a hospital bed they bought used from a supply shop. Ryan finally had something that Kevin didn't—life. And, if he was honest, there was something nice about that.

Now that Kevin was back, though, it was like everyone forgot that he only had a few days left. His grandparents were prioritizing spending time with the newly awakened Kevin over the soon-to-be-sleeping Ryan.

Ryan started to shuffle out, when he heard footsteps coming toward the room. He looked up and saw his mom with Chandra from next door. Chandra squatted down in front of him.

"Hey, Ryan. How are you doin'? Give me a hug, young man," she put her arms around him and pulled him close as he imitated a dead fish. She let go and stood up, her hands on her hips as she looked at the bed. She looked back down at him. "Isn't it amazing that your big brother's awake? Miracle of miracles, I tell ya. Miracle of miracles. Thank Jesus."

"I was in here when he woke up!"

He wasn't sure why he said it. He just opened his mouth, and it came flying out like a sea of bats soaring off the belfry at sunset. Maybe he just wanted *someone* to be impressed by *something* he said or did. Wanted *someone* to pay attention to him. If it couldn't be his own family, maybe it could be Chandra. She bent down and put her hands on her knees.

"You *were*? What were you doing in here?"

Ryan shrugged and looked at the floor.

"Did you say or do anything?" she asked, then put her hands

on his arms. "This could be very important, Ryan. What was happening when Kevin woke up?"

Ryan's eyes met hers, and he froze. Suddenly, all the eyes in the room were focused on him, laser beams boring holes in his body. Now that he had their attention, he didn't want it anymore. He just wanted everyone to go back to what they were doing, back to ignoring him, letting him play his games and go about his day. He had towers to defend, barbarians at the gate to block. The people in the castle were counting on him. He couldn't let them down. Why couldn't everyone just let him go?

He shivered loose of Chandra's grip, then ran down the hall and into his room. He launched head first onto the bed, and yanked the covers up over his body, a cocoon where he could hide for a bit.

He didn't want to think back to the moment when Kevin awoke. Didn't want to think about it for another second.

16

Rolling over in bed, Laura tried to avoid looking at the clock. Through the curtain, she could tell the sun was just peeking over the horizon, at most, and that gave her a good enough gauge that she had no business being awake yet.

Getting her mind to shut down long enough to drift off had been nearly impossible, though. More than a few times, she'd nudged the covers off and padded lightly across the hall to peek in on Kevin. She didn't know what she was expecting to see. From across the room, there was little observable difference between a coma and a peaceful sleep. She tried to watch his chest. Was it rising more than before? Were his breaths deeper, more full of life?

Standing just inside his door, it occurred to her how much she wanted to hear him snoring—what a wonderful sound that would have been. Just a gentle purr, showing he was taking air in, and he was going to be fine.

Now, lying in bed, she was trying to resist another check-in on Kevin when she thought she heard a noise from outside, in front of the house. Not just a sound, but a variety of them. Metal clanging against metal. Car doors slamming. Murmuring voices.

She peeked at the clock, and it read 6:51. She wasn't sure why there was so much commotion on the street this early in the morning, and she was debating checking. If she got upset, she knew sleep would never come. On the other hand, maybe she needed to give up on that at this point anyway. Until she saw Kevin's eyes light up again, stress was going to win.

She looked over her shoulder at Stephen, lying on his right

side, a gentle wheeze from his throat suggesting he was sleeping soundly. *At least someone is*, she thought, a slight sneer crossing her lips.

Out of the corner of her eye, a bright light flashed, and she spun her head back around. It was coming from outside, cutting through the purple twilight. It wasn't shining directly on the window, as it appeared to be coming from ground level, but it was plenty strong enough to be noticeable from the second floor.

She swung her feet around and shoved them into her slippers by the bed. Cinching her nightgown tight across her chest, she padded over to the window. She grabbed the curtain and pulled it back just far enough to see outside, keeping her body hidden from view.

Even though Brent had warned them, and it was probably inevitable, it was still a shock to see—five news vans with large satellite dishes mounted on top, men with shoulder-mounted cameras, women with impossibly well-styled hair for the crack of dawn, and glaring lights making it look like midday in their front yard.

Two of the women were holding microphones, their backs to the house, cameramen a few feet in front of them. Laura couldn't hear what they were saying, but she figured she could probably recite the words: *"The medical community, and the world, is stunned today after hearing that, yesterday morning, in this house behind me, a child named Kevin became the first to wake up from The Sleep. He had been in a coma for approximately fifteen months, and he has a younger brother whose tenth birthday is approaching in just three days, according to sources. We've yet to hear anything directly from the family, but we'll bring it to you as soon as it's available."*

Word was definitely out. She guessed it would have been wishful thinking to imagine they could have kept it anything close to private. This was going to be just the beginning of the fishbowl they'd be dealing with for quite awhile, and she knew it.

She gently pulled the curtains back together so as not to draw any attention to the window, and walked back around to the other side of the bed. She nudged Stephen's shoulder, and he woke with a jolt.

"Stephen, the media's here. They're out front."

He rubbed his eye with the heel of his hand. "What? Already? What time is it?"

"It's seven. They've built a camp out front. It's what they do. But they only have whatever story we give them, okay? They can't make us say anything. We can keep Ryan and Kevin out of this, and I think we should. Things aren't gonna be easy for a while, but we can do this. It's gonna get worse before it gets better, but we'll be okay. Got it?"

Stephen pushed himself upright, and shook his head.

"Oh, and one more thing," Laura said. "Remember what I said about not letting this turn us into hermits?"

"Yeah."

"Well, we may have to be a little hermit-like after all."

"You wanna wake him up, don't you?" Stephen stirred a swirling circle of milk into his coffee.

Startled, Laura spun around, lifting her hand to her chest.

"Oh! You scared me." She was leaning against the wall next to the stairs, one foot on the first step, looking up toward Kevin's room.

A crooked grin crossed Stephen's face, and he took a sip. It burned against his lips and tongue as he swallowed, and his grin morphed into a puckered grimace.

"No. I don't want to wake him up," she said. "I was just…I was only looking up the stairs."

"And why were you looking up there?"

Her head turned toward the stairs, then back to him. "I don't…" She ground her teeth into her lower lip. "Okay, fine.

Yes, I want to wake my formerly comatose son up to make sure he's okay. Does that make me the world's worst mother?"

Stephen laughed and sat down in a stool on the other side of the island. "No. Not at all. It's actually kinda cute."

"Are you saying you *don't* want to? This isn't killing you?"

He nodded and took a sip. "It's...turning me inside out," he admitted. "I'm just trying not to think about it."

"I mean, we *could* go wake him. Just to see."

"When the CDC guy examined him last night, he told us not to. He seemed pretty serious about that. Said we need to let him get his rest, or we're going to exacerbate any problems he might have."

"Yeah, I know. It's just weird. The little guy's been lying in that bed for over a year. How much more rest could he need?"

"It's not like he's just been peacefully sleeping the whole time. He's not Rip Van Winkle."

"Sure. But it's hard. He's still the first. There's no one to look at and say, 'Maybe he'll be like that kid.' He *is* 'that kid.' *He's* who everyone's going to compare themselves to, if this thing is finally ending."

"Is it?

"Is it what?" she said.

"Finally ending."

She looked up the stairs and was quiet for a moment. Then: "I've been waiting over the past day, expecting we'd start hearing news of more kids waking up. Ya know? I was thinking...*hoping* he was the start of something. Maybe he still will be. Maybe those media vultures outside will tell us. But nothing yet. Of course, word hasn't been out long about Kevin, so maybe we wouldn't hear about it right away. Not unless the family starts telling people."

"Like we did?" Stephen smiled, and she laughed, slapping him on the shoulder.

"Sure, smarty. Like we did. I mean, people were gonna find out. I don't know what happens from here. But I do know, assuming he wakes up again, he's gonna give hope to a hell of a lot of families."

"Yeah, he will. I just hope that hope is well founded." He sipped his coffee. "You going to the brewery today?"

"Maybe I'll need to cover my head with a jacket like they do with perp walks on TV."

Stephen laughed. "That'd be fun to watch."

"But, yeah, whatever I do, I won't be going anywhere until that kiddo wakes up, I'll tell ya that much."

"What do we do if he doesn't?" Stephen put his coffee down and looked at her. His chest throbbed thinking about it.

"If he doesn't?"

"If he doesn't wake up. If…" He shrugged. "If yesterday was a fluke. Hell, maybe it's happened to other families, and they just haven't talked about it. I mean, nobody knows how this crazy Sleep works. What if he's *not* the first? What if other kids have awaken briefly, given their families fleeting hope, then fallen right back out again?"

Her eyes narrowed. "I don't like where your head's at this morning."

"I'm just trying to be realistic. What do we do then? What do we do if this is a cosmic tease of some kind? Can we handle that?"

Laura's eyes rolled around in her head, and she lowered her chin to her chest, taking in a deep breath. She swallowed hard, then looked back up.

"I don't know. Probably. Maybe. Technically, it doesn't have to be any different than it was before. We've been doing this for over a year; we could fall right back into that rhythm."

"But…?"

She nodded. "But it'd be hard. Probably harder than the first time. At least then, we *knew* it was coming. I mean, absolutely *knew* it. That was the deal. That was what we signed onto when we had these kids in the first place. We *knew* that was part of the contract."

"This is different, though."

"*Very* different. Now we don't know what to expect. He could go right back to the coma, or he could be a relatively normal kid from now on."

Upstairs, a bell clanged, the sound carrying downstairs. Laura and Stephen jumped to their feet and ran toward Kevin's room.

Stephen got there first, and turned the doorknob. Ryan came moping around the corner in his pajamas, rubbing his eyes.

"What's that noise?" Ryan said.

Stephen put his finger to his lips as Laura came up behind him. He could see the whites of Kevin's eyes through the darkness.

"I put a little bell on his chest while he was asleep," Laura said, a smile creasing her cheeks.

Stephen looked back at her. "Well, I guess that worked."

Laura tapped her temple with her finger and raised her eyebrows.

"Morning, tiger," Stephen said to Kevin, who gave a slight nod. Stephen walked to the bed; Laura and Ryan followed close behind.

Kevin looked like he was trying to say something. His lips were quivering a bit as he moved them, and he seemed to be struggling to make them work like he wanted. He pursed his lips, then let his mouth fall open. He did it again.

"Are you trying to tell us something, sweetie?" Laura said. "Do you need something?"

Again, his lips pursed, like he was preparing for a kiss, then they fell apart. There was the slightest sound of air being pushed out from between them, a quasi-whistle.

"Are you trying to say 'one'?" Stephen said, looking back at

Laura, who shrugged. "One what? One something?"

"Is that it, honey? One? Are you counting?" Laura turned to Stephen. "This has to be so frustrating for him. He can't say the word, and he doesn't have the strength to write. It's heartbreaking. I feel helpless."

Ryan's voice came from behind them. "He's saying 'Water.'" Their heads swiveled.

"What'd you say?" Stephen said.

"He's asking for water. Wa…Wa. He's thirsty."

They looked at each other, then at Kevin. His nod was barely perceptible, but it was there.

"I'll be damned," Laura said. "How'd you know that?"

"Lucky guess," Ryan shrugged and walked back out of the room.

"I'll get the water," Stephen said.

"Maybe get us some liquor while you're at it."

Laura smiled at Kevin and raised an index finger. "Your dad will be right back with some water, baby. Okay? I'm just gonna step out for a minute. So glad you're up."

She bent over and brushed his hair back from his forehead, then kissed him. She rose and walked to the doorway to look out and see Ryan go into his room and flop down on the bed, facing the ceiling. He quickly pulled out his phone and woke it up.

Laura glanced back at Kevin, then walked to Ryan's room and knocked on the doorframe.

"Can I come in, kiddo?"

He shrugged, not taking his eyes off the phone.

She sat down on the edge of the bed, feet pressed against the floor, trying to make eye contact with Ryan. His eyes weren't budging from the game.

"I think we should talk," she said, sitting down on the edge of the bed.

"Sure," he said, his eyes still on his game.

She kept trying to get his attention, but he was engrossed, his thumbs moving at blinding speed against the phone screen. She reached up and put her hand on the top of the phone to push it down, but he resisted, holding it where it was.

"You're gonna have to put that down, Ryan."

His shoulders slumped. "But I'm in the middle of a game!"

"I'm not asking. Put it down, or I'll take it away for a while. You want that?"

He frowned and tapped the Pause button, then laid it at his side. He crossed his arms tight against his chest.

"You have anything you want to tell me?" she asked. "You've been acting strange lately. Is there something wrong?"

Still frowning, he shook his head lightly. She took a deep breath.

"You were in the room with your brother when he woke up. We heard you scream. What happened? Do you know what made him wake up?"

He looked at her for the first time, his eyebrows pressing together, eyes narrowing. She thought he looked immeasurably older than his not-quite-ten years. His face gained lines she'd never seen before, carrying the weight of a life much more lived than his.

"Why?" Tears welled up in his eyes. She laid her hand on his.

"Why...what? What do you mean, honey?"

"Why me?" They were trickling down both cheeks, and he sat up to face her.

"Oh, baby. I...don't understand your question. I want to help, but I can't unless you tell me more."

He grabbed her shoulders to pull her toward him. She leaned in and wrapped her arms around him, lifting him into her lap and rubbing his hair as he sobbed.

"Shh...Shh...It's okay. It's all right. You know your dad and I love you. We'll do anything for you. Just hang in there, okay?"

Laura felt helpless, holding her youngest son as he wept, and not only not knowing how to fix his problem, but not even knowing how to figure out what the problem was in the first place. Ryan wasn't all that talkative to begin with, but he'd become even more withdrawn in the twenty-four hours or so since Kevin had woke up from The Sleep.

Was it just shock at seeing his brother back awake? Concern over his own fate? She didn't know. And there was still the weird episode he'd had prior to that, when he nearly threw himself out the window. Did that tie into this somehow? She would have thought Kevin waking up would have brought elation to her family, and it did, but that seemed to have been short lived. Now, she was feeling her son's tears soak through to her skin, watching his chest heave as he sobbed, and Kevin was a long way from even leaving his bed.

Both of her sons were trying to communicate with her, but she couldn't understand either one. She felt disconnected, from her children, her life, her marriage, the world around her. This wasn't the life she'd planned as a little girl, playing with dolls between her chemistry set and beating the boys at basketball. Lots of adults called Laura a tomboy growing up, but she'd loved playing house when she was alone in her room, dreaming of a big family, a house full of her own kids. She'd be the smart mom, the one who could whisk away problems in the blink of an eye, cook a delicious meal, then also teach her daughter how to take a jump shot. Super Mom, with a lab coat and a pair of gym shorts. She'd do it all.

And she had her brewery. She'd made a career out of chemistry, lived the dream of a devoted husband and two kids she loved more than anything in this world. But as she approached the end of high school, The Sleep had changed everything when it began to take hold around the world, to the point that the decision to have kids at all had been a tough one. She couldn't honestly say she never regretted it. It was a decision she questioned herself about nearly every day, and there was no shortage of people in the world who considered it irresponsible to have kids. And if you, as a parent, didn't question yourself on your own, they'd make sure to plant those questions in your head.

The suffering her sons were going through, and her inability to help, made it so much worse. For much of their lives, Laura and Stephen had been able to act like The Sleep wasn't all that real, that it was just this thing in the far-flung future, something they didn't have to worry about. They'd cross that bridge when they came to it. Then it came, and they planted Kevin in a bed, closed the door, and tried to ignore it as best as they could, hiding the reality of it from Ryan to whatever extent was possible. They told themselves that was for the best, that Ryan wasn't equipped to handle it, that they'd just be causing him unnecessary worry.

Of course, that didn't prevent Ryan from knowing what was going on. That didn't do anything to keep him from seeing his brother lying there, wires and tubes coming out of him like he was more machine than boy. Maybe confronting it head on would have been the better choice. Maybe they'd made it worse by trying to shield him from it. Maybe. That decision was behind them, though.

Stephen peeked his head into the room. "I got Kevin his water. Everything okay?"

"Call Nathan. Get him over here ASAP."

"What's wrong?"

She looked down at the top of Ryan's head and kissed it, pulling him tighter to her chest, then looked back at Stephen, shaking her head.

"I have no idea."

17

Lying on a brown plush leather couch, her head sunk deep into a feather pillow and her knees bent in front of her, Denise read through the most recent posts in the fifty-seven-page "Knoxville Neighbors" message board thread about the Frasers and Kevin's awakening.

KnoxTitan87
Are we still sure this kid's the only one who's woken up? Would we even know if random kids in some backwater Middle East or Africa country suddenly burst out of the coma? Maybe he's just the only one the news has any clue of so far.

ScruffyJoeyN
The government controls this whole thing. Anybody who's paying attention knows that. They're choosing who lives and who dies. You think they couldn't have cured this shit a decade ago if they wanted to? Of course they could have. They've been sitting on a cure for years. But this is good for business. We're all so focused on this one so-called "disease" that nobody pays any attention to all the corruption going on in Washington. It's a huge distraction, while they steal the country out from underneath us. All of you are playing right along with it. If we wait them out, they're gonna have to put the cure out there soon just to keep the human race going. Mark my words: They'll "find" the cure just in the nick of time, and they'll hail themselves as heroes. Fuck them all.

PuffPass2017

@KnoxTitan87 Believe me, this has been the biggest story in the god damn world for two fucking decades. If there were other kids waking up, we'd hear about it. This Kevin kid's the only one so far, and there's no sign of it spreading. And, I mean, good for him and his family. But it's also kind of ridiculous. Why just him? It just doesn't make any fucking sense. After 20 years, this one Knoxville kid just wakes up? There's something weird going on, I'm sure of that much. As always, I think @ScruffyJoeyN is smoking something even stronger than I am, but that doesn't mean he's not at least thinking in the right direction.

HarrySignfeldTime

I can't believe what I'm reading here. Shouldn't we just be happy for the family? It's a damn miracle, is what it is. We shouldn't be jealous or make up all these crazy conspiracy theories. Maybe this is a sign from God that he has good work to do in Knoxville. Maybe more kids will wake up, if we give it a little more time. Or maybe there's something we can learn from this kid, and this family. Are they Christian? Is there something they've done that we should emulate? We should embrace them as our friends and neighbors, and see what they can offer. I worry about the tone we're setting here. Just my 2 cents.

DMshallWin

@HarrySignfeldTime I don't know how well anybody else on here knows the family, but I can vouch for the fact that they're not good Christian people, and I don't know of anything we can learn from them. I've been to their house. The husband and kids are OK enough, but the wife has problems. You know? Mental. Seriously. I've seen her scream at the top of her lungs at her kids for nothing. Just stuff like not putting the dishes away as quickly as she wants. It's nuts. And, not to gossip or anything, but she sleeps around like it's nothing. Her husband has no idea. None. He's pleasant enough, but he's clueless. I'm pretty sure they don't even go to church. I've never seen them say grace before a meal, or heard them mention going to service. I get what you're saying, Harry, but this isn't the family for that.

PaulBetweenYall
I don't know this family at all, but this can't just be a fluky thing, can it? I mean, if this kid really is the only one in the whole damn world who woke up, that can't be a coincidence. Haven't the doctors said this could be about the kids not having hope for the future, and their bodies shut down? Nobody really understands this, but that's the closest to an explanation we've gotten. It was documented many years ago in Sweden, I think, that can happen. So does this kid have some sudden reason for hope? If so, what brought that on? What changed? I think that's the question.

KnoxTitan87
@PaulBetweenYall That is a good question, honestly. If we assume he's the only one, why? To pretend it's just random occurrence doesn't make much sense. There's got to be a reason that one out of hundreds of millions just suddenly woke up like it was nothing. Of course, I don't have much confidence the doctors know shit. But if it actually is a matter of hope, does this kid have some now? He clearly didn't a year ago, or whenever he dropped out. He does today, though? Why?

TheInBetween
@DMshallWin You shouldn't talk like that about that family. That's really mean. How would u feel if someone said that about u?

PaulBetweenYall
@KnoxTitan87 Exactly. But here's the thing…They've said nothing publicly since this happened, right? Maybe they even know, but they're hiding it. They've got another kid heading toward The Sleep himself. Are they afraid if they give their secret away that their next kid will fall victim? I'm just asking questions here, but the key is that it's essential that we get this answer for the sake not just of our kids, and not just the world's kids, but all of fucking humanity. And I'm not being melodramatic. Those seriously are the stakes. If they were to disappear without telling us what they might know, our entire species goes extinct in another 10 years.

IAmTheWalrus69
@KnoxTitan87 @PaulBetweenYall Honestly, I think some of us should go over there and check them out. See what they have to say. I'm not suggesting we do anything crazy, but a show of solidarity couldn't hurt, to impress upon them how important this is, and how many of us there are. How many of us have kids who have been impacted by this? Or will soon? Or have loved ones whose kids have been? Pretty much all of us, right? If they're sitting on the secret to solving this puzzle nobody else has solved, we need to know. Like, right fucking now. There's no time to wait for them to get their house in order, or celebrate with their kid, or whatever they're doing now. They need to be confronted.

DMshallWin
What are you guys gonna do? Break the door down? Do you actually think they'll just let you inside? I wouldn't let some mob inside my house, especially if I had kids. I hate that woman's guts, but she's not dumb enough to open the door for a bunch of crazies practically marching up there with pitchforks. You might want to be a bit more subtle.

@TheInBetween How would I feel? If I were the tramp she is, I'd feel like I deserved it. That's how. The rest of the family, I've got no beef with.

KnoxTitan87

@PaulBetweenYall I think @IAmTheWalrus69 is onto something there. We don't know them. If we sit back and wait for them to do the right thing here, we might be waiting a long damn time. I'm not saying we should do anything rash, @DMshallWin. We don't need to go in there looking for a fight. We just need to get some answers. We owe it to our own kids, and the kids of parents around the world. They can't all make a pilgrimage to Knoxville. If there's some information the Frasers have that could help, I think we have a responsibility to get it.

PuffPass2017

@KnoxTitan87 @IAmTheWalrus69 @PaulBetweenYall I'd be in for going over there. We should try to get together a good group of people. Anybody you know, especially those who have kids, let's get them to head that way. I say we organize this ASAP. Like, today. There really isn't any sense wasting time. But I do kind of agree with @DMshallWin in that we shouldn't just march a bunch of strangers up to their door like we own the place. At best, we're gonna spook them. At worst, who the hell knows? Do they have guns in the house? I know I'd be itching for my shotgun if a big gang of people started gathering threateningly in front of my house, and asking questions about my kids. We need an in with them. Who would they trust? Maybe somebody else can get us in.

DMshallWin

@PuffPass2017 I don't know about getting all the rest of you in, but I can talk myself in. I'm sure of it. They know me. Even the wife doesn't know I want her to drop dead. I can smile through gritted teeth with the best of 'em. Maybe I could just go up there and see for myself, and report back here.

PaulBetweenYall
@DMshallWin No offense, but I'm not convinced that's enough. We need a show of force, or we risk losing everything. The stakes are too high to leave this up to chance. I mean, look, I agree with everybody else here that we don't need to be armed or anything. Let's not freak them the fuck out. But we need more than just one person there, or they can just blow us off. I agree with @IAmTheWalrus69 on that. Just a calm group of concerned citizens. If @DMshallWin feels like she should be the one to go up to the door, that's fine by me. The rest of us can hang back, or she can bring one or two people with her up there. But I'm not leaving this up to some message board person I've never met before. These are our kids. This is our future. We're gonna be a part of it. We're taking a stand. I'm making some calls right now. You guys with me? Let's shoot for 2 pm.

DMshallWin
@PaulBetweenYall I should be able to do 2. Their street, Cannondale, is short. So let's all meet on Penwood, the next street up, and we can coordinate from there. Get whoever you can to join us. See you guys in a few hours.

18

Laura pressed the top of the glass down against the rinser, and water shot up, cascading down the sides of the glass. In addition to rinsing it clean, this also made the inside of the glass more slippery, helping the next beer pour more evenly with a thick, fragrant head on top. These are the details Laura was obsessed with and, she believed, were part of why her brewery had persevered—and even, at times, thrived—in a tough business environment.

She tilted the glass at a forty-five-degree angle underneath the tap, letting the beer flow against the side, allowing the head to gather diagonally from the bottom. Around halfway through the pour, she brought the glass back to vertical to finish it off at the top with a clean, white head. She had done this tens of thousands of times, but she still got a lot of satisfaction from getting it right, then presenting it to the customer.

"Brownlow Brown," she said as she put it down on the bar. "Tab's under Walter, right?"

"You got it."

After the difficult morning with Ryan, she knew she had to get out of the house for a while. Stephen told her he'd catch Nathan up when he got there, and she was thankful for the escape, though she worried the brewery wouldn't be a refuge too much longer. The spotlight on her and her family was going to get brighter over the coming days and weeks; that much, she knew. The question was how overwhelming and intrusive it would become. Police had even called with an offer to station an officer outside the house as protection—given the importance of keeping Kevin safe—but

Laura declined, not wanting their home to feel even more like a prison than it already did at times.

This afternoon, there was no crush of media frenzy and people wanting to tear off a chunk of her to take home as a souvenir, but there were a few choruses of "I saw the report about your kid this morning. That's amazing!" And, out of the corner of her eye, she was sure she saw several people sneakily snapping pictures of her, no doubt going straight to their Instagram page so they could brag to their friends they were looking at the mom of the world's only conscious 11-year-old boy.

Laura felt like she was being watched by everyone, like she was losing control, and that was a feeling she despised. But if this was as bad as the public attention got, she figured she could deal with it—for a few days or weeks, at least. If nothing else, it was nice to look out over the bar and see the place as busy as it'd been in awhile.

Her staff was in controlled-chaos mode, filling out flight cards for those who wanted to sample six small pours, changing out kegs after one kicked, pulling out crates of clean glassware from the back, and washing some by hand when needed. One typical aspect of a bar that they didn't have to deal with was changing television channels, because she'd made the decision from the outset not to have TVs at Palmyra. She took a hit occasionally, though it was less every year as the quality of professional sports eroded with no young players coming up to fill in for the older ones retiring. Still, sometimes, someone would sit down at the bar and look around, puzzled, asking where their TVs were. When staff would tell them they didn't have one, that person—almost always a man—would sometimes huff and walk out. Laura was willing to live with that because she felt like there needed to be a bar in town that took a stand for lively conversation and being present in the moment. She thought her regular patrons would appreciate that, and she'd attract a crowd that wanted to escape the reduced but still-present whine of sporting events in the background. That Palmyra would provide at least one oasis for the people who didn't care about staring at a screen, who just wanted to enjoy a pint with their friends or meet a few new ones. And on that point, she'd been right.

Laura also felt it was important that the staff saw she was willing to do the grunt work when needed—pour beers, wash glassware, switch out a keg, bus a table—because it quashed any excuses they had not to do it themselves. She could set the example. If the owner's working *that* hard, I better bust my ass even more. And they typically did.

No matter how long she owned the place, she hoped she'd always be grateful for her crew working hard, making the place run. When she first started Palmyra, she never took a day off if the brewery was open. She kept it closed on Mondays, mostly because she—and the staff—needed a day to rest, and that day sure as hell wasn't going to be a weekend. Mondays were slow days in the hospitality industry anyway, and she was far from the only bar in town to take that day off. They wouldn't open until five on Christmas and Thanksgiving. Other than that, they did normal hours throughout the year. It had been brutal on her, physically and mentally, but this was her baby, and it was going to rise or fall on her hard work, not someone else's. After close to three years, she finally felt comfortable enough with her staff to take off on her tenth wedding anniversary. She'd resisted calling and checking in throughout the night, as she enjoyed a lobster tail for dinner, and gasped when Stephen slid a green sapphire ring on her finger. Laura didn't wear jewelry outside of her wedding ring on a regular basis—and she even typically slipped that off at work, when she remembered—but she took every opportunity she could to wear that ring. It was simple, with no diamonds, and the deep green that could nearly pass for a sparkling black was her favorite color. He'd done well.

When she'd walked into the bar the next morning, everything was in its place. There were no fires to put out. No complaints lodged. In fact, she'd remarked to Stephen later that the place looked cleaner than it had been since it first opened. She suspected the staff stayed later than usual, making sure everything was spotless so she'd know they had her back. That was when she learned to trust and let go—just a little bit, of course.

Stephen brought the spoonful of applesauce to Kevin's mouth, and slid it between his lips. While Kevin wasn't ready for solid foods, he'd taken fairly quickly to food he didn't have to chew. Brent told Stephen that was a good sign, and they could keep the IV out as long as Kevin was willing to eat *something*. So, Stephen went to the store and got all the applesauce, yogurt, and fruit drinks he could fit into the basket. They were going to do all they could to build his strength back up.

It was hard seeing his son like this, but he kept reminding himself how much worse it could be. And, all in all, Kevin seemed to be in good spirits, for a kid who could barely move and couldn't talk. He was breathing normally without the respirator, and could control his head enough to make a slight nod or shake in order to communicate Yes and No. He could move his fingers a little bit, and he could slowly wiggle his toes. Brent had been pleased with the progress so far, and said it was about as much as they could have hoped for this soon. He was going to continue making regular stops by the house just to check on how Kevin was doing, but he liked where they stood.

Stephen was looking forward to the day he could get Kevin into the gym downstairs and get his muscles some work. He'd worked with some patients who required deep rehabilitation before, but nothing on this level. In the back of his mind, he'd always wanted to try, to see if he had the skill, discipline, and bedside manner to coax a body back from the brink of death like that. For his first attempt to come with his own son felt daunting, but he was sure the sense of accomplishment would be beyond what he'd experienced before.

Then there was Ryan down the hall. Stephen didn't get much of an explanation from Laura before she'd left, only that Ryan was stressed and needed to talk to Nathan. Stephen called him, and he said he had another patient to see in the afternoon; he'd come over to speak to Ryan after that. Stephen worried about Ryan; he didn't always understand or feel close to his youngest son. Their personalities seemed similar, but he still didn't have a sense of what Ryan was thinking most of the time. When Stephen had been a kid, there were no cell phone games to immerse yourself in. He came of age curled up in a ball in the corner of his room, reading *Huckleberry Finn* and *Tom Sawyer* a dozen times, imagining what it would be like to hop on a raft and float down the Tennessee River, letting the current grab ahold of you, soaking in the sour fragrance of the cypress as you coasted through a swamp, the air so thick you felt you had to dodge it. It was a life he'd spent countless hours fantasizing about. Even so, he didn't think he'd ever felt as isolated as Ryan sometimes acted. On the other hand, he also didn't have anything weighing as much on him at nine as Ryan had, with the reality of effective death stalking him like a shadow, never leaving his side; the sun might duck behind a cloud, but the disappearance of your shadow was merely a temporary illusion. It was always there, waiting for its next opportunity.

So, they tried to understand the challenge Ryan had to face, and Stephen learned to give him his space, with Laura's help. And that was what he was trying to do while feeding Kevin. He hoped Nathan would be able to give him some more answers.

Stephen was lifting the spoon up to Kevin again when the doorbell rang.

Hopefully, it's Nathan, he thought as he pushed the spoon into

THE LITTLE TRAGEDY

Kevin's mouth, put down the jar and started walking downstairs. *And hopefully that horde of media didn't tackle him in the grass on the way.*

From the bottom of the stairs, he could hear the commotion coming from the front yard, the desperate TV reporters and bloggers spotting a person approaching the house and looking to get some sort of sound byte or video clip that would go viral. The sound swelled and got closer, and Stephen winced at the idea of Nathan having to elbow his way through the crowd. But he'd warned Nathan about the situation, so maybe he'd been prepared to stay silent and keep his head down.

Stephen raced across the front room and peeked between the curtains; he could tell the amount of media had grown, maybe double or triple what it'd been when Laura left. They were crushing together into one amorphous blob, at least twenty men and women, cameras and microphones outstretched, pushing toward the front porch, yelling over each other. It was surreal. Stephen wondered how long this would last, and how long they could take it. Just a few days before, they'd have never imagined they'd be this damn interesting. He longed to be dull again.

Wanting to rescue Nathan as soon as he could, Stephen scampered toward the door and opened it. But it wasn't Nathan he saw standing on the porch. His chest tightened, and his vision turned into a thousand blinding lights as cameras clicked.

19

Nathan hit his turn signal and moved into the right lane, approaching the I-140 exit for the Frasers' house. His previous patient had run long, but he was anxious to get back to check on not only Ryan but Kevin too.

For the child psychologist of his time, this was basically the jackpot. He'd put in the work for many years with this family, and now they happened to be the first ones to have a kid wake up. There were opportunities for celebrity for him. He'd be the child psychologist who worked with the first child who was cured; people would ask him what he did with them, what the family was like. He could see a book deal in the future, and plenty of chances to tell his story.

Not that his only focus was on cashing in on the Frasers' good fortune or anything. Of course he cared about Ryan and Kevin, and the whole family. He was determined to do his job, and try to help them deal with the stress that had to be building.

But this was also a big challenge. There was no textbook written on how to counsel children in a household where one of the siblings emerged from The Sleep. The basic step of simply trying to provide a comforting environment for them to speak their mind, and offer advice where needed, would help. But Nathan was going into these conversations without an idea of where they might lead. There was no profile for this. It was an opportunity to confront a completely new situation, for him to become an expert in a unique aspect of abnormal psychology. For a geek of the human psyche, that was exciting. And he couldn't help but also anticipate the attention that might come along with it.

As he turned the corner onto Cannondale, he saw a crowd spilling into the street in front of the Frasers' house, and the growing sound was carrying up the hill. There were media trucks with various TV station logos—some he recognized as local, but many he'd never seen before—parked along the street almost to where he'd stopped. He could see people being interviewed, some sitting on curbs, a few looking angry. Down the street, he could see neighbors outside, sitting on the porch taking in the show or standing on their grass, mouths agape, phone pressed to their ear.

Stephen had told him to expect a media throng, but this was far more of a circus than he'd anticipated. Who were all these people talking to the press in front of their house? Surely it wasn't just curious neighbors. All he knew was that Ryan needed him, and he needed to get inside the house, even if he had to fight off a crowd to do it.

His head wrenched away from the cameras and tucked into the crook of his left arm, Stephen extended his hand toward Denise, and she grabbed it. He pulled her inside and slammed the door shut. He could still hear the questions being yelled from outside as he bent at the waist, trying to get his breathing back under control. Denise stood straight and smoothed out the wrinkles in her red dress, then walked over and pressed the curtains together to make sure they were tightly shut on the window by Nathan's chair, and did the same for the other window in the corner of the room.

"That should give us some privacy," Denise said. "They'll calm down after a few minutes if we don't give them any faces to look at. Are you okay?"

Stephen could feel his head starting to pound, but his heart rate was slowing to something approaching normal.

"I...think so." He stood up straighter, and took a deep breath. "I hate that you had to fight your way through that. It's a surprise to see you. I assume you're not just stopping by to chat."

"Well, yes and no," Denise said. "I'm not here to swap recipes or anything, ya know? But it *is* important that we talk. Today. Now."

"I guess so, if you were willing to go through that to get here. Is something wrong? I mean, something other than the obvious." Stephen cocked his head toward the window.

Denise closed her eyes and licked her lips. She took a deep breath, the air whistling lightly into her nose, and she sat on the couch.

"There's a group of people on their way here. Knoxville people. Neighbors. I'm serving as a liaison of sorts, trying to help...let's say, smooth out the situation."

Stephen's heart began to pick up its pace again, and his head throbbed. He swallowed hard.

"You're leading a *mob* to my house?"

"No, no." She raised her arms in front of her and waved her hands dismissively. "Nothing like that. This is neighbors talking to neighbors. Everything's fine."

"Then why are they coming here?"

She sighed, then smiled wide. "Well, of course, it's about Kevin. We're all thrilled for you that he woke up. Such a miracle! You must be the happiest you've ever been."

He nodded. "It's been a good couple of days, having him back. We never expected it. But what does this have to do with a mob coming to my house?"

"There's that word again: 'mob.' Let's not look at it that way, Stephen. Really. This doesn't have to be negative. We're all on the same side here. I promise."

"When is this happening, Denise? Today? Tomorrow? Do I have time to get the kids out of here?"

The noise that had calmed down outside was picking up again. This time, though, it seemed to be moving *away* from the house. The shouts and stampeding feet were going toward the road.

Denise's smile was becoming nauseating.

"Okay, Stephen. I understand that you're upset. But I came here as a courtesy, because you're a friend of our family. I wanted to get out in front of this."

Stephen's head pivoted quickly to the window. "They're coming now, aren't they?"

"I understand your right to and desire for privacy. I get that. If it were my son—" She paused and shut her eyes, looking down and taking several quick breaths, followed by one deep one. "If it were my son, I'm sure I'd want the same thing, ya know? But many of these people have *their own* children. They can sympathize. They're concerned with the future of our entire *species*. Your story could save not just lives, but the world as we *know* it. Your story needs to be told."

"What do you mean 'our story'?" Stephen's voice raised an octave as he tried to resist yanking the curtains open. "There's nothing to tell!"

"Think. Not just for your concerned neighbors. For every kid, *everywhere*. Tens of millions of families. If you can come up with *anything*, think about the impact it could have around the world. You could change the course of history with a few words."

She stood and walked over to him, staring into his eyes.

"I understand. I really do. It's been crazy. I get that. But think. Is there *anything* you can come up with that *might* have triggered him waking up? Anything at all?"

It wasn't as if the question were completely new to Stephen. They'd pondered it. In fact, it was a question that had hung over their head for the previous thirty hours or so—Why Kevin? Why them? He didn't have any answer he felt remotely confident in. The only clue he had was that Ryan was in the room when Kevin woke up. Ryan had been acting strangely before that. And one thing had stuck with Stephen since that day when he pulled Ryan back inside. When he asked Ryan why he had been climbing out the window, he said, "To get to Kevin."

That phrase still ate at him. What had Ryan meant? What was driving him to nearly plummet to his death? Did he actually think Kevin was out there? If so, was it as simple as a stress-induced hallucination, or was there something more going on?

What Stephen didn't want to do was put more stress on Ryan. If he told Denise that Ryan may have had a part in Kevin waking up, there was no telling how many more people might find out. Stephen didn't think Ryan could handle that. Especially not in his current state. But Ryan was an introvert anyway. It was Stephen's job to protect his children, and he didn't want their lives to be a circus. He needed to be their shield against the world. He needed an answer that had nothing to do with Ryan, so maybe they'd all go away.

"Well, there is one thing," Stephen murmured, the noise outside growing louder. "We've thought it was a long shot, so we haven't mentioned it. I don't know *why* it could've worked, but it's as good a guess as any, I suppose."

"That's great, Stephen. What is it?"

"A couple of weeks before Kevin woke up, we started reading nursery rhymes and singing lullabies to him each night. We didn't think he could even hear us. It was just soothing for us, I think. He'd been out for quite awhile, and Ryan's getting up there too, and we didn't know what the future held. So I thought it was more for us than for him. Just something to feel like our baby was our baby again, ya know?"

She nodded, both her hands resting on top of his.

"It was silly stuff like 'Hickory Dickory Dock' and 'Jack and Jill' and 'Rock A Bye, Baby.' That kinda thing. I can't think of any good reason *why* it would have caused him to wake up. It doesn't make any sense. But it's something we did that was different from what we'd done. There's no medical reason that I know of for that to be effective. But the result is…" He smiled and paused for a moment. "We've got our son back."

Nathan began walking down the hill toward the Fraser house, staying on the outside of the TV vans for cover, skipping quickly from one to the next. The closer he could get to the house before anyone saw him, the better a chance he thought he'd have to make it to the front door. As he crept toward the front of the WBIR-TV van, he was at the Frasers' driveway, and he could get a full picture of the craziness unfolding there—reporters running from one person to the next, getting quotes and photos. He could envision the headlines: "Chaos Reigns After Fraser Son Wakes."

He got out his phone and dialed Stephen's cell number, but hung up when he got no answer after the eighth ring. He considered going back to his car and getting the hell out of there, but he felt an obligation to Ryan, to the family. He'd been with them through so much, and Stephen was clearly worried when he called earlier. There was something wrong, and that was what Nathan had signed up to deal with. Any doctor could handle problems that were easy. The true test of anyone's mettle was how they handled situations that challenged them. Nathan believed that.

The sound of quiet conversations interspersed with shouts reverberated around him as he pressed his back against the news van. One peek around the corner made him think there was no way he'd make it to the front door without being harassed, blocked, and possibly even assaulted; these random people in the yard didn't look like they were there to have a picnic and fly a kite. He knew there was a back door behind the fence that they usually left unlocked when they were awake to encourage the reclusive Ryan to play outside. It was possible they'd locked it when they saw a horde gathering on their front lawn, but it was also possible they hadn't thought about it.

He inched quietly to the rear of the van and looked over to the side of the house. The chaotic scene seemed mostly confined to the front yard. There was some spillover to the side, but the path over there looked far less daunting. He crouched and slipped along to the next van up the street in order to get a better angle at the fence he knew he'd probably have to scale. One more peek around the back of the van helped him plan his route, as straight as possible around the outer edges of the crowd, hopefully unnoticed by most of the people, who'd be too distracted to see a man dashing across their peripheral vision. He was wearing suede loafers—not the greatest running shoes, as he hadn't exactly been planning a sprint at any point that afternoon—but they'd have to do.

Nathan took three deep breaths, counted to three, then ran, eyes fixed on the fence maybe fifty feet in front of him. He could feel some eyes turn toward him, and a couple of men spun in his direction, one pointing at him with his mouth curled in a scowl. That man began moving into Nathan's path, possibly to knock him off his feet, but Nathan bowed out a little further, skirting the man's right shoulder by inches. As he reached the side of the house, he could feel eyes staring him down; he started timing his steps to be able to jump up the side of the fence. A few feet away, he leapt and stretched his arms over the top of the fence, pressing his feet against the bottom half of it in order to secure himself; a couple of men ran for him. He hoisted himself up, bringing his chest above the top of the fence, his feet pushing against a notch in the wood below. He could hear the men approaching, but he didn't want to look back.

He lifted himself a little higher and then felt a tug on his foot. One of the men had ahold of his right shoe and was trying to drag him back down. Nathan shook his foot, trying to loosen the man's grip or maybe kick him in the head. But he couldn't see where he was kicking, and nothing was connecting. He could feel the shoe starting to shake free. He pushed down with his toes, forcing the shoe down off his heel. The man's grip freed from his foot, the shoe fell to the ground. Nathan quickly lifted both his legs as high as he could, getting one knee on top of the fence and turning until he was lying prone against the top of it. The men were jumping for him, but he was holding his left leg as high as possible, pressing it against the fence for extra support.

Nathan saw one of the men take a couple of steps back and wave his arm to clear himself some space to jump. Nathan knew he only had a couple more seconds. He let his right leg hang limp over the inside of the fence and rolled in that direction, his left leg coming up with him as the man leapt, his arms hitting the fence where Nathan had been. Just as the man's hands gripped the top, Nathan let himself drop, and he hit the ground with a thud, falling backward and his tailbone connecting harder than he expected on the dry, packed soil.

He stood, brushed himself off, and ran to the back door. He heard another man hit the fence in the same way as the last, and he figured he didn't have much time before more would be over it behind him. He got to the door and turned the handle; the door pushed open. He pulled it shut behind him and turned the lock, then closed the curtains on the door's window.

Nathan navigated the back part of the house, shuffling through the kitchen and coming around to the living room, where Stephen and Denise were standing, looking at him in alarm.

"What the hell are you doing here?" Nathan asked his wife, eyes narrowed, feet frozen in place.

Denise stood, her limbs stiff, eyes firing wildly, looking across the room at her husband. For several seconds, she said nothing, just meeting his eyes, the two of them barely moving.

Then, finally: "I'm trying to deal with a situation. You might have noticed it's not the most normal of days around here. But I got what I needed. You do what you need to do, Nate."

She pivoted and walked to the front door, grabbing the doorknob, then stopped. She spun back to look at Nathan.

"Despite what you saw out there, we're on the same side here. I want you both to know that. I don't want any of this to get ugly. Keep that in mind, Stephen." She locked eyes with Stephen for a moment and nodded slightly, then turned her head. "Nathan."

Without waiting for a response, she opened the door and stepped out to the front porch. A few minutes later, Stephen could hear the crowd mumbling as the people wandered back where they came from, reporters still shouting questions.

"How's it going, big guy?" Nathan said, pulling a chair up beside Ryan's bed.

His phone set beside him on the blanket, Ryan leaned forward. "Not bad." He shrugged. "Just another day."

Nathan smiled. "Just another day? There was a good bit of commotion downstairs just a few minutes ago."

Ryan raised his eyebrows. "Was there?"

"You didn't hear anything?"

He shrugged again. "I was playing my game before you came. I get pretty into it."

"Yeah. Yeah, I know. Still playing tower defense?"

Ryan looked down at the bed and scratched his leg. He offered no answer.

"It's okay. I'm not judging or anything. It's just...a lot of out-of-the-ordinary stuff has been happening. You're not scared by any of it?"

Ryan shook his head, keeping his eyes down.

"Not a lot of people know you like I do, Ryan. And I'm not buying this. Your mom says something's bothering you, and I think you're holding out on me. You know that whatever we talk about in here stays in here. That's our deal, right? I don't tell your parents anything you don't want me to. You trust me, right?"

His shoulders first jolting, then relaxing, Ryan's eyes dropped again.

"There's *something* you're not telling me, Ryan. Does it have to do with Kevin? Look, if him waking up is stressing you out, I understand. You're in a weird position. It's not telling you anything you don't know to say The Sleep isn't far away for you. It's totally understandable for you to be worried about that. That doesn't mean you don't love your brother. I'd be worried about it if I were you, too. But you've got to talk about it. If you bottle everything up, it's only going to make it worse."

For several moments, they sat quietly. Ryan rocked slightly on the bed, his legs crossed in front of him, arms dropped like anvils between his knees. Nathan leaned back in his chair, trying to look casual, like he could wait a year if he needed to.

Ryan ran a hand through his hair, then pounded the bed three times with a fist. Nathan jumped slightly, but made it a point to keep his composure, as if he expected exactly this. He didn't want to let Ryan know he was surprised.

"Is that anger you're working out, Ryan? Or frustration? What is it? You can tell me."

Picking up a pillow and placing it in his lap, Ryan dropped his head forward and wrapped his arms across the back of his neck.

"Your dad said you were in the room when your brother woke up. What was that like? Did something happen?"

Ryan shook his head. "*Of course* something happened."

"What? What happened, Ryan?"

"You don't know?"

"You were the only one there. You're the one who can tell us. Maybe we can help if you do."

Ryan bolted upright, and tossed the pillow to the side. He rose up on his knees and looked straight at Nathan.

"Kevin's been awake a lot longer than you think, Doctor Nathan. He's even talking…if you'll listen."

Ryan collapsed on his side, then rolled over to face the wall at the back of the room, opposite Nathan. He pulled the blanket up over his body, tucking his shoulder inside.

20

"You seriously could have called me, Stephen," Laura said as she sipped on her coffee, the rising morning sun tossing scattered bands of light across the kitchen around her. "I would have come home and helped out. You shouldn't have had to deal with all that shit by yourself."

"No. It was fine, really. I probably got more nervous than I needed to. And we don't need the brewery to suffer. I'm already having to cut back on patients now that Kevin needs so much attention. I also know how important that time is to you. It's okay."

Laura put her mug down and reached across the island to grab Stephen's hand.

"I do appreciate you handling it. Denise was some sort of ringleader?" She laughed. He joined her.

"I don't know. It seemed that way. Never thought of her as leading a lynch mob before."

Laura brushed her hair out of her face, the dark brown strands glistening against the sun.

"What did they want, anyway?"

"She was insistent that I give her some theory on why Kevin woke up."

"Hell, I'd like to hear one myself."

His lip curled in a smirk. "I mean, all I've got is Ryan. He was in the room. Did something happen with them? But I wasn't going to tell her that, with that mob of people outside. The last thing we need is for them to start zeroing in on Ryan."

"Jesus. No. We've got enough problems already."

"Right." He brought some green tea to his lips, but it was still too hot. He could barely sip it, and it burned on the way down.

"So what'd you tell her?"

"I told her about how we started singing lullabies and nursery rhymes to Kevin every night a few weeks back."

Laura tilted her head and looked at the ceiling. "Just to be clear…we *didn't* sing any lullabies to Kevin, did we?"

"Not a one."

She stifled a laugh. "I guess that'll work as well as any other lie to get them to go away."

"That was the plan. We'll see how long it holds them off. Lots of parents are gonna be Googling nursery rhymes over the next few days."

They looked at each other, smiles slowly creeping across their mouths. Then they burst out laughing; it overflowed from somewhere deep in their stomach, their lungs, bent over at the waist, tears trickling from their eyes. It was an emotional release from stress of the previous few days, when they'd dealt with so many highs and so many challenges. This was a moment for that all to escape. It was a release they needed, and Stephen stepped around the island closer to Laura, still laughing.

He put his arms around her and pulled her close; she covered her mouth and ducked her head, trying to control herself. Stephen put two fingers under her chin and lifted it, then leaned forward. They kissed, longer than they had for some time. It dawned on Laura as her lips opened and closed again, wet against Stephen's mouth, that she wasn't sure how long it had been since they'd kissed passionately. Like they *wanted* each other. Even before Kevin woke up, there were so many demands to taking care of a comatose child and running a business that there hadn't been much time to put into caring for their relationship, treating each other like they were newlyweds every once in awhile, exploring their bodies like it was their first time in the back seat of an old

Chevy. A quick morning peck had become all that either of them could muster. This was nice. She'd missed it. She wrapped her arms around the back of Stephen's neck, and he pulled her tighter against his chest.

"Ewwwww," said Ryan, bounding into the kitchen, jolting his parents out of their kiss.

Laura wiped her mouth with the back of her hand and smiled at him.

"Nice to see you up and about. How ya doin'?"

He shrugged. "Okay, I guess."

Visions of Ryan's birthday flashed into Laura's mind. Two days. What was going to happen to him?

"You should go out back and sit outside," Stephen said. "When was the last time you went out? Doctor Nathan said getting fresh air is important for you."

"I *could*."

"Yeah, it's nice outside," Laura hopped off her stool. "Go ahead out back, and I'll join you in a few minutes. We'll play a game or something."

"Can I take a drink out?"

"Sure. I'll pour us all something. Lemonade sound good?"

"Okay."

Laura was glad he didn't put up much of a fight. As Ryan trudged out the back door, and they heard it shut behind him, Laura turned back to Stephen, who was smiling behind her. She tapped his nose.

"We've maybe got ten minutes till he misses us. Quickie in the kitchen for old time's sake?"

He laughed. "Can I take a rain check?"

"I provide those on occasion. Go check on Kev. See how he's doing. I'll keep Ryan occupied for a little bit."

Stephen turned to walk up the stairs. "Love you."

"Love you too."

It was about three in the afternoon when Laura parked at Palmyra. Sometimes, she didn't come in on Mondays since they were closed to the public, but she often liked to at least swing by and check on the place, maybe touch base with her brewmaster to see how some of the new beers were progressing.

As she approached the front door, she saw something glittering on the sidewalk. The closer she got, the more spread out she saw it was. Then she noticed that windows on both sides of the front door were smashed in, with glass scattered both inside and outside the brewery.

She opened the door and saw her brewmaster, Haley, standing behind the bar with a phone to her ear.

"What the hell?" Laura said.

Haley pulled the phone away from her ear and pointed to it, mouthing the word "Police."

Laura began looking around to see if she if anything was missing. This was the first break-in they'd had in years. Back when she first opened the brewery, this North Knoxville neighborhood Fourth and Gill had been pretty rough around the edges, so much so that she'd kept one of her handguns behind the bar just in case someone pulled something; she was determined to be ready. She'd never had to use it, but the neighborhood at least made her anxious enough to keep it there. She saw its charm, though, and she got a terrific deal on rent at first, so she took a chance. And, while it still had its sketchy moments, she was pretty comfortable there by this time, enough to not bother with a gun. She'd become embedded in the community, and had fallen in love with the people, the walkability of the streets, the small locally owned businesses that banded together against lots of odds in those early years. She enjoyed being part of a neighborhood renaissance of sorts. And, as she had become more a staple of the community, she'd found the break-ins and other problems grew less and less frequent. Sure, there was the occasional drunk patron making a scene, or a homeless person wandering in asking people for money, but it rarely rose to the point that she had to address it. People around here looked after each other, and would often find a way to get the drunk guy home, or to invite the homeless person to sit with them and have a drink. She was always proud to see that.

So, it was a shock to see the broken glass strewn across the ground. Not only had Laura begun to feel safe in the neighborhood because of her ties to the community, but crime in general had fallen considerably in recent years. Petty stuff like this was far less frequent than it had been before The Sleep began, or in the first five to ten years after it started. There weren't a lot of positives to children falling into incurable comas, but one of them was a significant drop in common crime—muggings, break-ins, robberies, pickpocketing, assault. A look at pre-Sleep crime statistics showed a bell curve with those sorts of crimes most frequently committed by males in their late teens, then early twenties, peaking around age twenty-three, then dropping rapidly in their late twenties. By the time a man reached thirty, such crimes had been quite rare, and women of any age committed those crimes at such low rates as to not be much of a problem.

And, at this point, there was nobody in the world who was awake, and younger than thirty, other than kids who hadn't yet reached ten—with the lone exception of one Kevin Fraser, who was probably eating some canned peaches his dad ground up in the blender as Laura stood there thinking. Who would have done it?

"You were my next call," Haley said. "I went out to grab a late lunch, and came back to this. Wanted to go ahead and get the police on their way."

Laura glanced back at the glass. "Yeah, you did the right thing. I guess you didn't see anything."

"Just glass everywhere. At least it's not cold."

"There's always that. I was playing with Ryan outside before I came. Have you seen anything missing? I haven't noticed anything out of place."

"Nope. Nothing that I can tell. We might want to inventory those bottles in the cooler, though. I suppose it's possible they grabbed some beer and bolted." Haley hesitated for a moment before continuing. "There was one thing that was kind of weird, though."

"Besides someone breaking into the brewery in the middle of the day?"

"Yeah. Besides that. The door was still locked when I got back. If people broke in, I'd have expected them to come inside and unlock the door. Makes it a lot easier to run in and out to grab stuff, rather than having to duck through those windows that can't be more than four feet tall."

"Four and a half, actually."

"I'll trust you on that. But you see what I mean?"

"Yeah," Laura said, scanning the scene. "I mean, they could have gotten through those windows, but you're right. If you're making a smash-and-grab, why not unlock the door for a quick exit once you're inside? I'd have expected it to be wide fucking open when you got back."

"Right. Theoretically, they could have crawled back inside after they were done, re-locked it, then crawled back out along broken glass just to confuse us. But I kind of doubt that."

"And since they did it in the middle of the day, that means they probably knew we were closed on Monday. Though I guess that's no big secret. Since they did it when you were gone for lunch, though, that suggests they were watching you, waiting for an opportunity. How long were you gone?"

"Forty minutes, at most. Still got to check the attenuation on a few beers, and I've got to move the IPA to the bright tank.

Couple dozen kegs need to be cleaned. So I wasn't taking a long lunch. Just grabbed a sandwich down the street."

"So, unless they just got really lucky, they saw you leave, and either knew you'd be the only one here, or guessed pretty well."

"That's kind of creepy to think about."

"Damn right, it is."

21

As someone who worked with people for a living on helping them overcome physical limitations to heal their bodies, it was fascinating for Stephen to watch Kevin's physical progression since waking up from the coma. Now on his third day since emerging from The Sleep, Kevin's eyes were more active. He could move his lips and even say some words at the level of a whisper, with some considerable effort. He was moving his fingers slowly, and he could lift his arms and head slightly.

If this rate of improvement kept up, Stephen thought he might be able to get Kevin out of bed and into a wheelchair in a matter of a few days rather than months. And once Kevin was at that stage, it wouldn't be too long before they could start really working on his range of motion, strengthening his legs and arm muscles, and eventually walking. Several other therapists he knew had already called to volunteer their time to help work with Kevin, which he knew would take a significant burden off him. While there was a part of him that wanted to do the work with his son himself, he also knew how long and intense this sort of physical therapy could be, and that it wasn't something he had real experience with. He'd worked with people who'd broken bones and ripped tendons apart in car crashes or while pushing their bodies beyond their limits, but he'd never essentially had to teach a grown person how to walk again, or to hold a glass of water. It seemed likely that Kevin would have to relearn a lot of what he had already known, and it was a daunting mountain to climb. Stephen was anxious to start climbing it, but he also needed to make money by treating other patients, and he could use the help wherever he could get it once the time came.

As Stephen rolled Kevin onto his right side, he heard footsteps from behind him.

"What are you doing?" Ryan asked, walking into the room.

"I'm turning your brother so he doesn't get sores from lying in the same position for too long. You've seen us do this before."

"Yeah, I guess. You still have to do that now that he's awake?"

"Until we can get him out of this bed, we sure do." Stephen bent down and looked at Kevin, their noses nearly touching. "And we're gonna get you up and out of this bed just as soon as we can, aren't we, champ?"

Then Stephen turned to Ryan. "You wanna say something to your big brother? He's starting to be able to talk a little bit, but you have to get close to hear him."

Ryan waved, but didn't move any closer. "Hi."

"Come on up here where you two can hear each other."

Stephen crouched and picked Ryan up, lifting him into the chair with him. For the first time since the morning Kevin woke up, Ryan was looking him dead in the eye, their faces just inches apart. Kevin gave what looked like a crooked smile. Ryan squirmed in his dad's arms, trying to get free. His feet slid out from under him on the chair, and he crashed into Stephen's legs. Stephen grunted loudly.

"Okay, okay. I'll let you down," Stephen said. "Man, that hurt. You're gettin' big, kiddo."

Ryan's mouth wrinkled, and he turned his head behind his shoulder, away from Stephen. He was just staring up with big eyes, his feet slowly shuffling backward.

"Hey, Ryan," Stephen said. "You know what we haven't talked about in a little bit? What do you want to do for your birthday? It's just two days away. We'll do whatever you want!"

Tenth birthdays were odd events these days. Decades before, it had been a little bit of a milestone, moving out of the single digits and a little closer to the teenage years; now it was tempting for it to be more of a funeral than a celebration. How do you properly acknowledge a birthday that's essentially a death sentence? That was the question so many parents and children faced as that fateful day approached.

Celebrating it and treating it like any of the nine previous birthdays was difficult for everyone involved. And Ryan wasn't stupid. He knew what his turning ten likely meant for him. But Stephen and Laura felt it was important to celebrate it, to treat it as normally as possible. If it was going to be his last birthday celebration, they wanted it to be a good one. If nothing else, he'd have that day. That one special day, awake and alert, able to run and jump and play. They'd done the same for Kevin on his tenth. He wanted to play baseball on his birthday. It was early December, and fairly cold, but they'd reached out to the parents of every friend of his they could track down, and organized a huge baseball game at the local park. Dozens of kids showed up, despite it being forty-four degrees. Some of the parents dressed up like umpires. They set up a scoreboard in the outfield. Seeing Kevin have a great day on what they assumed was his last had been a huge comfort to Stephen and Laura.

They wanted to give Ryan the same sort of day, but they weren't sure what to do, and Ryan hadn't been much help. He didn't really have friends, and his main activity was playing games on his phone. But they were trying to be encouraging, telling him he could do anything he wanted, go wherever he wanted. They'd make it happen, even if there were only two days left for them to put something together. Laura's parents could keep an eye on Kevin for the day. If Ryan wanted to take a day trip somewhere, or see a museum, or just sit and watch birds fly across the sky, they were ready and willing to do it for their final day with him.

Ryan shrugged and his eyes dropped to the floor. "I dunno."

Stephen got out of the chair and dropped to his knees in front of Ryan, trying to get to eye level.

"Anything you want. We'll go anywhere. Do anything. If you had one wish, what would it be?"

Still looking at the floor, Ryan's feet began to shuffle. He scratched his head, his dirty blonde hair tangling between his fingers, then falling forward in front of his face.

"Why don't I ever get to be big like you and Mom?" he said.

The question hit Stephen in the stomach. "I...don't know. I wish I knew."

"It's not fair. It's really not fair. You guys get to do whatever you want. You get whatever you want. I don't even get a door on my room. I'll always be a little kid with no friends and nothing to do. I just sit around this house and wait for my turn to end up like *him*. Like all of 'em. It's not fair. I want to be big. I want to have friends and make money and kiss girls. You get to do that stuff when you're big. But I'll always just be small. I don't get to grow up, but you do. Why? Did I do something wrong?"

Stephen was trying to stay strong as he listened to this, but tears trickled down his cheeks. He wiped his sleeve across his face. His throat tightened, and he swallowed hard.

"You're right. It's not fair. I don't know why it has to be this way. We all want to know. And we're trying to figure it out. We're doing everything we can. But the adults haven't solved the puzzle yet. We've let you down. I know that. You shouldn't have to deal with this. There's no answer to why we got to be adults other than we're just lucky. It's not anything you did wrong, and it's not anything we did right. It's just...not fair. Like you said."

It was a heart-wrenching conversation to have with your son. What Ryan was saying was right. It wasn't fair. All these young children, who'd barely gotten a chance to get their lives going, who weren't that far removed from diapers, having the lights go out so prematurely. They didn't deserve this, and it made the world a hard place to live in. It was enough to make you question the purpose of it all. This senseless waste of so much potential, so many young lives that could have gone on to make a positive difference in society. Entire generations now, snuffed out before they got the chance to make their mark, to make new discoveries, to build relationships, to give birth to other people who would have made an impact. Ironically, by this time, it was possible that the person who would have discovered the cure to The Sleep fell victim to it before they ever had the chance.

Kevin waking up was an amazing gift, and Stephen hoped he and Laura could honor that gift. He hoped maybe they *could* use his awakening to, in some way, help to end this plague. And, if they ever lost motivation to find that solution, they didn't need any more reminder than the one here in this room.

There was just one full day left before Ryan's tenth birthday, and Ryan didn't know how to feel as he walked into his room and flopped down on his bed, wedging his head between two feather pillows.

On one hand, this was the only world he knew—his parents, this house, the jagged winter trees scattered in the yard under an impossibly blue sky. He had a hard time imagining anything else. What else could there be out there? What would it be like not to be here?

Nine years old or ninety-nine, it was the question people inevitably encountered as death loomed—What would the experience be like? A coma wasn't exactly death, but the likelihood seemed low that two brothers would be the only two kids in the world to awaken from one. Ryan was every bit as good as dead in a couple of days, and he was scared of it.

He didn't have the capacity to grasp the idea of not existing, of falling asleep never to come back to being himself. He clearly knew the world had existed and history had marched on long before he'd ever even been born, but that was all in the abstract.

This was more real, the idea that one day soon the world would carry on and he wouldn't be aware of any of it. He'd fall asleep on the night of his tenth birthday and never again open his eyes, never see his mom's smile, play his games, or watch tree limbs fluttering in the breeze out his window.

He didn't know how to process any of it. A nine-year-old maybe shouldn't have to, in a fair world. But he was understanding more and more that fairness was a concept nature didn't adhere to. The universe was uncaring, and unbound by human ideas of what was right or just. He, just like all the other children for the previous two decades, was on an inexorable march toward the end. Had he been born any time before around 1989, he'd be an adult, maybe with a family and kids of his own. But he had the unfortunate luck of the draw to be born in 2009, and that meant he was subject to the same morbid inertia as every other such kid.

Still, he was haunted by Kevin's words, coming to him in his dreams, telling him this wasn't the end but a new beginning. The dreams had stopped since Kevin woke up, but he still glimpsed it when he was awake, or whenever he looked into Kevin's eyes. They were the same half-dead eyes he saw in his dreams, the same crooked smile, same pale skin.

He didn't know how to explain it to anyone. It all seemed so real, but also surreal at the same time. How could Kevin have reached out to him through his dreams? That couldn't have happened. But how did Ryan know what Kevin would look like when he woke up? And did Kevin speak some sort of code to him when he stumbled over "water" a couple of days earlier? Was that his way of letting Ryan know the dreams weren't dreams at all? Or was it just a weird coincidence?

Then there was the morning when Kevin woke up. It still wasn't something Ryan was comfortable thinking about, and he was afraid what people would say if he told them what happened.

He didn't think he'd done anything wrong, but others might see it differently. He'd never forget that morning. Never forget the moment when Kevin's eyes blinked open.

If Kevin had once been living in some alternate kids' world, he seemed intent on staying in *this* world for now. But why? In the dreams, he'd been trying to put Ryan at ease about his impending coma, telling him about the wonderful world he'd be entering, but now he was back in this "real" world himself. If it was so great across that chasm, why wouldn't he stay there and wait just a few more days?

In two days, Ryan would either be essentially dead, or in this other world Kevin told him about. If there was no other world, the worst thing about the coma would be the purgatorial nature of it all. Heaven only awaited the dead, while this world held the waking. Those in a coma had no natural place. They weren't in this world, or the next. That was part of what made the idea of children creating their own kingdom so intriguing. It meant they'd sidestepped purgatory, with a new place where they could live together and not suffer the sins of the adults, where they were outside heaven and Earth. A world of their own creation. A new place, where everyone could run and jump and play. Where nobody was picked last, and every kid could hit a curveball.

Ryan desperately wanted it. But some part of his brain wouldn't let him fully commit. Some part of him said to be skeptical, that it was too good to be true, and his mom had always told him to look critically at any idea that flattered him too much. "Don't be a sucker," she'd say. That was the scientist in her talking—measure twice, and cut once. Don't let the enticement of a pleasant idea lead you down a bad path.

He didn't know what to think. There were so many competing thoughts rattling around his head, and he didn't feel like he had the mental tools to sort through them all in the short time he had left. The Sleep beckoned. It wouldn't be long now before he'd see what the other side looked like, if there indeed was one. Soon, he'd know.

22

Walking downstairs and flipping on the kitchen light, Laura was the first one in the house to wake up. With her typical late nights at the brewery, it wasn't too often she got the chance to beat all the boys out of bed, but she relished it when given the opportunity. Tuesdays were usually the time when it was possible to pull it off; with the brewery closed on Monday, she could curl up with Stephen and a good book by nine o'clock and be up before sunrise if she wanted.

There was something about being the only one awake in the house on a chilly mid-spring morning, darkness still blanketing the kitchen window, the silence hanging heavy over the house. She had no responsibilities. Nothing anyone was expecting of her. The world was hers. Whatever she chose to do, she could do it, from listening to some jazz to looking over the previous day's test numbers from the brewery to streaming an old movie on her computer. There were no distractions, and the whole day was laid out in front of her like a map. She could survey it from here and make plans, figure out what challenges she might face, and get pointed in the right direction. The possibilities just seemed endless before six a.m. Not even the sun was standing in her way.

She started to put on a pot of coffee and heard a noise from the back of the house. She froze, her eyes darting, waiting to see if she'd hear it again. Would one of the media people have gone over the fence? Surely, they weren't going to those lengths. She couldn't keep them from camping out on a public street, but she'd damn sure fight them breaking into her backyard. It was barely past five-thirty in the morning. Were the media even out there this early? But, as frustrating as it would be if it were some reporter snooping, the thought crossed her mind that it'd be much scarier if it *wasn't* the paparazzi.

She tiptoed to the back door to make sure it was locked, and confirmed they'd secured it before going to bed. Then she stood there waiting, not daring to move. She didn't want to look out the window, afraid of what she might see. Now she was thinking that it might have been nothing. Between the media, the mob, and the brewery break-in, she was on edge. She figured it was hard to blame her. It wasn't that she was paranoid; these weird things *were* happening to them. Her boys were upstairs, and she'd do anything in her power to protect them from whatever showed up at their door, but she also didn't want to barricade the place like some sort of prison. This was a home. It needed to be welcoming. They were in suburban Knoxville, not some crime-infested neighborhood. She knew she shouldn't have to jump at every shadow that crawled across her sightline. This should be a safe space for her, and her family.

It was also possible it was just a squirrel, or a cat that scampering around. She didn't hear anything else, so she returned to her coffee pot, carrying it to the sink to get some water. Then she heard it again, louder this time, and her mug crashed to the surface of the island, coffee sloshing over the edge and pooling on the white ceramic. Her head spun quickly in the direction of the back of the house, the rest of her body still. She couldn't identify the sound, but she was sure it was there this time. This wasn't a mistake. She heard *something*. Footsteps? Something banging against the door? An object crashing into the house's facade? She couldn't place it.

Part of her said she needed to rush to the door, throw it open, and see what it might be. But a big part of her wanted her to stay right where she was. If it was a person out there, that person probably wasn't doing a social call this early in the morning.

Should she go upstairs and get Stephen? Was it worth waking him up for a little noise she heard outside?

But, no. She could handle this herself. She didn't need Stephen to protect her. She hated the cliché of being the damsel in distress, hiding behind her man to shield her from harm. She was an independent woman. She was smart and resourceful. She could let him sleep, and deal with whatever was out there.

She got up and reached above the sink, where some pots and pans hung. She grabbed a large cast-iron skillet in one hand, then pulled a butcher's knife out of the block on the counter behind her. If it was a reporter, they'd deserve whatever they got; if it was anyone else, she was going to need the protection. Slowly, carefully, she stepped toward the back door, landing softly with the balls of her feet, ears alert, eyes fixed in front of her.

As she approached, she could see out the open curtains on the window near the door, and there was nothing but darkness. The sun was still hiding, as was anyone who might be lurking in the shadows. Her heart beat faster. Not knowing was the worst part. She'd have rather known there was a serial killer waiting for her than to not know anything at all. That left anything as a possibility. She could open the door and feel silly for ever worrying, or a gunshot could pierce her skull the moment she showed her face.

Laura had never been like this before, and she didn't like it. She'd never felt so unsure of herself, so unsafe. She'd been through so much with one child falling into a coma and the other rapidly approaching his own, but it was the one waking up that was threatening to send her on a descent into madness.

The doorknob was within reach, and there was nothing but silence. It weighed on her shoulders like anvils, holding her to the ground, freezing her hand against the knob, refusing to turn. But she had to know. She had come this far; she couldn't turn back. She had children to protect. She didn't have the luxury to be a coward, to turn tail and flee upstairs, hoping her ears and her instincts had failed her. She had to push forward.

She twisted her wrist, and the knob turned slowly, then clicked in the lock. The door popped open just a hair, and she pulled carefully, keeping the door between her body and the back patio. Little by little, she peeked around it to the outside, only allowing one eye to slip around the door's edge every couple of seconds. Still dark, she saw nothing.

The door fully open, Laura looked around, listening for anything that could explain the noises she'd heard. A few scattered birds called to one another, but there were no more breaks of the silence that surrounded her. Now standing fully in the doorway, she wondered what she'd been afraid of. There were no signs of anything. Not so much as a stray cat. The world was quiet and still. The morning held no surprises for her.

She reached behind her and flipped on the light switch, her breath crystallizing as she exhaled in the chilly air. The light above her snapped on, drowning out the dark and revealing the cold concrete just beneath her feet.

Feeling foolish, she breathed deep, taking in the cold air, then glanced downward. Against the gray concrete, she saw streaks of red. It was sloppy, like spray paint. Rounded and slashed shapes, there were letters, but upside down. Her chest tightening and her breath suddenly short, Laura stepped across the patio, turned and looked back at the door. Her mouth dropped open, and her hands covered it. She let out a small gasp as she read the message staring back at her in scarlet: "A WHORE LIVES HERE."

23

Page 134 of the Knoxville Neighbors message board thread continued:

PaulBetweenYall
I'm assuming this lullabies thing isn't working for anyone yet, or we'd have started hearing about it. My wife's all about it. I think she liked getting the chance to sing something, just for the sake of doing something while sitting with our kid except cry. It's a little haunting for me to walk past the room and hear her singing "Ba Ba Black Sheep" through obvious tears. But if it gives her something to do, great. And if it helps the kid, even better. Anybody else trying it?

PuffPass2017
Oh, come on, Paul. You're smarter than this. Are you really falling for this lullabies bullshit? I'm certainly sympathetic to your wife. I know she's been through a lot, like a bunch of us have. And if it helps her stay sane in this absurd world we're living in, more power to her. But you can't actually think there's any chance this is gonna help. Singing? After all the studies and papers and tests and medical trials and failures, singing poorly is suddenly gonna wake them all up? I get why you'd *want* to think it'd work, but I can't imagine you *actually* believing it.

DMshallWin
@PuffPass2017 Be a skeptic if you want, but that's what the man said. So, if this worked for his son, maybe it'll work for

someone else's, ya know? Who are you to tell Paul or anyone else what they should believe? Be the Doubting Thomas all you want, but God has a plan for this, I can guarantee you that. He's doing all this for a reason. Maybe He wants us to reconnect with our kids, or our childhoods. We aren't here to question why, we're just here to follow where He leads us. The father of that family is a good man. You all know how I feel about his wife, but he's never done anything to make us doubt him.

ScruffyJoeyN
The lullabies are a code, guys. It's amazing to me that more people don't get that this is a government conspiracy. Lullabies and nursery rhymes? Are you serious? You mentioned "Ba Ba Black Sheep." That's basically promoting racism from the 13th century. "Jack and Jill" is about King Louis XVI and Marie Antoinette getting beheaded. "Mary, Mary, Quite Contrary" talks about a murderous psychopath queen they called Bloody Mary. "Ring Around the Rosie" is about the god damn plague killing children, for Christ's sake. Wake up, sheeple. These things are some dark shit. Even bringing them up is code. What you're probably doing when you sing this stuff is implanting some orders into their system. These kids are being controlled from a command center. The government is building an army, and they're just waiting for the moment to unleash them. They didn't know how they were going to get the code sequences to them, but then they came up with this, and you're all falling for it, hook, line, and sinker. Amazing. Truly amazing. And they call me crazy!

PaulBetweenYall
@PuffPass2017 You can fuck right off with your condescension about me "being smarter" than to not agree with you on something. And my wife doesn't need your permission to do whatever she feels she can to possibly bring our kid back.

Look, I'm not saying I think this is gonna work. I honestly have no idea. But what alternative do we have? You think we should all just ignore what the only father of an awakened kid said to do, and sit on our hands? What's your great solution to all this, huh? You're too afraid to commit to doing anything because you're afraid of feeling foolish, or helpless. You'd rather put your kid's life at stake than to risk maybe doing something that doesn't help. Well, damn it, we're at least gonna try it. And if it ends up working, I'll go give that father the biggest damn hug I've ever given another human being. And if it doesn't, well, we're no worse off than we were before.

TheInBetween

They don't sing anything. I can't tell you how I know that, but it's true. This whole thing is a lie. They don't know anything, but I do.

DMshallWin

@TheInBetween With all due respect, unless you actually live in that house, there's no way you can know any of that. You're just guessing along with the rest of them. This isn't speculation. It happened. And the CDC has confirmed the boy's awake, so that's that. The father had no reason to lie. The wife may be wanting to keep everything to herself, but her husband has more class than that, thank the Lord. If we still had our boy, I'd be singing my God-loving butt off right now. If you have kids (though I somehow doubt it), you should be singing too.

ChanjoBanjo

You know what's interesting to me? I've got a friend who lives very near them, and she said she stopped by a couple of days ago to see the kid who had woken up—I think she may be the only one outside the family who's seen him—and she had a weird run-in with the other boy. That other boy said he was in the room with his brother that morning when he woke up. When she asked him more about it, the kid bolted out of the room like lightning. That sounded weird. I just watched him run down the hall like the devil himself was chasing the boy. Now, my friend has been suddenly seeing the younger boy sitting outside sometimes, just sort of staring. Sometimes, with a parent, but also by himself. His 10th is coming up really soon. Tomorrow, I think. What's gonna happen then?

IAmtheWalrus69

@ChanjoBanjo That's interesting about the brother, Chanjo. I didn't know his 10th was coming up so soon. That could make for an awkward situation, if one kid wakes up right before The Sleep takes the other one. Or, what if the younger kid just stays awake? What would that tell us? That'd be wild. I'm not sure what my reaction to that would be. If that floozy wife wasn't ready to talk then, she'd have a fight on her hands, for sure. Also, Chanjo, you seemed to slip from third person to first person there for a second. You might wanna clean that up, or someone's gonna think your "friend" is actually you. lol

24

"I think we're almost there," Amanda said, hitting an "E" with water from a pressure washer. "Won't even be able to tell any paint was here."

Stephen was on his hands and knees, dripping wet and cold, scraping at bits of paint with a heavy wire brush. He wiped his forehead with the crook of his elbow. It was barely fifty degrees, but he was sweating. Or, at least, he thought he was sweating. It was hard to distinguish between sweat and hose water by that point of the morning.

"Thanks for bringing the pressure washer. You're a lifesaver. That thing seems like it could take the paint off my car."

She gritted her teeth as the "E" slowly dissolved in front of her.

"Hey, when my best friend gets called a whore, I don't mess around," she was nearly yelling so Stephen would hear her over the roar of the water jet. "Whoever did this, I'd like to have a few minutes with them and this puppy."

The last little bit of the "E" loosened, and Amanda turned the hose off while Stephen scrubbed to sweep away the scraps of paint stubbornly hanging onto the concrete where they were sprayed. Amanda dropped the pressure washer and shook her arms.

"Man, that thing's no joke," she said. "I hadn't used it in awhile. It's not light."

"I could have helped." Stephen kept scrubbing, looking for any remaining red.

"Nah, I was good. Now I won't need to go to the gym today.

So there's that."

Stephen smiled. "I really do appreciate it. I know Laura does too."

"How's she doin', anyway?"

Stephen bent at the waist, getting his eyes as close as possible to the concrete, trying to spot any paint specks he might have missed before.

"Well, she's been crying since she woke me up." He put down the scrubber and stood up, his right knee cracking as he did. "I get it. She's been through a lot lately. You heard about the break-in at the brewery?"

Amanda frowned and nodded her head.

"Yeah," he said. "Well, there's that. And Kevin, of course. Ryan's been struggling with all the craziness, and now *his* tenth is tomorrow. We still don't know how we're gonna handle that, or what's gonna happen. There's the media attention, that weird gathering on our front yard, and this morning was the second time she's had to deal with cops in two days. I know business has been a struggle lately. It's just…a lot."

"No, I get it." Amanda leaned against one of the side of the house. "How do you even think someone got back here?"

Stephen looked around the back yard. "Climbed the back part of the fence, I guess. Nathan climbed it yesterday. I wonder if someone who was there got the idea from watching him. Hell, it's one blessing of the media throngs out front—if not for them, this might have been on the front porch for everyone to see. If it could be worse for Laura, that would have done it."

"That's true," Amanda agreed. "She's tough, and I always figure she can handle anything. But you wonder if there's a breaking point. Ya know?"

"God. I don't even wanna think about that. She's the engine that drives this place."

"We both know she's been your rock in the past. Remember

when you lost your job a few years ago? And when you had your shoulder surgery, and weren't sure if you could do physical therapy anymore?"

"Sure." He shrugged. "Of course I remember. She was always there for me."

"Yep. And maybe it's your turn to be strong now. In case she needs to have a weak moment. Ya know what I mean?"

Stephen nodded. Amanda began pacing and studying the patio.

"It looks pretty good. I'm glad she won't have to see that again. What'd the cops say, by the way?"

"I don't know. Took a report, whatever that means," Stephen muttered. "I mean, what do ya do? We don't have any cameras back here. Nobody saw anything. Not even the media out there, and you know they'd have jumped all over it if they had. Nobody was hurt. Nothing was stolen. It's…low-level vandalism, I guess. They're not exactly gonna form a special investigative unit to hunt the bastard down."

"But this combined with the break-in? And the mob on the front lawn? Doesn't that make it more suspicious?"

"I mentioned that. They just shrugged and said they didn't have any reason to think it was related. There's no obvious evidence for any of it. They're not bringing guys in to dust for prints like this is the movies. They've got bigger fish to fry, I'm sure. I asked them if we could clean it up. They basically said we could do whatever we wanted. So, I called you, and here we are."

"Damn," Amanda said. "Any idea who might have done this shit? What kind of crazy fuck would do that?"

"No idea. Who in the world would say something that cruel about Laura?"

"Hell, not just *say* it. Climb a fence twice to spray paint that junk bright red on her patio. That's ballsy. Batshit crazy. But ballsy."

"It's nuts. I don't know what to think about it. It just feels like this house is coming apart, and we're not at all ready to deal with tomorrow."

"Ryan—right. I know she's worried about it. She's texted me plenty. It's like a freight train headed toward you guys, and you're tied to the tracks. There's nothing you can do. It's gotta be a helpless feeling. Hell, *I* feel helpless, and he's not even my son. Though it sorta *feels* like he is."

"You were probably the smart one, not having any." Stephen sat down on a lawn chair next to the patio. Amanda pulled another chair over and sat next to him. "We just…wanted to feel normal. We wanted to have that family, and give them the best life we could. And look where it's led us. Kevin's bed-ridden. Ryan's on the verge of falling into a probably incurable coma. Or, at least, we have no idea what cures it. And we're struggling to deal with the fallout of it all. It makes you wonder if we just weren't meant to have kids at all."

"Oh, fuck *that*. You guys are awesome parents. Those kids are lucky to have you both and, even if this is all Ryan gets, he's had a hell of a run. Ten years isn't great, but it's longer than a lot of kids have gotten over the years. You guys did everything you could, and I'm sure Ryan knows that. So does Kevin. Hell, you guys fucking *brought Kevin back from the dead*. What other parents can say *that*?"

Stephen laughed, and Amanda put her arm around his back.

"So be proud. Whatever happens from here, you two kicked ass as parents. And you're gonna keep kicking ass for awhile to come."

Behind them, they felt the breeze from the front door coming open, and they both swung around to see Laura standing in the doorway in her bathrobe.

"Is Ryan out here with you guys?" she asked, her voice strained and breath short.

They looked at each other. "Um, no," Stephen said. "I assume he's in his room."

"Well, he's not. He's nowhere. He's *gone*, Stephen!"

25

Stephen darted into Kevin's room. As he did, he straightened up and smiled at Kevin, waving calmly to not tip off that anything was wrong. The last thing the boy needed in his state was more stress and worry. Kevin gave a smile—his smile was starting to look less lopsided and more controlled—and Stephen crouched behind the bed to look underneath it. Dust bunnies danced and fluttered as he lifted the bed skirt, tumbling over each other. Sweeping under the bed clearly hadn't been high on their priority list for a while. More importantly, there was no sign of Ryan.

Standing back upright, Stephen smiled again at Kevin, whose brow was a bit furrowed as he looked back. Stephen patted his feet lightly as he walked to the other side of the bed, peeking around the corner to see if Ryan might be hiding in the back of the room. There was nothing there except an old rocking chair and a large chest that had belonged to Laura's father. It was a rich mahogany with strips of wood nailed horizontally across the top of the lid and each side. Brown leather handles were bolted to the sides, with silver metal clasps that looked like they could hold the world itself in place. On the front were handmade black metal fasteners, with a large oval-shaped one in the center with a hole meant for a padlock. The story went—and Stephen figured by this point that everyone who knew James had heard it at least once— that he'd saved the life of another deckhand when the man fell overboard, and James was the first man to leap over the railing and into the water. The man was unconscious, but James' strong knot-tying right hand was able to grip him under his arm, while he coaxed them both back to the surface with his other arm and legs.

When they emerged, he looked up and saw most of the crew leaning over the edge of the boat, and a cheer broke out when they saw their heads poke out of the water. He swam them both to the edge of the boat, and they pulled him onto the deck. As one of the crew did CPR on him, a couple of the others grabbed James' arms and lifted him up, soaking wet. After a few seconds, he heard the man letting out a watery cough, and the men flipped him onto his side, smacking his back to clear his airway.

The man survived, and this chest was James' reward at the end of the summer. The captain said he would have given a monetary bonus, but the fishing wasn't good enough that season. But James loved the chest, and gladly accepted it. The chest had character, and it was already close to 100 years old when it became his in the 1970s. He'd made a vow to pass it on as a family heirloom, and hoped to see it last many more generations—generations that now would likely never exist. But here it sat, just feet from Kevin, quite possibly its final resting place, after however many adventures.

They kept some blankets and toys inside, but something about it struck Stephen in the moment. It was big enough to hold a ten-year-old. Ryan might have to curl up, but he could get himself in there if he took most of the stuff out. This was silly, though. Where was the stuff? If he'd cleared out the chest, where'd he put everything? The room was clean. Or could *someone else* have put him in there? No. This was dumb.

But, if he's not in there, where is he, Stephen? Where is he? The thought bounced into his brain from out of nowhere. *This isn't that big a house. Laura said she looked in the front yard. There aren't that many places he could be hiding, and this is one of them. You're just scared of what you might find.*

That much was true. This would be weird behavior, though, even for Ryan. Why would he jam himself up into an old sea chest? Was he alive in there? Did any kids fall into the coma a little bit early? He didn't think so, but he couldn't think of any logical reason it couldn't happen. The odds seemed good that it *had* to have happened at some point, given twenty years of this. And it would certainly be solid karmic retribution if they got one kid back unexpectedly after they thought that was possible, then lost the other unexpectedly *before* they thought it was possible.

He looked back and at Kevin, who was merely staring at the ceiling, his eyes glassy and cold. He looked less like himself than Stephen could remember since he'd awaken. He seemed relatively peaceful, just very still. A mannequin, pale and lifeless. Stephen thought maybe he was just looking at him from too far away, and his mind was playing tricks on him a little bit. Whatever the case, he felt a chill run up his back and splinter across his shoulders, making him shake. He spun back to the chest, aware of his heart pounding faster. It didn't make any sense that Ryan would be in there, his hands wrapped around his knees, his face blue, a plastic bag tied around his neck, but he also couldn't rule it out unless he opened it. Why was that image even coming to his head? What was wrong with him?

Stephen began walking back toward the door when he caught movement out of the corner of his eye. His legs froze, head slowly turning that direction, toward Kevin's bed. Kevin was rising, just bending at his waist, his entire torso lifting as if he were doing a sit-up. Very slowly. But there was no struggle. It was like he was being pulled up by skilled puppeteer strings, smooth, effortless. Stephen's blood ran cold.

Finally, Kevin was sitting straight up, the first time he'd been in that position in well over a year. His legs, ramrod-straight in front of him, hadn't moved an inch. His pupils were dilated, and he didn't blink. His eyes looked twice their normal size, like they were trying to leap out of his head. His arms hung stiffly at his sides. Then his mouth began to open.

"Out," he said, softly, but clear as day. That was Kevin's voice. No one else's. It didn't sound muddled or raspy. It was Kevin saying a word. Stephen's heart leaped in his chest.

"Out!" Louder this time. Raising his voice a full octave. What did that mean? "Out"? Did he want out of his bed? Did he want Stephen to leave? What was he trying to say? Stephen stared, his expression blank.

"Out! Out! Out!" Kevin's face contorted into anger, he screamed, the room filling with his voice, a sonic boom that Stephen was sure could be heard blocks away. He pressed his hands to his ears to muffle the blistering sound, the word repeating over and over, spilling impossibly from Kevin's gaping mouth, swirling around him. "Out! Out! Out!" The words didn't soften. They seemed to grow even louder, an intolerable piercing wail. How was it possible Laura and Amanda weren't hearing this and sprinting up the stairs to find out what was happening?

And what exactly *was* happening? What did it mean? Something was holding Stephen there. He could move, but something was telling him not to leave. "Out" could mean for him to get out.

Or it *could* mean to get Ryan out.

He stepped quickly back to the chest and leaned over it, letting his right hand fall from his ear. The sound of Kevin's voice continued, rattling against his eardrum. Hesitantly, his hand dropped toward the chest's latch. He needed to know, but he was petrified of what might be there when he opened it. He started to lift the latch. Suddenly, Kevin's voice stopped. Stephen had never been in a room that felt more quiet, like a church in the morning before a funeral.

The lid creaked as it rose, a tomb being opened. He wasn't sure how long it had been since they'd opened it. Months? Definitely. Years? Perhaps. The lid was heavier than he remembered. As the opening cleared, he felt his heart could nearly explode. Then he saw it—catching a small glint of light from the nearby window, a steak knife that had gone missing from their butcher's block a few months earlier.

How could that have gotten in here? The puzzled thought echoed in his mind. Obviously, someone had to open the chest and put it in there. Stephen knew he didn't do it, and he couldn't think of any reason Laura would have. Which meant it had to be Ryan. Didn't it? But why would he steal a knife and stash it in the chest?

He bent over and wrapped his fingers around the handle, holding it up for a closer look. Inches from his face, he turned it and looked at the blade. It didn't look like it'd been used for anything recently. Had Ryan just been playing a joke? He shook his head and stuck the knife in his pocket.

He turned back to the bed, and Kevin was lying on his back, just as still as he'd been when Stephen entered the room. Then his head fell to his left, and he looked at Stephen. A perfect smile crossed Kevin's face.

"Stephen!" He heard the voice bellowing up the stairs. It was Amanda's. "Stephen! Come down here right the *fuck* now! I don't know what's going on."

Laura had seen Stephen go up the stairs, and she continued toward the kitchen, Amanda following close behind. She'd walked through here only a few minutes before and there was no sign of Ryan, but she was hoping she'd missed something.

"Ryan!" she said, trying to mask the panic in her voice. "Ryan, honey. Are you in here?"

Behind her, Amanda opened the pantry, but saw only boxes of cereal and cans of vegetables staring back at her. It was a narrow entry, and she thought it would be a tight squeeze even for a child of ten.

Laura turned the corner and opened the coat closet. Perhaps he was playing some sort of game with them. He wasn't really the type for those games, though. Kevin when he was younger, would have done this sort of thing. But it would have been out of character for Ryan. She heard Amanda saying his name as the pantry door slammed shut, and Laura thought Ryan almost couldn't possibly be in the house unless he was badly hurt, unconscious, or dead. He couldn't just ignore them like this.

Events of the morning flashed through her head—drying her eyes on a bathroom towel, then walking to Ryan's room to give him a censored version of what happened, and why the cops had been there. When she didn't see him, she figured he'd wandered downstairs to eat breakfast. She went to the kitchen, but it was quiet, no empty glass by the sink that Ryan might have used to drink his orange juice. No empty granola bar wrapper. No wet glass ring on the island. She peeked into the living room, but the couch was empty, as was the recliner in the corner. Everything was still. She looked out the window into the front yard, white media vans still lining the block, a few reporters standing outside smoking or chomping on granola bars. No Ryan.

Laura went back upstairs and re-checked his bedroom, looking around his bed, in the closet. It was as if he'd vanished, been beamed up from Earth to another planet. Then something caught her eye. His phone was on his bedside table. That was the moment worry turned to something more, buzzers sounding in her head, red lights flashing to spur her into some sort of action. He never went anywhere without his phone. That was his game room. His lifeline. His companion. If he had any friends, his phone was his best. She nearly tumbled twice on her way downstairs, then flung the back door open.

"Should we call the police?" Amanda said.

"For the third time in two days and second time in a few hours?" Laura's voice was strained.

"I get it, but this is your son. If he really is missing, every second counts."

Laura pulled at her hair with her hand, feeling the tug on her scalp.

"Sure. I know. It's just getting a little ridiculous. I hadn't dealt with the cops in years, and now I'm suddenly calling them like it's a bodily function. I don't want to get into a 'Girl who cried wolf' situation, and they start tuning me out."

"Okay, so what do ya wanna do here?"

"Look, I don't think he's inside. I've checked everywhere, and Stephen's checking upstairs again now. You guys have been in the back yard all morning, so he can't be out there. What's left? The front? The media'd be going nuts if he were out there. Let's give downstairs one more sweep. Then we'll call the cops if he's not here. I'm just hoping I missed something, and I'm an hysterical mess."

"All right. Deal."

Then the noise came from the front, hurtling toward the house like a wave.

Laura flung the front door open and was greeted by a flash of cameras and questions yelled from in front of the porch. Her eyes wide, she looked down and saw Ryan, knees pulled tightly to his chest, rocking slowly back and forth on the top step. She walked toward him, then stopped and looked at the vultures before her.

"Get away, or I swear to god I will sue every goddamn one of you for trespassing and anything else I can think of." Laura stood tall, swinging a stiff arm at a dozen reporters swarming her porch. "Don't you have any decency at all? Can't you see he's a *child*? Christ! Get back! Now!"

The reporters lowered their cameras and began to retreat, pulling back toward their vehicles on the street. The door opened behind her; Amanda and Stephen walked through it.

"Hey, baby. How ya doin'?" Laura sat next to Ryan, stroking his head. He didn't move, and his blank expression stayed the same. "You gave us a scare, ya know that? You shouldn't be out here without telling us. Your dad and I didn't know where you were."

He stayed silent, and she kept rubbing his head, her fingers gliding through his thick hair when something caught her eye. On his left wrist, she saw red, and her heart skipped. She reached down and rolled up his sleeve. Had he hurt himself? Could he be cutting himself on purpose?

She pulled his arm toward her so she could see it better. Then she touched it and noticed it was dry. She scratched with a fingernail, and it flaked off. Whatever it was, it wasn't blood. Red clay, maybe? Just a kid not bathing himself well enough? But she also knew there was *something* weird going on with him.

"What's wrong? Can you say something to mommy? Just let her know you're all right, at least? I know things have been stressful lately. We just want what's best for you, though. You know that, right? Your dad and I love you very, very much. And we'll do anything to help you feel better. What can we do, baby? What do you need?"

"Has he been out here the whole time?" Laura heard Stephen say, and looked back to see him standing there.

"Excuse me," a reporter's voice came from across the yard. She was walking gingerly toward the front porch.

"If you try to ask us questions right now, I…" Stephen said, his chest tightening.

The reporter raised her right hand. "No, I understand. I'm Elizabeth Cassels with the Knoxville *News Press*. I'm not looking to ask anything. I just thought you'd want to know more about what happened with your son, how he got here."

Laura looked back at Stephen, then at Ryan again, and kissed his forehead.

"Okay," Stephen said. "That might help."

"First, I'm sorry about everything that's happening with your family. It probably doesn't mean much coming from one of us out here, but I know it has to be hard."

"And you're one of the ones making it even harder," Laura said. "Just tell us if you know something that can help."

"Sure." Elizabeth nodded. "As far as any of us could tell, he's only been out here a couple of minutes. At least, we didn't see him before then. He came walking out from the side of the house. It was strange. I said walking, but 'stumbling' is probably more accurate. He looked dazed. Confused. Just out of sorts. I felt for him. Then he sat down on the porch, rolled himself up into a ball, and it initially sounded to me like he was trying to say…something. I couldn't make out any real words, especially over all the other reporters. I didn't know what to do, and then you were out here."

Laura stood up and turned to Stephen and Amanda. "He won't look at me. There's something weird going on with him. Maybe it's the stress of everything. I don't know. But I'm afraid something's wrong. We need to do something."

"Yeah. I'm just not sure what." Stephen sighed. "Some crazy stuff went on upstairs, Laura. I don't even know where to start. Let's get him inside, and I'll do my best."

Laura bent down to pick Ryan up, and the three of them turned toward the front door.

"I hope your son feels better," Elizabeth said.

Stephen turned and gave her a slight nod, and they went back inside.

26

"Do you think you should just talk to them?" Amanda sipped on a chamomile tea, cradling the mug in both hands and just touching it to her lips, the heat flowing across her tongue into her throat.

Laura laid a half-full bottle of vodka on the island and looked across at Amanda.

"Talk to who?"

"Them," she motioned her head toward the front of the house, and took another careful sip. "The reporters out there. Isn't that what they want? Maybe they'll go away."

"I'm not sure that's how it works," Laura laughed slightly. "Give them a taste, and they'd get even more hungry."

Amanda nodded, leaning on the island. "You may be right. I could see that. They've got a job to do, and I guess you guys are that job for the time being."

Laura threw back a shot of vodka, then lifted the bottle again. "And quite a job they're doing."

"But even if they wouldn't leave, there might be some value in it."

"And what would that be?"

Laura turned as she heard Stephen step off the stairs into the kitchen.

"Still resting?" she asked.

"Yeah, he's out like a light. Thankfully. Nathan said he's tied up today, but we should call him back tomorrow if Ryan doesn't seem better, and to try to get him some sleep. So we're successful on that front, at least."

"Small miracles," Laura said. "Let's keep checking on him." Stephen nodded.

"So…" Amanda said, then paused as she took a bigger swig of her cooling tea. "You asked what the value of talking to the press might be."

Laura swung her chair around and propped her elbows on the island. Stephen sat down next to her.

"Well, don't they always say to get out in front of a story? I mean, I know none of us is a PR expert or anything, but we've all heard that. It's Politics 101. And, in a way, that's what this is—politics. Or PR. Whatever. You guys are in the midst of a public relations crisis. It's almost like you need a media relations manager to handle this stuff. You don't have one, though. All you've got is me."

She smiled, and Laura threw a side glance at Stephen, who rolled his eyes and stifled a laugh.

"And," Amanda said, pausing for another quick drink, "I think you should tell your story. Get some sympathy from the community. They've heard nothing from you. And I know you guys have been avoiding most of what's been written, but I'm gonna go ahead and tell you it hasn't exactly all been positive. In the absence of real news, people are gonna make up bullshit, whether it's to get viewers or clicks or just to try to make sense of things. You can fill that gap between what's real and what's not with your own words, if you want."

"I appreciate what you're saying. I really do," Stephen said, then wrinkled his nose. "I just don't think either one of us wants to stand out there and have all those cameras and microphones pointed at us."

Amanda sighed. "I get that. So what about just one of them? We do it in the house. On your home turf. I could even be your liaison of sorts, and you wouldn't have to go out there at all."

Laura ran a hand through her hair and looked at the ceiling for a moment.

"But who would that one be?"

Amanda took a big gulp and smiled.

"Elizabeth Cassels seemed nice."

Laura carried a rocking chair into the living room and set it down near the recliner with both facing the couch, a small coffee table between them. Stephen was scooping magazines off the table and then used a white cloth to wipe some dust off its surface.

He tossed the magazines in the recycling bin, wiped his forehead with the back side of the cloth and looked at Laura. "Are we ready for this?" he said apprehensively, leaning against the wall.

"We're ready. We've been over it. We're gonna be fine."

"I'm just nervous I'll say something I shouldn't. The media can twist anything they want to, even if just by the words they choose to use or leave out."

She walked across the room and put her hands on his shoulders, then met his eyes with her own.

"It's been a rough few days. I'm stressed as hell. I know you are too. But I think Amanda's probably right. Getting our story out there is the best thing for us at this point. If we can tell what happened, honestly, no bullshit, I think we'll get people on our side. This is a loving, supportive community. They want to be behind us, I'm sure of it. They're just scared, and desperate. Can we say we wouldn't feel the same way if it were another family in our position?

"I know I'd do *anything* for those boys upstairs, and so would you. Other parents feel the same way about their kids. They want to save them. They want what we already have, and they're willing to put pressure on us in order to get it. What we have to do is get them to understand that we know the way they feel, that we sympathize with them and want to do anything we can to help them. But, right now, we just don't know, and we've got a family of our own to think about too."

He nodded. "Are we gonna stick with the lullaby story?"

"Wouldn't want to make a liar out of you, would we?" She grinned, and he laughed. "But let's not get too carried away with it. Okay, Little Boy Blue?"

Amanda peeked her head through the door and made eye contact with Laura. "We ready?" she asked.

Laura looked at Stephen, mouthing the words "We got this," and walked to the door. Amanda pushed through the door and motioned for Elizabeth to walk inside.

"Hi, Mrs. Fraser. Pleasure to meet you. I'm Elizabeth Cassels with the Knoxville *News Press*," she extended her hand, and Laura shook it. "This is Peter Leigh. He's here to take pictures if you don't mind. We wanted to get some shots without that harsh lighting outside, help show you're a regular family just like anybody else out there. We'd particularly like some shots of Kevin while we're here. Show that miracle of yours off to the world."

"I guess that's fine. I can take you upstairs really quickly to get a couple shots of Kevin," Laura said, shaking Peter's hand, then gesturing toward Stephen. "This is my husband, Stephen. Oh, and call me Laura."

Stephen stepped forward, greeting them with a handshake.

"I apologize for the limited seating, but we don't sit in here as a big group all that often. We spend a lot of time in the kitchen, where the food is."

Elizabeth laughed and settled into the rocking chair, next to Amanda in the recliner. "That sounds like me when I get back to my apartment at night. A splash of bourbon and some PB and J over the kitchen sink at two a.m., then off to bed. Barely even think about the living room."

"You're a girl after my own heart," Laura said. "I'm pretty sure hard liquor and PB and J are staple foods of a healthy diet."

"The surgeon general recommends it."

Laura hoped the laughter would break the tension a little bit. She knew Stephen didn't deal well with stress, but she appreciated him trying. She was holding it together, but not as well as she wished she were; she wished she had the vodka bottle sitting next to her, but she didn't think that'd be the best look. Laura was doing the best she could to mask the fact that there was a constant knot in her stomach, at least partly because she thought Stephen needed her to. She knew him well enough to know he probably wanted to be strong for her, but he didn't have it in him. She still saw in him the man who made her heart flutter years ago, and he was a terrific father, but he was no action hero. He'd thought reasonably quickly to come up with the singing lie to get those people off his back before, but she wished she'd have been there to maybe think up something more plausible. If people found out he lied, it could give their credibility another hit, and she didn't know what the reaction would be. She was hoping this interview could help get that narrative under control.

That was one of the biggest challenges for her—she craved control, and she felt like everything in her life was spiraling away from her. She had no control over Kevin falling into a coma, or him eventually waking up. She couldn't control what would happen to Ryan. And now, she couldn't even control her little world at the brewery or her own home. This was her chance to take a modicum of that back. She'd rehearsed the words in her head. She knew the message she wanted to get across. They'd be sympathetic, thankful to God, puzzled by what was happening, and eager to help. People would put themselves in her shoes, and feel like they'd handle it much the same way. And if she could accomplish that, maybe she could start to get her family and the sanity of her life back.

"We'll just be a minute," Laura said, tilting her head to signal Peter to come with her.

Elizabeth nodded. "So, shall we begin?"

"Shoot," Stephen said, hoping he was ready for this.

"Let's talk about the current situation a little bit," Elizabeth began. "What was it like when you found Kevin was actually awake?"

"Well, I was the first one up there," Stephen said. "It was in the morning. Laura and I had been downstairs chatting, and we heard…"

He paused, not sure of the next words. A *scream* is what they'd heard. Ryan's, he had assumed. But, after hearing Kevin yell at him the morning of the interview—or did he imagine that?—he wondered if they'd actually heard Kevin on the morning he woke up. That wasn't physically possible, though, to wake up from more than a year in a coma and immediately scream. And, after all, he could still barely whisper, and only a word or two. Or, well, that was what Stephen had thought, anyway.

What was the right answer? If they had been right that it was Ryan, was that information they wanted out into the world? Did they want to expose Ryan to that sort of scrutiny?

"…a noise," Stephen said, after pausing a few seconds. "We didn't know what it was, but we thought it came from Kevin's room. Which was, of course, pretty unusual. We raced up the steps, threw open the door, and there he was. You could see the white of his eyes for the first time in so long. The feeling was indescribable. Truly. We didn't know what to do with ourselves, whether to cry or laugh or just collapse in a heap on the floor. What did we do to get so lucky, ya know? I think it's fair to say it was the best moment of our lives."

"It really was," said Laura, stepping off the stairs, Peter close behind her. She sat down next to Stephen on the couch. "It sounds cliché, I'm sure. But we're the first parents to experience this. It was a mixture of the most amazing elation and relief you could ever feel, along with a feeling of bewilderment and..."

She scratched her head, looking at the ceiling as if the words she was looking for might be scaling up the walls. She threw her hair back and shrugged her shoulders.

"...just *thanks*, I guess. We aren't special, or more deserving of this than any of the millions of wonderful parents out there who agonize over their child's fate every day. It's heartbreaking to think about. We know exactly how they feel, because that's how *we* felt. It's easy to get numb to it all. But I think it's important that we don't let this become *normal*. That we don't just accept it, like this is reality, and the human race is doomed to march toward extinction. We need to keep that sense that The Sleep is wrong, and fixable. We're hoping Kevin's awakening can give people a jolt of hope.

"And, well, two of those people are me and Stephen. Along with our other son, Ryan."

She gave a melancholy smile to Elizabeth, who returned a sympathetic frown.

"Yes, absolutely," Elizabeth said. "I know a little bit about your younger son. Ryan's tenth birthday is tomorrow, right?"

"That's right," Laura said.

"That has to be challenging for all of you. What should be a time of happiness is weighed down by this huge unknown. What have you done to prepare?"

"Well, it's tough," Stephen admitted. "Emotionally, you can try to shield yourself from it, but it's comin' for you whether you're ready or not. We've been through this before, so we know the steps, so to speak. That can only prepare you so much, though."

"Of course." Elizabeth nodded and scribbled in her notebook. "And have you been singing the lullabies to him too?"

Stephen felt sweat begin to bead on his forehead. He hoped it wasn't noticeable, as Peter snapped a picture of him from his right.

"What was that?" Stephen said.

"Lullabies. Nursery rhymes. We'd heard you sang them regularly to Kevin leading up to his waking up. That's what you told neighbors a few days ago, right?"

Stephen nodded tentatively.

"Right," Elizabeth said. "So, I was just wondering if you were continuing that with Ryan, maybe trying to preemptively head it off in case that helped with his brother."

The sweat on Stephen's head got colder.

"Um, yeah. Yeah," he said. "Sorry, I didn't understand the question at first. Yeah, we've been doing the same with Ryan recently."

"Great," Elizabeth said, leaning forward, her notebook resting in her lap, pen between her fingers. "So you think that was what caused it?"

"We aren't doctors, Elizabeth," Laura said, smiling widely. "We'd hate to speculate. The truth is, we really don't know. We're just trying anything we know how. Did we accidentally stumble upon the solution everyone's been looking for? Maybe. If so, nobody would be happier than us. There's just no way to know right now, though."

"Sure. Yeah," Elizabeth said. "It's just that, we've talked to a number of experts, and none of them seem to think that could have any real effect. Do you have any reason to think it did?"

Stephen's head was pounding, and his heart's rhythm was picking up. He didn't know why she was pushing this line of questioning. He had hoped this would be an easy way for them to get a feel-good story out in the media, but now he worried she was going to set a trap for them. Maybe Laura's instinct hadn't been right.

"Are you accusing us of—" Laura started, but was interrupted by a noise from behind the couch. It was Ryan stepping onto the kitchen floor from the stairs. Elizabeth was facing him; she smiled and motioned him into the living room.

"Hi, Ryan!" she said. "I'm Elizabeth. How are you doing?"

Walking beside the couch, he stared quietly at her.

"Okay, Ryan. We should get you back in bed," Amanda said, standing up to take him back to his room. "Wave to the nice lady, Ryan."

"Are you looking forward to your lullaby, Ryan?" Elizabeth asked.

Ryan stepped forward. "What?"

Amanda reached down and put her arms around him, but he slapped at her arms and yelped, stiffening his back and falling to the floor.

"They sing a song to you every night," Elizabeth said. "Right?"

Ryan stood back up and looked back at his parents. Stephen wiped his head with his shirt sleeve.

"Where did people get the idea that they sing?" Ryan said. "They never sing anything. Why do people think you guys sing?"

"All right. That's it. Too much excitement for you for one day, Ryan." Amanda scooped him up and threw him over her right shoulder while he kicked and screamed. "I'll just take him upstairs so he won't be in the way. You guys continue."

Amanda half-jogged to the stairs. Stephen could hear Ryan's yelling fade as she got him up to the hall, then down to his room. He swallowed hard, and looked at Elizabeth.

"Is there a reason you're lying about the singing, Mister Fraser?" she asked. "It seems like a small thing. Why the lie?"

Stephen stared back at her, breathing fast. He didn't know how to answer. She was right. It *seemed* like a small lie. The thing was, he didn't even know what—if anything, really—he was trying to conceal. Maybe something about Ryan. Or Kevin. Maybe nothing, except Kevin woke up, and that was really damn weird, and there was no good reason. All he knew was that every instinct he had was telling him to protect them. He came up with that lie on the spur of the moment. He could come up with another one here, but what good would that do?

"Mister Fraser?" she said, after he didn't respond. "What are you trying to hide?"

As sweat dripped down to his cheeks, Stephen could only think that he wished he knew.

27

Frasers struggle to explain son's awakening

By Elizabeth Cassels
News Press Staff

They've been asked the question dozens, maybe hundreds of times. They've asked it to themselves even more. They still don't have an answer.

Laura and Stephen Fraser were stunned when their oldest son, Kevin, awoke five days ago after more than a year in the grip of The Sleep.

Other parents in the community continue to demand answers—there must be something different about them, about their home, the way they cared for Kevin. Or something about Kevin himself. But no breakthroughs have come so far, despite the research of doctors from the Center for Disease Control and the reflections of the family members themselves.

"We aren't special, or more deserving of this than any of the millions of wonderful parents out there who agonize over their child's fate every day," Laura said. "It's heartbreaking to think about. We know exactly how (the other parents) feel, because that's how *we* felt."

The Frasers know first hand the feelings of the other parents not only because of their own personal experience, but because people of the community have been persistent in getting their message to the Frasers.

Recently, a large group of concerned citizens gathered on the Frasers' lawn in West Knoxville, and one of them, Denise Marshall, was invited inside to have a conversation with Stephen, who told her they suspected the reason for Kevin's awakening might be that they'd been singing nursery rhymes to him each night for several weeks.

After a number of medical professionals said they doubted that could be the case, Stephen on Tuesday acknowledged he lied about the singing after his youngest son, Ryan, said it never happened.

"I don't know why. I just don't know," Stephen said. "It's all been so hard. I don't know what the right thing is anymore."

In addition to the unprecedented awakening of Kevin—he's still the only known child to have come out of The Sleep coma since the plague began in 1999—the family has experienced a break-in at Palmyra, the downtown brewery that Laura owns and operates, vandalism at their home, and Ryan's 10th birthday coming up on Wednesday.

That birthday has been weighing heavily on them, as it does with every family. They say they don't know any better than anyone else what Kevin's awakening means, for themselves, Ryan, the community or the world at large.

"Emotionally, you can try to shield yourself from (The Sleep), but it's coming for you whether you're ready or not," Stephen said. "We've been through this before, so we know the steps, so to speak. That can only prepare you so much, though."

By Thursday morning, they'll know more—at least about if Kevin waking up has any impact on Ryan's impending Sleep. Because there's no precedent for this, doctors and child psychologists haven't reached any sort of consensus on how it might affect Ryan.

Nurse practitioner Brent Harris, who's been working with the Frasers since The Sleep took Kevin, said there's plenty of speculation, but few concrete facts to draw on in this case.

"There's just not much to say about it, from a medical perspective," Harris said. "We've never seen this before. Every bit of information we can gather from Kevin is helpful, and Ryan's fate could take this in a new direction once we know what it is. But, for now, no one knows what any of this ultimately means. It's fascinating, and it's been amazing to witness, but we're still very much in the dark, as a medical community."

Laura looked over the top of her laptop at Stephen, who was still looking down at his screen on the other side of the kitchen island. She looked at the top of his head, trying to will him to look up. Finally, his eyes rose to hers.

"What do you think?" she said.

"It's…not as bad as I worried it would be."

"No, that was probably about as fair as we could have asked for. And the picture of Kevin looks better than I expected," she said. "I just wish she could have left the lying part out."

"But there was no way she could. She's a reporter."

"I know." Laura sighed. "Why did Ryan have to pick that moment to get talkative?"

"Say what you will about him being an introvert, he can be sassy sometimes when he knows something somebody else doesn't."

"Yeah." She lowered her head, and looked toward the floor. Then she slammed her hand into the island. "Fuck! Fuck. God damn it. Maybe we shouldn't have done the interview. I just thought, everything was spiraling out of control, and maybe this was a way for us to—"

"I know. I know, babe. It's fine. Amanda was right. It made

sense. It's not like that wasn't gonna come out anyway. The lie bought us a little time, but that was all. If I hadn't screwed that up, there wouldn't have been any problem."

She reached across the island and grabbed his hand. She put her other hand over the top of it.

"You didn't screw anything up. You did your best," she said, trying to force a smile. "We're gonna figure this out. We're not gonna let this destroy us. We're stronger than this. Okay? We can do this."

"Ya know what we've gotta do first? There's a birthday boy upstairs, and we need to do something for him."

"Yeah. That. The day's here." Laura walked to the refrigerator and opened the door. "We could wake him up with cake," she said. "I had them build a tower with soldiers charging toward it."

"He's gonna like that."

"Probably the last time he wakes up. Might as well do it with icing on his face."

Her phone rang, and Denise picked it up off the table next to the couch.

"Hello?" she said. "Of course I read it. It keeps getting crazier, doesn't it?"

She stood and grabbed her pack of cigarettes from the coffee table, leaving the local news playing on the TV as she walked toward the back of the house.

"Oh, Laura put him up to it, ya know? I have no doubt about that. Stephen wouldn't come up with a lie like that on his own. That's just not the way his mind works, from what I've seen. He really is a good guy. Seriously. That story was all her doing."

Denise opened the back door and stepped out to the patio. It was a chilly morning, but the yellow coating of pollen on the concrete and the plastic chairs strewn across the yard told her spring was on the verge of becoming more than just a function of the calendar.

"Yeah, that was cool getting mentioned in the paper, huh? I'm famous. I bet Nate's jealous. They're writing about the family he's been working with for years, they quote some *other* psychologist, and then I get name dropped. It's hilarious. Can't wait to see his face when he reads it."

Pulling one of the chairs toward her, she swept the yellow dusting off with her hand, then swiped her hands together, trying to shake the pollen free. She took one more look at the chair, and sat down, then crossed her left leg across her right knee.

"You're not on the Neighbors message board, are you?" She stuck a cigarette between her lips and struck her lighter, the flame springing to life as she listened. "That's right. Well, it's really a hoot. You should get on there. So much gossip. Anyway, people on there are getting seriously impatient. Did you know they've denied every doctor and scientist who's called any access to Kevin? Yeah, I know. I read that on the board. No, I don't trust the newspaper. They just sensationalize everything. It's crazy, right? That's what's driving people nuts."

Denise leaned the chair back on two legs, resting against the side of the house as she blew smoke into the cool air.

"Well, yeah. Right. If they hadn't been so defiant, maybe we'd all have an answer, ya know? But you can't *make* parents have their kid examined by a doctor for not being sick enough, I guess. So we all sit here twiddling our thumbs while they stay holed up in their little bunker. From what I hear, Laura's the only one who leaves the house, so she can go to her brewery. She's basically locking the rest of them inside."

Out of the corner of her eye, Denise saw Nathan peeking out the window at her. She wondered what he was thinking, watching her smoke in the back yard.

"Sure. Yeah. I mean, my feelings on her are well documented—She's a conniving, cheating little bitch who doesn't have an empathetic bone in her body. She's been blessed with two healthy sons, which wouldn't make sense in a totally fair world. God has His reasons, I know that much. But, for the life of me, I can't figure out why she was chosen for this. Maybe it's going to ultimately be her downfall. I can't say I wouldn't get some satisfaction out of that."

Denise slid off her slippers and walked into the grass barefoot. She loved feeling the damp coolness, letting her toes stiffen up and a shiver creep up her calves. The grass twisted and turned beneath her feet, cushioning and cradling them as she strolled her yard, the phone pressed between her ear and shoulder.

"I really don't know what happens next, but people on the board are pissed about the lie, ya know? I know that much. They feel like they've been played. I'm trying to be a bit of peacekeeper, mostly because Stephen and the kids didn't do anything wrong, and I don't think riots around here are gonna be good for anybody. But there's only so much that can be done, ya know? I just know they didn't help themselves there."

Denise tossed the cigarette down on the patio and slid back into her slippers. She walked to the back door and paused with her hand on the doorknob.

"Yeah, that's right. Today's the other kid's tenth birthday. Shit's gonna get interesting, isn't it? It's a good question—What happens if The Sleep doesn't take him? Maybe one could be some weird fucking fluke. But two? Within a week or so of each other? There'd be no way to dismiss that as some unknowable mystery. They'd have to come clean. They'd have to let the doctors come in and run whatever tests they needed. For the good of the human race, they'd have to give up. And if they won't, well, I don't know what the consequences might be. I just know patience is wearing thin around here, ya know?"

"All right. Well, I'm goin' back in. We'll see if Nate's still here. Maybe I can rub my newfound fame in his face. Take care, girl."

28

Laura glanced at her watch. It was nearly three o'clock; the day was mostly over, and she was struggling. On one hand, she wanted it to go on forever, drag into infinity. This could be Ryan's last day alive and awake, being their quiet, smart, loving little boy. She tried to remember how they'd done it before, watching Kevin's final potential hours and minutes tick away. Knowing that, no matter what happened, the media swarm seemed likely to get worse. The dread and uncertainty. The boulder that settled into her stomach and sat there, turning into cramps and keeping her from eating.

Had it been this bad with Kevin? Although it was just a little over a year earlier, but she couldn't recall. She knew it had been a rough couple of days, but she didn't remember the sheer physical pain the stress was putting her under. Maybe having another kid with time still left helped give her some solace then, knowing the house wouldn't go completely quiet just yet.

And that was definitely part of it—the coming silence in their home. Even a relatively soft-spoken little kid was prone to outbursts and pattering around, tap-tapping down the stairs to get a snack or lie on the couch. Losing that was unfathomable to her. Their house turning into a near-morgue, death peeking around the corner and mocking them from the other side, unwilling to fully take their children but unwilling to let them go either. Ryan would be in purgatory of death while Kevin was in purgatory of life. Neither anything resembling a normal, living child, but neither gone enough to be buried and mourned.

That was even more the case now that *everyone* could point to the Frasers and say that could be them next. The news was reporting that parents had virtually stopped surrendering their kids to be put down humanely in the days since word spread of Kevin waking up. The government couldn't justify continuing the program anyway in the face of public backlash, so they'd put it on hold until they could learn more.

The eyes of the world were on their home, on what might happen in the coming days. As Kevin had approached his tenth birthday, they were just a normal family dealing with the same problems everyone else was as their child approached their The Sleep. But now, that had all changed. Now they were inspirations. Models. Carriers of the flame for every family still holding out hope that change could come in their lifetime. And, now, liars. Selfish hoarders of the secrets of life itself.

Sitting on the couch, Laura looked down at her mom and dad playing Crazy Eights with Ryan on the floor, a half-eaten cake with a few headless soldiers next to them. They'd spent much of the morning with Kevin in his room, but he said he was tired, so they left to give him some rest. He was getting bursts of a raspy voice back; his energy level was still low, though. He'd be awake for a few hours, but then his eyes would get heavy. Laura sometimes wondered if much of it was frustration at not being able to do more than just lie there and watch, so it was easier for him to kick them out and be alone at some point. If so, she couldn't blame him.

Downstairs, Ryan's tenth birthday carried on. He never gave them marching orders for the day. He didn't have any hobbies they could all participate in, and he didn't have any friends he wanted to join the celebration. With the media camp outside the house, they doubted anyone would have wanted to come over anyway. Laura's parents showed up before 5 a.m., while most of the media people were either asleep or lethargic; they brought some board games and a box of playing cards. They knew Ryan well enough to know they could keep him happy for a good portion of the day with the right combination of cake and games.

If Ryan wanted to play cards with his grandparents for much of the afternoon, Laura was perfectly content to sit there and nurse a gin and tonic—along with the rock in her midsection—and not breathe a word of complaint. At least she still had a life ahead of her. Any little smile she got out of Ryan, she'd try to treasure it. Her eyes rarely left him. Not as he ripped the shiny wrapping paper off a box that held a gray striped polo shirt and a pair of jeans that were a size too big. Not when she saw him sneak a third piece of cake, but she didn't have the heart to call him on it.

In a way, it was a perfect day, the whole family being together, Stephen hoisting Ryan onto his shoulders and carrying him around the house, and Laura's parents watching the latest YouTube video he'd been laughing at for days. Everybody played their part, as if this was just another birthday, another day in their lives. As if everything wasn't about to change forever.

She felt the couch jostle, and noticed Stephen had flopped down beside her.

"How ya hangin' in there, hon'?" he said, laying his hand on her knee while Ryan laid another card into the discard pile.

"Barely," she sighed and raised her glass to her lips. "Pretty much been going back and forth between watching Ryan and my fucking watch all day."

"I know what you mean. Really thankful your mom and dad came up. Took a lot of pressure off us."

"Wild horses couldn't have kept them away today. You know that. They know they got a lucky gift back with Kevin; they're not gonna waste a second with Ryan. The challenge is gonna be getting them to leave at some point."

"Hey, they can stay as long as they want, as far as I'm concerned."

"They gonna take our bed?"

"Sure." He smiled. "We'll get out the tent and go backyard camping. It'll be an adventure."

She stifled a laugh. "They got central heat and a hot shower out there?"

"I'll keep you warm."

"I'm sure you'd love to try."

She gave him a playful shove, and he clutched his shoulder, acting like she gave him a roundhouse kick, falling backward against the arm of the couch. She laughed and smacked him with a throw pillow that was lying behind her, while he curled up to block the blows.

For a moment, Laura did forget about Ryan and Kevin, about the chaos threatening to envelop their lives. For a moment, she was able to just be a woman who loved her husband, and enjoyed being around him. Those moments didn't come nearly as often as they had in the early days of their marriage. There were times she looked at Stephen and wondered what the future had in store for them, if they could weather the storm ahead. But occasionally, light shone through that. Occasionally, in moments like these, she remembered what it was like to truly enjoy being with him, and recognize how well he understood her.

From the table behind her, Laura heard her phone ring. She dropped the pillow and leaned back to pick it up. She didn't recognize the number, and she hesitated before answering it. She looked at Stephen and sucked in her breath. He pointed at her as if to say "Your call."

She tapped the button and put the phone to her ear. "This is Laura."

"Hello, whore."

Her chest tightened, and her neck tensed. Her head felt as if it were collapsing in upon itself, the pressure growing from the top of her spine. She could feel her fingers clutching the phone tighter, squeezing it like it was the last life raft in the sea. In the seconds following the words on the other end of the line, her actions were involuntary, unconscious. She couldn't control them anymore than she could stop the tide from coming in. The rage and helplessness was too much. Her body reacted with intensity.

She knew, though, she had to maintain *some* measure of control. She didn't want to derail Ryan's birthday, and she didn't want her parents to worry. She took three deep breaths and rose from the couch, raising an index finger to Stephen as she walked to the kitchen.

"Who the *fuck* is this?" she spoke in a seething whisper. "I swear to god, I'm gonna find out."

"Is Ryan enjoying his birthday?"

The mention of Ryan's name turned the pressure in her head into a full-body ache. She tried to concentrate, think about who it could be. Did she recognize the voice? Her first instinct was to assume that it was the same person who spray-painted the message on their porch the previous morning, but there was no way to know that. In all likelihood, word of that had spread to virtually everyone in the town and—given their celebrity status— to untold masses around the world. In theory, it made sense that this could be the same person. It could be basically anyone who wanted to terrorize her.

"Don't you say my son's name," she hissed, her teeth grinding together with each word. "You don't know us. You don't get to talk about him."

"Oh, but I *do* know you. Everybody knows *you*, the little whore of Knoxville. Do you like lying? Is it something you're good at?"

"I don't know who this is, and I don't know what you're talking about. Don't call again."

"You know *exactly* what I'm talking about. You lie about your kids just like you lie about messing around behind your husband's back."

That got her attention. Did this person actually know something, or was he just trying to get a rise out of her? Either way, this was starting to sound personal. That could make it more likely it was someone in town, someone she even perhaps knew; the area code wasn't the local 865, but that didn't mean much in the days of cell phones. Maybe someone who was disguising their voice somehow? It sounded like a man, but it also sounded somewhat artificial, like it might be run through some sort of computerized filter. The possibility still existed, though, that this was just some random person from wherever taking a wild guess. She didn't want to assume too much.

"I'm hanging up now and blocking your number. Have a nice day."

"It's gonna be worse than spray paint next time you—"

She hit "End Call" and threw the phone down the island, where it slid off and crashed into the linoleum floor, smashing into the wall. Stephen had been standing a few steps away, and he hurried over to her, placing an arm across her back.

"Hey, hey, hey. What was that?" he said, as she buried her head into the crook of her arm and began to cry. He rubbed her shoulders. "It's okay. Everything's gonna be fine. Who was on the phone?"

Laura shook her head, still wrapped tightly in her arms.

"All right, babe," he said, his hand moving across her back. "It's fine. Just take whatever time you need. I'll be right here."

She sucked in a deep breath, then raised her head. Beyond Stephen, she saw her parents looking on, frowning, flanking Ryan at the edge of the kitchen.

"Oh, god, I'm a mess." Laura wiped a sleeve across both eyes and shivered. "You guys go back to your game. I—I'm okay. I'm fine. Really. It's Ryan's birthday. I don't need to be going on like this."

James walked over to Stephen and patted his shoulder. He whispered in Stephen's ear, and they traded places. Stephen took Paula and Ryan back into the living room.

"What's wrong, sweetheart?" James asked. "I know these past few days have been stressful."

"Everyone hates us, dad." The tears started coming again. "I just don't understand how this happened. In a few days, we've gone from another random family trying to prepare for our second kid to fall into a god damn coma to the most hated and scrutinized family on the fucking *planet*. Now I'm getting threatening phone calls. People are vandalizing the house, breaking into the brewery. I feel like I'm losing it."

He nodded and put his arms around her, pulling her close while she wept on his shirt.

"I know," he said. "You two have handled this as well as you could. There's no script for this, just like raising kids. You remember what I told you when Kevin was born? You asked me how to be a good parent. You remember?"

She raised her head, tears choking in her throat. "You said, 'The script for Kevin hasn't been written yet.'"

He smiled. "You remembered."

"Of course, dad," she buried her head back into his shoulder, her arms pulling tight against him.

"Well, it's the same here. Just like millions of parents haven't had Kevin, or Ryan, nobody's gone through this before. Unfortunately, you're the first, and you're having to make it up as you go. You two have chosen to wrap your arms around your boys and try to shield them from whatever you can. I think that's a valiant and noble choice that people should respect. But people are selfish, and they want to know what's in it for them in any situation. They don't put themselves in other people's shoes. This world would be a hell of a lot better place if more people did."

She sniffed loudly and squeezed him tightly one more time

before standing on her toes and kissing him on the cheek.

"Thanks, Dad. We appreciate you guys always being there for us. With Stephen's parents not being around, I don't know what we'd do without you and mom."

He put his hand on her shoulders, and looked into her eyes. "Whatever you all need. You know that, right? There's nothing we won't do for you. We love you, and we're always just a phone call away."

She nodded and kissed his cheek again. They hugged, and then pushed apart.

"Now, you wanna come play some cards?" he said. "There's still cake left."

For a brief moment, she didn't feel the boulder in her stomach.

"That sounds nice."

The four of them surrounded the bed, with Ryan lying looking up at them, the blankets snug beneath his chin. It was a few minutes before midnight. Laura kneeled beside him and rubbed his forehead as his eyelids struggled to stay open.

"You're not gonna be able to stay awake much longer, sweetie," she said. "Have you had a good birthday?"

He nodded slightly, but it was easy to see he didn't have much energy left. At any point, his eyes could close for the last time. Stephen looked on, wanting to make the most of these final moments. His mind flashed back to a little over a year before, when much the same scene played out with Kevin, the four of them saying goodbye, Ryan struggling to stay awake as late as possible so he could spend a little more time with his brother.

That time, they all knew what was coming. And even then, there was a sliver of doubt. Even after two decades of children across the world falling into a coma, as parents, you wondered—It had to end at some point, didn't it? And, if it did, why not with our kid? You knew you wouldn't sleep that night. You knew your mind would be racing too fast, going over scenarios in the coming days, obsessing over every memory of the first time the kid walked or talked or said "Daddy." Thinking none of that could ever happen again, though still with that lingering doubt.

That was partially because the whole phenomenon was unfathomable. A ten-year-old boy, full of life, healthy, laughing, running around the yard enthusiastically, snuffed out for no apparent reason. No accident. No brain injury. No trauma. Stephen felt like the absurdity of it clouded your mind as a parent. Maybe the other kids hadn't been this happy, hadn't been this full of life. Maybe your family was special. Maybe it could be different.

But then it wasn't. And you wept, screamed, cursed God, fell into a depression. Some parents just ended it right there, slumped over their child's comatose body. He understood the instinct, but he didn't have the fortitude for it. Looking down on Ryan there in the bed, his wife talking to him, willing him to stay a few more minutes as her quirky little son, he *really* understood the instinct.

Still, though, if any parents had reason to at least have a glimmer of hope headed into this particular evening, it was him and Laura. If any grandparents had a *rational* reason to think maybe it could actually be different this time, it was the ones standing on the other side of the bed from him on this night, as the last minutes of Ryan's tenth birthday ticked away.

That was because an eleven-year-old—amazingly, an *eleven-year-old!*—was asleep down the hall, and they were pretty confident he'd wake up the next morning. They'd feed him and spend some time talking to him, testing out his vocal chords to see how he was coming along there, seeing how his motor skills were improving.

Stephen still didn't know what to make of the incident with Kevin's screaming and the chest in the room; part of him thought he imagined the entire thing. Part of him was scared it would happen again. With everything else going on, he still hadn't talked to Laura—or anyone—about it. He figured she'd forgotten to ask by this point.

The important part, though, was Kevin was awake and part of their lives again. And that gave them at least *some* reason beyond a mere wish to think maybe there really *would* be something different this time. Maybe they really *had* cracked the code, whatever that code was. Of course, that was going to make it even more devastating the next morning if Ryan didn't wake up after all. Hope is a dangerous thing that isn't easily extinguished, and Stephen feared it could be the spark that lighted the fuse that sent them spiraling deeper into madness.

He knelt beside Laura and put one arm around her, rubbing Ryan's leg with the other. The boy kept forcing his eyelids back open every time they'd nearly go shut.

"I don't want to go to sleep," Ryan said, in a voice that sounded younger than he was, borderline pouty. "Am I gonna wake up again?"

Laura's head fell toward the bed, and she raised it back up again.

"Yes. Of course you are, baby," Laura's voice cracked. Stephen could see she was struggling to look confident.

"You think so? What about all the other kids?"

"Your brother's awake, isn't he?" she said. "You talked to him this morning."

"Yeah."

She swallowed hard. "Well, there's your answer then. We've got this figured out, kiddo. Don't worry at all, okay? Just…Just go to sleep. We'll see you in the morning, and Daddy will have a nice, big breakfast ready for you. How's that sound?"

"Good. Why are you crying, Daddy?"

Stephen hadn't realized tears were dripping off his cheeks. He quickly wiped them with his hand.

"No. No, big guy. I'm not crying. Just a little tired. It's past my bedtime. We should all be getting to sleep."

Stephen watched Ryan's eyelids flutter, then squeeze together. His head fell to the side, resting against the pillow. His limbs went limp, and he was lightly snoring within seconds. At 12:03 a.m. on the day after his tenth birthday, Ryan was asleep.

29

Lying on the couch downstairs, Laura stared at the ceiling.

"You know there are a hundred and thirty-six squares in each section of this ceiling?" she said, then counting the larger squares. "Well, except those that get cut off against the wall. Those aren't as big."

"God, you're delirious," said Stephen, leaning back as far as the recliner would go. "What time is it?"

She fished her arm out from between couch cushions to check her watch.

"Quarter to six. Have you slept at all?"

"Not sure. Don't think so. It's hard to tell. Sometimes, I feel myself drifting, and then I think about taking Ryan on his first hike in the mountains, and I'm wide awake again."

"You should try counting the ceiling squares."

"Sounds scintillating. Is it anything like counting sheep?"

"I don't know. I'm eventually gonna run out of squares to count. I suppose sheep can go on as long as your mind can keep tossing 'em out there."

"So the sheep win, I guess," he said, rolling over to his side, trying to find a comfortable spot.

"I hope Mom and Dad are okay in our bed," said Laura, letting her eyes go out of focus, the squares getting fuzzy and blending together. "Dad's probably up there snoring right now."

"We really need a fourth bedroom."

"We were able to use the old garage until you turned it into your therapy room, smart guy."

"Ah, that's right," he said. "Well, I guess this chair is more comfy than a squat rack."

Laura picked up one of the pillows she kicked to the floor earlier in the night, and shoved it underneath her feet, trying to get them elevated, hoping it might make lying on the faux-leather couch more bearable.

"I'm *really* tempted to go up there and wake him up," she said. "I swear, this night's never gonna end."

"You know that doesn't help. The kid didn't go to bed until after midnight. If you wake him up too early, he'll just fall back asleep and the coma will hit then."

"Yeah, I know all about the studies and everything. We've been through this shit before. Doesn't change how I *feel*, though. The temptation is insane, even if I know it's pointless."

"What are we gonna do, Laura? I mean, about all this. Assuming Ryan's out."

"Well, since Kevin woke up out of nowhere, we obviously have to keep Ryan going. As long as humanly possible. There's no other option."

"I get what you're saying. But *how*? How do we afford caring for one child in a coma and another trying to rehabilitate from one? That'd strain the budget of even a fairly rich family. And we're *far* from that."

"*Fuck*, Stephen. I don't know. Bank loans? Second mortgage? Take equity out of the house? Sell plasma? My parents could probably help us some. I could go wait fucking tables somewhere. I don't know, but we're fucking *doing* it. We'll figure it out."

"We already took out a second mortgage to get money for—"

"Then a third, damn it! Or a fourth! Or a fifth! *Whatever it fucking takes*." Laura sat up and faced Stephen, speaking in a hard whisper. "This *really* isn't what I want to be discussing right now."

"Okay. Fine. We've just been putting off the conversation for awhile, and we're out of time."

"You don't think I *know* that? Jesus, Stephen. It's six in the fucking morning, the day after his tenth birthday. I *get it*. The walls have closed in. We're broke. You're struggling to find clients. Business has been spotty at the brewery the past few days. All this shit with Kevin waking up has thrown everything out of whack. I *get it*. I know."

She sighed. "Ryan's either gonna wake up, or he isn't. And there's not a damn thing we can do about that. Assuming he doesn't, we don't have the money to keep him alive but—I swear to God, I'll strip or be the highest-class hooker you've ever seen if it seriously comes to that. It was one thing when them waking up was just a wish on a rainbow, but now we *know* this can happen. And that means we find a way."

Stephen pushed his feet down and sat up straight in the chair, feeling just how exhausted he was.

"It's not that I disagree, babe. It's just—"

"No, I know what it's 'just.' Put it out of your head. We're figuring it out. But *later*, okay? We're both way too fucking tired and irritable to do it now. We need some sleep."

"I'd say we've got a better chance of a million bucks landing in our lap."

"Try counting money. See how that works for you, since sheep and ceiling tiles aren't doing the trick."

They both laid back down, Stephen stretching out as far back as the chair would go, Laura laying her head against the arm rest, her feet propped up on two pillows.

"How long do we have to wait?" Stephen said, after a few minutes.

"As long as it takes," she said, rolling onto her side, facing the back of the couch. "As long as it takes."

Laura stepped off the stairs into the kitchen, and Stephen looked up at her over a cup of coffee at the island.

"How are your parents doing?" Stephen asked, taking a sip of coffee.

"Fine. Nervous. It's..." She looked at her watch. "...a few minutes past nine, and no sign of anything from Ryan's room. They said they wanted to visit with Kevin a little longer."

"So he's awake."

"Yeah, but he wasn't up past midnight. And who the hell knows how well Ryan actually slept. How would you sleep if you knew you'd probably never wake up again?"

Stephen nodded and lifted the cup to his mouth again. "Man, this is hard," he said. "Probably even harder than with Kevin."

She looked over Stephen's head to the window above the kitchen sink. Green leaves were gathering on the spruce tree's limbs, and it was still. Not a hint of wind. It was statuesque in the morning sun streaking across it into the window from the east. A few wispy clouds crawled by, the only imperfections in a stunning blue sky.

Laura still had hope. She wouldn't allow herself to completely let that go. But every minute that passed diminished that hope a little bit. Every minute without hearing that bed creak or his footsteps tapping down the hall was one minute closer to The Sleep. She didn't want to believe it was going to happen; hope had a way of holding you hostage. There was little you could do to completely escape it once you'd surrendered to it. It would invade every pessimistic thought, every bout of logic and reason. It was a constant back-and-forth in her head, debating if depression or cautious optimism was more appropriate, for reality and her own sanity.

She wanted to go into Ryan's room and shake him, try to pull him out of his sleep. But all the medical opinions—including what the CDC doctors had stressed on their recent visits—was that waking them before they had eight hours of sleep would do nothing to help matters. There were many stories of children waking up early, even getting out of bed and eating breakfast, much to their parents' elation, then falling out, their head buried in a bowl of cereal, never to wake again. Researchers had also made attempts to ply these children with caffeine and amphetamines in the hopes of keeping them awake through the night. They'd work in shifts, playing games with the kids, watching movies, eating snacks, just generally occupying their attention in order to get them to the other side of the night. But, every time, once the child did fall asleep—and that could only be postponed for so long—the coma was waiting for them there. There was no cheating The Sleep, it seemed.

So, they knew the best bet was to let him sleep until he awoke naturally. The waiting was unbearable, though. They'd made it through the longest night of their lives, and now the morning threatened to drive them even crazier.

Stephen got down off his stool and hurried past Laura toward the stairs. She turned and saw her Dad at the top, motioning toward Stephen. When he reached the top of the stairs, her dad whispered something to him, and he looked back at Laura.

"Grab the wheelchair," he said, his hands cupped around his mouth. "Kevin wants to come down."

Laura pulled the wheelchair out of a corner in the living room, and rolled it back into the kitchen. Cradling Kevin across his midsection, Stephen came down the stairs and placed his oldest son into the chair, strapping his limp feet into the holds.

"You're set," Stephen said. "Want something to eat?"

Kevin's head bobbed, more of a semi-circle than a normal nod, but a good bit better than he'd been able to do a few days earlier. Stephen opened the pantry and pulled out a small bowl of microwaveable macaroni and cheese off the top of one of several large piles of them he'd apparently purchased.

"Did you clean out Knoxville of microwave mac and cheese?" Laura asked.

"Most likely," Stephen said, adding a little bit of water, then popping it in the microwave. "It's quick, easy, and Kevin doesn't have to chew it much. It also has the added benefit of him loving it."

She looked back at him, and he smiled something very close to his old smile. He was starting to be recognizable as the old Kevin, the Kevin she—and pretty much everybody else—loved. She hoped he'd eventually get his old personality back, even if he wasn't entirely there physically. After all they'd been through, she'd take that. She'd take it in a heartbeat.

The microwave dinged, and Stephen pulled the plastic bowl out. He peeled the lid off and stirred the contents, blowing lightly on it as steam rose from the watery cheese sauce. He brought it over to Kevin and scooped a spoonful, lifting it to Kevin's mouth. His lips parted slightly, and he took a bite, then smiled as cheese dripped down his chin.

It was a scene that, not long before, Laura never would have imagined she'd see—Kevin, eating macaroni and cheese in their kitchen. It was so simple and sweet that she wanted it to linger as a memory she could call back to when she got sad or couldn't find hope. Just the sight of her son enjoying a little bit of food was enough to give her a warm feeling that took her mind away from Ryan for a brief moment.

In between bites, she could see Kevin was trying to talk. Stephen leaned in closer.

"He's saying he wants to go outside," Stephen said. "Out in the backyard. I guess we can finish the mac and cheese out there."

"Sure," Laura said. "I could use some fresh air. You guys want to stay inside just in case we have a visitor?"

Her parents nodded and sat down at the island.

Stephen pushed Kevin's wheelchair toward the back door. Laura held it open for them. He pushed Kevin through the doorway and to the left onto the side of the patio.

Laura stepped outside to follow them, but noticed a flash of color to her right. She turned that direction, and a scream crawled up her lungs, exploding from her throat.

"Ryan! Oh god, it's Ryan!" She looked up at the house and saw Ryan's window open. "Call nine-one-one! Now!"

Stephen dug in his pocket for his phone, while Kevin sat silently, staring straight ahead.

30

Laura's hand shook as she held the pen, trying to fill out a form the receptionist handed her when she got to the hospital's waiting room. When they carried an unconscious child into the emergency room and told them he'd fallen out of a second-story window, the doctors immediately took him back to an exam room. The form affixed to a brown clipboard stared up at her, laughing. When she got to the question about Ryan's age, "10" didn't seem like it could possibly be the right answer.

Her mind rattled and hummed with questions, unanswerable except by a child who lay unconscious a few rooms down the hospital's frantic hallway. The irony of the morning was that the open window and his body lying broken, face down in the grass seemed to indicate that he woke up, and now he might be stolen from them again. How else could he have gotten out the window? They were sure it had been locked when they put him to bed; it had been far too cool that night for them to open it, and he couldn't have opened it himself without the key.

Of course, that raised more questions. The key to the window was hidden in their closet, on a shelf that even Stephen needed a step stool to reach. Would Ryan have grabbed the step stool from the kitchen without anyone hearing him, snuck into their room, past her sleeping parents, climbed to that shelf, and retrieved the key to open his window? How would he even have known it was there in the first place?

Or were the locks not installed properly? Perhaps that made more sense. But Stephen had tested both windows. Laura watched him. He pulled as hard as he could, the muscles in his neck straining to open them. They wouldn't budge until he unlocked them. Ryan wasn't even awake when they were doing any of this; Laura thought he barely would have even noticed the locks, much less known how to get them open.

Tickling the back of her mind was what Ryan had told her during lunch at Tomato Stand a few days earlier—that Kevin was speaking to him from some world beyond theirs, where adults weren't allowed, and he wished they could all be together there. She still wondered what he meant. The more space she got between that afternoon and this moment, the more she'd wanted to ask him about it again, probe a little deeper. But she'd just never gotten up the nerve. Besides, it was almost certainly just strange dreams that he couldn't separate from reality as he headed toward an eternal sleep.

To know he woke up, though, and potentially fell to his death afterward made Laura shake. The fear and guilt were strong enough to cause physical pain, that boulder settling back into her stomach, her back and shoulders twisting into raging bulges of swollen cartilage trying to strangle her from the inside. How could they have let this happen? Their little boy had come back, but they somehow let him die anyway. They had to scoop up his mangled body, still donning his Spider-Man pajamas he refused to go to bed without, and pass him off to the hospital's doctors, hoping maybe they could do something. *Anything.*

The cruelty of reality hit her like a a sledgehammer. Laura felt like they were being toyed with. If there was a higher power, was he having fun torturing them, watching them suffer? Were they ants under a magnifying glass for some god-like figure, trying to see just how much they could take before they were transformed into a greasy spot on the ground? She'd always thought of herself as tough, but this wasn't a reality she was ready for. She was on the verge of giving up. Uncle. Done. Standing eight count.

It was impossible not to question herself. Question *themselves* as parents. Think about every mistake they'd made. Did it all lead to this place? To a doctor walking out in a minute or an hour or half a day to tell them, "I'm sorry, ma'am. We did everything we could"? Then there'd be the judging looks and whispers from everyone in the neighborhood—and, with the notoriety they'd gained, the fucking *world*—who would examine their every action, talking about how they didn't deserve to have Kevin if they couldn't keep their other kid alive. That they obviously didn't install the locks correctly, or had left the window open and just didn't want to admit it. The police would come by again to inspect the room. There would be pressing questions for why they'd let him stay up so late, why they didn't hear anything when he'd gotten out of bed and opened the window. They'd be skeptical of Laura and Stephen's story, however true it might be.

One of the biggest questions, of course, was just how hurt Ryan was. She was no doctor, but he looked shattered, like a crystal vase tossed in the air and crashed into a slab of concrete. His right arm was bent backward, and it looked like a bone was trying to poke through the skin on his left. His head was bruised, and his right foot looked like it was dangling precariously from his contorted ankle. He had broken bones, of that she was sure. There was no sign that she could see that he'd even tried to break his fall. The way his body was splayed out on the lawn looked like he'd taken a swan dive, belly-flopping to the ground.

From her left, she saw a man in a long white coat walking into the waiting room, and talking to the receptionist. Laura's breathing picked up speed, and her shoulders got tighter, constricting against her spine and neck. She saw the receptionist point in their direction, and the doctor made eye contact with her. He walked across the room to where they were sitting. Laura grabbed Stephen's hand and stood up.

"Mister and Mrs. Fraser," the doctor said, his arms behind his back. "I need to have a word with you about your son."

Stephen stared into space, vaguely watching nurses in stark white shuffling around the waiting room, sometimes ushering bleary-eyed people down the hall, other times delivering folders to the receptionist before hurrying back in the direction they came from.

He was only barely absorbing what was going on, like a dream that you can't quite remember from the night before. He could see the basic physics of the scene in front of him, but the connectors weren't quite there for him to put it into functional thoughts. It was all just background noise surrounding the cacophony in his head.

He thought that no parent should have to deal with the emotions of carrying his shattered, broken son to the car, fearing one limb or another might snap if he didn't support it. That lifeless body felt held together by string and duct tape, a life-sized ventriloquist's dummy smashed to bits.

While Laura drove to the hospital, frantically pressing the gas pedal and weaving them through traffic, Stephen had sat in the back seat, Ryan's twisted body next to him, his head cradled in his lap.

It had reminded him of that afternoon several days before, when he'd pulled Ryan in from the same window he eventually ended up leaping from. He had yanked the boy back and dropped to the floor with him, holding his head in the crook of his arm, wondering what could have possessed him to do something so reckless. He'd said then that Ryan could seriously hurt himself if he'd fallen out, but he wasn't sure Ryan even heard him.

Stephen had asked him why he'd done it. Why was he trying to climb out the window? Sitting in the waiting room, Ryan's answer came back to him, reverberating. He remembered the dazed look on Ryan's face, the way he looked like he was halfway between this world and some other place. The answer hadn't made sense then, and maybe it still didn't. He wondered if it should, though.

"To get to Kevin."

Those had been Ryan's words before he collapsed into Stephen's arms, and then Stephen called Laura before carrying him to bed, wrapping him up in blankets and then shutting the window as tightly as he could. Nathan later confirmed what Stephen had suspected—stress was the likely culprit. Just a bad dream. Lots of kids had them as their tenth birthday approached. It was a difficult time. The best they could do as parents was try to carry on as close to normally as possible, and show him whatever attention he needed before The Sleep came to take him.

But was there more to it? Stephen looked over at Laura's mournful expression and quivering hands as he remembered Kevin sitting up as straight as an arrow, screaming over and over at him. He had yelled "Out!" There was no good reason—and still wasn't any—to think he was physically capable of producing those decibels. Days later, he could still barely make low screeching sounds that vaguely resembled words. Yet, somehow, just hours ago, he bellowed like a banshee, a deafening, sinister sound that overwhelmed all of Stephen's senses as he made his way back to the chest. He'd thought "Out!" meant for him to get Ryan out of the chest, but Ryan wasn't there. Maybe "Out!" had meant something different, though. Maybe "Out!" had meant outside, which was where Laura and Amanda found Ryan around the time Kevin finally went silent again.

Did this all have any connection to Ryan leaping out the window and crushing his body on impact a couple of floors below? He had no idea. He couldn't help but wonder, though. This was the first time Kevin had suggested getting into his wheelchair downstairs. Then, he had suggested they go outside, where they found Ryan. There was no telling how long he'd been there. But did Kevin somehow *know*? Was that why he'd insisted they go to the backyard? How could he possibly have known?

Something strange was going on, and Stephen didn't have the first clue what it might be. And it wasn't a conversation he had any idea how to start with Laura, who was struggling just to deal with reality, much less some weird supernatural crap he was considering laying upon her.

He felt Laura clutch his hand and start to stand up and noticed a doctor approaching them, so he stood beside her.

"Mister and Mrs. Fraser," the doctor said. "I need to have a word with you about your son."

"How is he?" Laura asked, her eyes red and swollen.

The doctor glanced at his feet, then back up at Laura. "You said *yesterday* was his tenth birthday, correct?"

"I...Y-Yes," she stuttered. "It was. *How is our son?*"

"Ryan's fine, Mrs. Fraser." The doctor shook his head, frowning slightly. "And given what you're telling us, frankly, that's what has us confused."

Laura rushed down the hospital's hall, still clutching Stephen's hand, and the doctor's words echoing through her mind.

Fine? He's not fine. He's a broken mess. If he's awake but in a full body cast, I'll be beside myself with happiness.

But the doctor insisted there was nothing wrong with Ryan. He was sitting up, eating ice cream the nurses had brought him, and telling them it was his birthday. When they asked him what year and he said "Ten," they assumed he was joking. Then they recognized his face and name from the news, and it clicked.

The doctor wanted to know why they'd even brought Ryan to the hospital. Laura tried to explain that he'd fallen out of the window, and he looked badly hurt. The doctor shrugged, though, and told them he didn't appreciate them wasting the time of his emergency room staff when there were people who truly needed their help.

Stephen said nothing, but Laura could hardly blame him. The moment was surreal. More than anything, Laura just wanted to get back to see her boy—who, apparently, was not only awake on his tenth birthday but healthy. She was willing to nod and say whatever she had to say to get the doctor to stop talking and take them to Ryan.

They entered a large room with a series of beds separated by curtains on rails that they could pull around for privacy. Some people had oxygen masks, and others had crowds of nurses around their bed, taking pulses and hooking up IVs.

Finally, they were approaching the last bed on the right side of the room, and the doctor stopped. Laura looked to her right. Sitting there, lifting a scoop of chocolate ice cream to his mouth and smiling, was Ryan.

"Oh my god, Ryan," she said, rushing toward him and wrapping her arms around him. Stephen followed in closely behind. "I'm *so* glad you're okay. You made it! It's your tenth birthday, and you're awake!"

As she held him in her arms, he continued shoveling ice cream into his mouth with a red plastic spoon. Stephen still hadn't said anything. The doctor pulled over a chair for him.

"How are you?" Laura asked Ryan. "You're not hurt at all? You feel fine?"

Putting another scoop of ice cream in his mouth, he nodded and bounced on the bed.

"This ice cream's good."

"I'm sure it is, sweetie."

Laura stood up and looked at the doctor. A nurse had walked up beside him.

"You're saying you examined him, and there's absolutely nothing wrong with him?" she said incredulously, shaking her head.

"When you said he fell out of a window and had several

broken bones, we brought him straight back," the nurse said. "But when we put him on the bed, his eyes opened, and we couldn't find any injuries. He didn't express any pain during any of our tests, so we didn't run X-rays."

"How can you be *sure* without running X-rays?" Laura was grasping for some sense of logic, but couldn't find it.

"Ma'am, maybe you just *thought* he fell out of the window," the doctor said. "Or maybe he's Spiderboy and can land without hurting himself. Either way, your boy is fine. And we need that bed, so it's time to take him back home."

None of this made sense. Laura was certain Ryan had been badly injured when he was lying on the ground. He was unconscious and didn't move at all the entire way from the backyard to the hospital. Not a flinch. Not a sound. Nothing. His bones looked like twisted metal from a scrapyard. But now, he was sitting there in front of her, the perfect image of a healthy kid, slurping on ice cream without a care in the world.

She knew she should be happy—thrilled beyond words, even—to have not just one but two kids back from virtual death, the only two they knew of in existence. In that way, she and Stephen were fortunate beyond measure. She didn't want to dismiss that or seem like she wasn't grateful for their amazingly good fortune that they most certainly didn't deserve.

But the foundations of logic on which she'd built her career in science and chemistry, then taking that knowledge over to beer, seemed to be crumbling beneath her. She prided herself on following evidence, looking for the answers that were best supported by what she could learn and replicate, and nothing was adding up to her at this point. It was confusing enough that Ryan had somehow gotten out of the locked window in the first place. Now, though, she had to deal with the notion that he got out of the window, fell to the ground, and didn't so much as sprain an ankle or knock out a tooth.

Meanwhile, Stephen hadn't spoken since they got to the hospital. He sat there, pale and ghostly, looking at his shoes, or the floor, or a spot on the wall. Was he so stunned by what was going on that he was going into shock? Did she need to check him in while they were at the hospital? Or was he just overcome by the stress of the moment? She knew he didn't handle these situations well, but this seemed like a new level for him.

"Okay," she said. "Come on, Ryan. Let's get going."

She signaled to Stephen to get up. His mouth dropped open slightly, and he rose slowly to his feet. When he took his first step, she thought he might fall, but he kept his balance. Laura grabbed his hand, then took Ryan's on the other side, and they walked toward the exit.

31

The Knoxville Neighbors thread hit 338 pages on the afternoon after Ryan's birthday:

PaulBetweenYall
Did everybody see on the news that the Frasers tore off down the street like a bat out of Hades this morning? Some reports said the youngest kid was in the car with them, but not the older one. Any thoughts on what that means? I think our poll had 95% saying he'd go into a coma like the rest of them. Surely we'll find out soon, unless they chain the kid to his bed or something. I wouldn't put anything past them at this point.

IAmtheWalrus69
@PaulBetweenYall Seriously, anybody who thinks that is nuts. Having one fluky kid wake up is one thing. But these people aren't witches. They haven't cracked some sort of code. I don't know why they drove off this morning. Maybe they were frantic, and wanted to give the kid in a coma a drive around the neighborhood. Fuck if I know. But the big question we should ask is what the hell they're gonna do once the younger kid falls out, because that's what's gonna happen. They're already paranoid as hell and getting hounded by the media. They can't have any money, unless they're fucking trust-fund babies. Have any of you been to that brewery she owns? Palmolive, or something like that? I don't remember. But it sucks. All these fancy-ass beers that all the 30-whatever hipsters like, sitting there in their skinny jeans and twirling their mustaches. But ya know what? Hipsters don't have

any money. They usually don't even have a damn job. They just like to turn up their noses at the rest of us. What's wrong with a regular beer? Not a damn thing, that's what. My daddy drank regular beer, and so did my granddaddy, and that woman will never make enough to support two bed-ridden kids on that swill.

ScruffyJoeyN
Of course he's gonna wake up. Come on, guys. How many ways do I have to lay it out for you? You don't have to be a genius to follow what's going on. The first kid wakes up for no good goddamn reason, right? No warning. No explanation. Nothing. He's just awake, out of nowhere, and none of the other kids are. Then they hide out, basically don't say a word except to antagonize all of us. That's because the government has silenced them. They're not *allowed* to talk, because they know a lot of top-secret shit. The government is setting us all up for something, and using this family as pawns or patsies or whatever you wanna call it. But this whole thing has been controlled, and now the younger kid's gonna stay awake. I'm telling ya. You just watch. And when he does, that's the final sign that they have full control over not just the kids, but probably all of us. Always have. Then it's checkmate, guys. See if I'm not right. I'd be gathering my survival gear and stocking up the bomb shelter if I were you right about now. You better be damn sure that's what I'm doing.

PuffPass2017
@IAmtheWalrus69 I don't know that I'd be so sure. I'm not saying I think the other kid will stay awake, exactly. But what could we possibly draw on to say he won't? Obviously, @ScruffyJoeyN is off his rocker, as usual, but he's not wrong that this is more of a possibility than you or a lot of others seem to want to admit. And that's just because this whole thing is unprecedented. Not a soul knows why the older kid woke up, and

he woke up just a few days before his brother's 10th birthday. And now they drove off from the house in a damn hurry. I'm hearing they took the younger kid to the hospital. Is that a coincidence? I mean, I guess it could be, but maybe it's not. It just seems like odd timing to me. Maybe there's a connection between the kids, and the hospital trip. None of us knows enough to definitively say there's not.

IAmtheWalrus69

@PuffPass2017 While I still think you're crazy if you say the kid's gonna stay awake (unlike every other kid for the past 20 fucking years!), that's interesting what you bring up about the timing of the older kid waking up. That honestly hadn't occurred to me. But what exactly would you be suggesting? In other words, yeah, let's say I grant you that it's strange, and that there could be a "connection," as you say. What's the connection? What would that even mean? Are you talking supernatural? Like, they have some sort of cosmic connection, and the older kid was coming back…to do what, exactly? I just don't get what it would be *other than* a coincidence.

PaulBetweenYall

@PuffPass2017 Yeah, I've gotta agree with @IAmtheWalrus69 on this one. The timing issue, while a little intriguing, doesn't seem like it has anywhere to go other than into some woo about other dimensions and them communicating practically beyond the grave or something. That's not a place I think many of us are prepared to go, but I'll give you points for creativity.

PuffPass2017

@PaulBetweenYall @IAmtheWalrus69 Those are all fair points. Maybe it's really nothing. The older kid was out for a little over a year. Maybe he just happened to wake up then. But none of that changes that we have no idea what's been going on in that house. They've given us precisely jack to go on. They sold us that crap about lullabies, people all over the place started singing badly to their kids, and then they admitted that was all made up. So what *is* the answer? Do they really have *zero* clue about why the older kid woke up? Their silence speaks volumes to me. And if the younger kid wakes up, it's not gonna prove some @ScruffyJoeyN-style government conspiracy. It's gonna prove there's *something* very different going on in that house than is going on in any other house on Earth. And, by god, we need to figure out what it is.

PaulBetweenYall
@PuffPass2017 On that point, you're probably right. The younger kid most certainly isn't gonna stay awake. But if, by some miracle, he avoids The Sleep, we've got to think there's something going on with that family. Part of me wonders if they've figured out something really key, and are trying to confirm it works before they sell it to the highest bidder. I mean, shit. You know how much that'd be worth? It'd be the greatest medical discovery in the history of mankind. It'd make curing polio look like kids playing doctor. This would literally save the entire human race. If they had the answer and put it out there for sale…to hospitals, governments, doctors, researchers…who wouldn't pool together money to be the ones to say to the world they made this discovery? You'd be the world's greatest hero overnight. So, yeah, if the younger kid, by some chance, were to stay awake, we need to do something. And it needs to make a statement. Not more child's play like the broken windows at the brewery.

TheInBetween
You guys don't think he'll stay awake? Your all stupid. What if I told you he's awake now? What would you say to that?

IAmtheWalrus69

Whoa. I'm 100% on board with @PaulBetweenYall and @PuffPass2017 on this shit. And be skeptical of @TheInBetween if you want, but you need to remember he was fucking on point about the lullabies being bullshit. And, as I recall, he also said somebody was gonna send a message to the family the morning "A Whore Lives Here" got spray painted on their porch. So, as bad as his grammar can be, he just may be credible. Does anybody know who he is?

DMshallWin

What are you guys talking about? It's starting to sound like a lynch mob in here. Look, I'm as sympathetic to you all and your kids as anybody, but I can't sit here and condone whatever "make a statement" is. There are two kids in that house, coma or not. And the husband hasn't done anything wrong. I think you all better get with Jesus, and pray for the strength to stay away from that family. I can go talk to them again if you think it'd help, but let's not go overboard, y'all.

PaulBetweenYall

@DMshallWin This isn't for you to decide. I know you like to fashion yourself as the moral police, but you're not the king (or queen) around here. This here's a meritocracy, and you've got no more claim to the high ground than any of us. Maybe if you had a kid of your own instead of handing him over to the gub'ment, you'd understand why we feel we've got to take action. Maybe you'd step up and help us instead of lecturing us on what you think is best. We're taking this shit offline. @IAmtheWalrus69 @PuffPass2017 You guys, let's set up a private chat. Invite whoever you think is with us.

32

Startled awake, Laura reached for her phone, glowing white in the dark of her bedroom, Stephen and Ryan snoring beside her. She tapped it to answer the call, and heard Haley on the other end of the line.

"Hey, Laura. I need you at the brewery."

Still shaking the sleep from her head, Laura ran a hand through her hair and sat up. She shuffled into the bathroom, then closed the door quietly behind her. She tilted her phone to peek at the screen.

"It's five thirty in the morning. What's wrong?"

Laura heard a deep sigh on the other end of the line.

"You should just see it for yourself. Words aren't gonna do it justice. Can you come? Now?"

"Um, sure," she rubbed her eyes and shook her head. "I'll throw something on and be there in thirty. Let me just ask, is this good or bad?"

There was a pause.

"My next call is to the cops," Haley said.

"Shit," she slid out of her soft flannel pants, kicking her slippers off on the cold bathroom tile. "I'm on my way."

Laura pulled into the narrow parking lot in front of Palmyra and was immediately struck by the sight of her sign, the white letters bloody with crimson paint, dried in drips in the cool spring air. It looked haphazard, like a bucket of paint was simply thrown up there, with no strategy other than chaos.

She got out of her car, and could already glimpse the carnage through the open front door. The glass they'd replaced there was broken again, glass strewn on the floor inside. It mixed with much more glass, large curved pieces scattered on tables, seats, and even out onto the pavement.

It crunched under her feet as she entered the brewery, and the sight sucked the breath out of her. Red paint was splashed across the bar, blanketing the tap wall, erasing sections of the mural of the view of downtown's Gay Street they'd had commissioned a couple of years earlier.

Broken beer glasses were everywhere—hundreds of them, by the looks of it. Stems lying lonely without the rest of the tulip, handles thrown wide from shattered steins. Much of it was swimming in beer, a thin film of which covered most of the floor, nearly flooding the area behind the bar. Broken brown glass from bottles also laid scattered around the brewery, but mostly in front of the tap wall, where the beer river looked nearly ankle deep.

Laura was in a daze, looking around at the ruin that had become of her life's achievement, her sanctuary. She'd always been able to walk through those doors and feel safe, in control, part of a community that embraced her and wanted her to succeed. She embraced it back, building her business on being proudly Knoxvillian, never even distributing beer outside the vicinity of the city. If you wanted Palmyra's Brownlow Brown, you had to come either to the brewery or a select few friendly bars in the Knoxville area. If you wanted to take home some Crozier Kolsch, you weren't going to walk into a Nashville beer store and pick up a bottle; you needed to make the pilgrimage to Palmyra or check out a local bottle shop.

And this was like a dismissal. Like the city was telling her that her love was unrequited. That everything she'd built was worth tearing down, regardless of how much time and energy she'd put into it. Regardless of how much time she'd lived there, or sacrificed to stay.

She saw movement from the back of the brewery and tensed up before she recognized Haley.

"Oh, you're here," said Haley, wearing a pair of work gloves and pushing a mop and bucket. "Sorry. Didn't hear you from back there. I'm so sorry, Laura."

Laura looked around, her mind trying to absorb the enormity of it all.

"What happened? It was like this when you got here?"

"Yeah," Haley's cheeks ballooned out as she exhaled and wiped her sleeve across her forehead. "Um, I was coming to mill in the grist for the new Crozier batch when I saw all this. It's awful."

"I see they broke glasses and bottles."

"All of 'em," Haley pushed the mop away and walked closer to Laura, laying her gloves on the bar. "As far as I can tell, anyway. Even dug into our boxes in the storage room. Glasses and filled bottles. Smashed 'em on the floor. They also emptied a bunch of the kegs. Good news is the tanks don't look like they were fucked with…other than the paint, anyway."

Laura looked over Haley's shoulder to the brewhouse in the back, and saw their previously gleaming silver steel brite tanks and lauter tun splashed with the same paint as the rest of the brewery, splattered from the bottom, like a red wave cresting on its way up.

"Jesus," Laura said.

Haley nodded. "I guess you saw the sign too. I just don't know what to say, Laura. I feel like I was punched in the gut. This is my home, too. I can't believe someone would do this."

"What about the cops? Are they on their way?"

"Already came and went. One was right around the corner, so she was here in, shit, thirty seconds, probably. Looked around, took notes on what I told her, then got a priority call she said she had to take. Hopefully, they'll come back."

Laura sighed. "God. What the hell is going on with my life?

Ryan's awake, by the way."

Haley's eyes grew wide, and she smiled. "Holy shit, Laura! That's incredible! First Kevin, then Ryan. What is happening with you guys? This is amazing. Do you think this is a sign that The Sleep might be weakening? Maybe you guys are just the beginning?"

"I don't know. Maybe," Laura looked down at her feet, soaking in sticky beer. "All I know is it's changed our lives dramatically in a really short time. It's something we asked for. We hoped for. But then it happened, and everything that's happened around it has been insanely stressful and…well, *this*." She gestured around them, at the wreckage of her business.

"So, yeah, I wish I knew. I *really* do," Laura said. "People think we know…*something*. Or *should* know something. I'm not sure. But it's getting desperate, and there's a lot of fear out there. It's primal when it comes to your kids. They're lashing out because they don't know what to do. They feel helpless against an enemy they can't see. Now, my family has become the enemy they *can* see."

"You think all this has to do with Kevin and Ryan?"

Laura kicked the bottom of a broken bottle across the floor. It skittered and clanged into the wall by the front door, shattering into three jagged pieces.

"That's what prompted all of this. Our life was normal. Imperfect, of course. But that's what *life* is. I wasn't always happy, but I didn't expect to be. Now it's all invaded. It's like the life I didn't fully appreciate before has been stolen, and I miss it more than I ever thought possible. I'd give anything to go back to just normal 'Go home sweating and smelling of beer, feeling like the least sexy woman in the world, sliding into bed next to my sleeping husband I can't remember the last time I had sex with, knowing the kids are gonna wake me up in four hours so I need to fucking fall asleep fast' bullshit. Your boring, mundane life seems boring and mundane until it's gone, and then it feels like fucking *paradise*. And now I don't even have *this* place to escape to."

Haley put her arms out and wrapped them around Laura's neck. Laura folded hers across Haley's back, then laid her head on her shoulder. Part of her wanted to cry, but no tears were coming. She felt too numb for that. Her emotions were becoming too complex for her to fully understand. Was she sad or angry? Hopeless or defiant? The answer, it seemed, was yes.

Laura heard murmurs coming from outside the brewery, sounding like an approaching group of people. It was a light hum at first, but she could tell it was getting closer, footsteps, light conversation. Her skin prickled, her shoulders tensing up. She pulled out of Haley's embrace and swung to face the front door. There was a back door they could get to if they needed to escape quickly, assuming the horde wasn't back there too. What could they want now? They'd already trashed the place. They probably thought nobody would still be there yet, though. It wasn't even six thirty in the morning. Breweries don't open until later, and most of these people would have no idea that much of the actual brewing got done in the early morning when it's cooler.

Laura looked around for a weapon, anything they could use to at least buy themselves a little time to get away; she wished she still had one of her guns behind the bar, but they were both locked up at the house. It was one thing for them to wreck her brewery, but it was quite another for them to hurt her or Haley. She wasn't going to let that happen without a fight. Things could be rebuilt, repainted. Insurance would cover most of the cost, though it was always a struggle to get the money. As difficult as everything had become for her recently, she still wanted to get back to her kids in one piece. She didn't want to die. In a way, that alone brought a measure of comfort. The fact she wanted to fight, was in fact desperate to do so, told her she hadn't given up. She wasn't going to leave her boys without a mother, her husband a widow. Even standing in a puddle of her life's work turned to ruin, she was going to stand her ground.

"Here," she said to Haley, handing her a broken bottle. "Take this. If we have to, we'll run out the back."

They both stood facing the front door, inching backward, jagged bottles held chest high in front of them. The crowd was close now. Probably just a few feet out of sight, coming off Broadway to their left. It had to be a large group, based upon the sound. She worried that if they were charged by a dozen or more people, there might not be much they could do to fight back.

Then she saw the first people come around the corner. The lump in her throat was so big she could barely swallow, her sandpaper tongue scraping the top of her mouth.

She recognized the first person, though. She knew that long black hair immediately—it was Matt, the owner of Knox Partners Brewing just down the street. His wife, Vivien, was beside him. Just behind them were Rick and William, the couple that owned Angry Squid Brewing downtown. From the looks of it, they'd brought most of their crews with them, and some familiar faces of people who regularly drank at Palmyra. Many of them were carrying tools—buckets, mops, gloves, paint scrapers, trash bags, push brooms, and shovels.

Laura shook her head and laid down the broken bottle. "What are you all doing here?" she asked.

"Oh, just figured we'd hang out. Nothing better to do at six in the morning," Rick said. "Got anything to drink?"

Laura threw herself at him, pressing her body against his and pulling him tight. He patted her back lightly. She could see people already starting to scoop up glass and drop it into bags.

"I may have made another phone call or two," Haley said. "Thought a hand or thirty could help."

Laura pulled one arm off Rick and gestured toward Haley.

"Oh, come here," she said, bringing Haley into a three-way embrace.

Those tears finally came.

33

The warm afternoon sun hitting him, Ryan sat in a lawn chair on the backyard patio, a wry smile creasing his face.

He'd beaten it. Whatever "it" was. There was no good reason he ever should have felt the sun again. Or, at least, not *this* sun. Whatever that other world held, he didn't know if it was anything like this one. But here he was, kicking back in his own yard, a golden orb casting heat down on him. A miracle of this particular world. He'd made it to the other side of The Sleep.

There was something triumphant about that, he thought. Like he was a young conqueror, basking in the glow of his victory. And the spoils of his win were this warm spring sun, and the boxed apple juice he had sitting beside him in a cup holder next to his phone in the armrest.

Of course, there was also the possibility that it was never his choice at all. That it was nothing he'd done, and not so much a victory for him as a rejection *by* them. Whoever *they* were.

And there was also this strange undercurrent he felt—"hate" wasn't exactly the right word, but maybe it was something like contempt. For not just this world, but also his parents, and all the adults around him. He couldn't identify any real reason for it. But there was something within him wanting to fight back against them holding him where he was. As if he were a captive longing for freedom. It was a feeling he couldn't quite touch, though. As if it were too heavy for him to lift by himself, but it might rise into sight at any time. It wasn't something that ruled his thoughts most of the time; he was aware of it, though, even if he didn't understand it.

He *thought* he was happy to be here, to feel the sun again, to spend more time with Kevin and his parents. It even looked like Kevin was improving, and might be able to have a real conversation soon. Ryan looked forward to talking to him about everything that had happened; if anyone could help him understand better what he was feeling, it was Kevin. Because Kevin had *been* there. He'd seen the other side, and returned. He was the only person alive who could say he'd ventured across, then come back to tell the tale.

The adults had no idea there even *was* another world out there. They thought this was just the kids falling asleep for a long time. When Doctor Nathan and Doctor Brent had stopped by that morning, he could tell they had no clue what was really going on. Neither did those other doctors whose names Ryan couldn't remember. He didn't know where they were from. They all wanted to jam things in his ears and mouth, stick him with needles, and ask him questions. None of them asked about what really mattered, though. They didn't have any idea.

But Ryan and Kevin knew. None of the adults would ever take them seriously, but they knew the truth.

"Ah, there you are," he heard his dad say from behind him, as the door swung shut. "Taking in a little sun?"

Ryan opened his eyes and looked at his dad, squinting. "Something like that."

"Mind if I join ya? Kevin wanted to take a nap, so I thought I'd hang with you a little bit."

"Sure."

His dad pulled another chair over from the other side of the patio and sat down.

"Beautiful day, huh?"

"Yeah, it's warm."

Neither of them said anything for several seconds, just leaning back and letting the sun hit them.

"Can I ask you something?" Stephen said, his eyes closed.

"Go for it."

Stephen swallowed hard. "What do you remember about yesterday morning?"

"I remember being at the hospital. And eating ice cream."

"Yeah." Stephen nodded and turned his body toward Ryan. "Is that all?"

He shrugged. "Pretty much."

"What do you mean by 'pretty much'?"

"I mean that's *pretty much* all I remember."

"Do you know *why* we took you to the hospital?"

"You thought I was hurt?"

"We did," Stephen said. "And that's because you—or, well, *someone*—somehow opened your locked window, and you apparently fell out of it, flat onto the ground. That's where we found you, looking like you'd broken every bone in your body. We thought you were dead. *That's* why we rushed you to the hospital. Do you remember?"

Ryan remembered it, but didn't know what to make of it all. He remembered waking up to the window being open, the cool air filling his room, like water filling up a sinking car. He felt desperate to escape. He rose from the bed and walked to the window, sucking the cool air into his lungs. As his head ducked outside, he wasn't cold anymore. It felt like an embrace, surrounding him, beckoning him to come further, like a thousand angels batting their wings. He didn't feel fully in control of what he was doing. Part of him did insist this was crazy, that it was a long way to the ground, and it would hurt if he fell. He was plenty old enough to know the basics of gravity. But another part was adamant that he could fly, that this one time there was something different. That he'd been interrupted before on his way to his destiny that lay out this window, and he had to complete the journey this time. He couldn't let fear of Earthly forces like gravity stand in his way. He had to push forward.

Then he jumped, and he *was* flying, or something close to it. He threw his limbs out, a flying squirrel looking for a soft place to land, and he could feel something pushing up from beneath him, a pair of invisible hands holding him up. He had no propulsion, but he was floating in the air, closer to the tree than his window, looking down on the patchy green grass below. He wasn't afraid anymore, even though his instincts told him a fall from that height would hurt badly. He was secure in the arms of an angel, flying, defying the world that held him. His dad said they found him on the ground, but that part he didn't remember. The last thing he knew, he had been floating, the most carefree he'd ever been.

"Nope," Ryan said, his eyes still closed, the sun warm on his face.

Back inside to check on Kevin and get some water for him and Ryan, Stephen was walking up the stairs when his phone vibrated. He pulled it out of his pocket and looked at the screen. There was a text message from a phone number he didn't have saved.

How well do u know ur wife? it said.

Stephen stopped on the third step, his breath catching in his throat. Part of him wanted to just ignore it. Maybe block the number. Don't give them the reaction they want. Just pretend you never saw it.

On the other hand, the question was intriguing. How well *did* he know his wife? They'd been together well over a decade, so he felt like he knew her pretty well. But did he, really? He didn't know a lot about her life at the brewery, beyond the stories she chose to tell him. They were sort of in completely separate worlds a lot of the time, with him working from home and keeping up with the kids, while she pulled fourteen-hour days at the brewery and climbed into bed well after he'd already fallen asleep. In some ways, he felt like the answer might be "Not as well as I'd like to think."

Stephen swiped right with his thumb on the notification, and waited for the screen to refresh onto the text message.

Who is this? he typed.

Doesnt matter. Do u love ur wife?

The question struck him in the chest.

Of course I do.

Wud u still love her if u knew shes a whore?

Stephen's face flushed, and he stumbled to the kitchen island to sit down. It was basically the same message that had been sprayed on their front porch a few days earlier. Was this the same person? If so, how did they get Stephen's cell number? The thought of whoever it was finding new ways to harass them made Stephen nervous. What might they do next?

I'm blocking you, Stephen typed, his thumbs shaking enough to making typing difficult. *Please lose my number, and don't ever come near my house again.*

He closed text messages and tapped "Settings" to navigate to where he could block numbers. He was trying to type the number in, but kept messing up while his hands quivered, when another message popped up.

Ask her about Nathan

He stopped typing and went back to the text message screen.

Ask her what about Nathan?

U know. Just ask. See what she sez

Who are you? Why in the world would I trust you?

U dont have 2. Ask her

Stephen's head was spinning. What could this anonymous person possibly know? And why would they tell him this via text message? Just to put doubt in Stephen's mind? Like he needed more stress at that moment. Nathan was basically part of the family. Surely neither of them would have betrayed him in that way.

But now that the suggestion was in his head, it was hard to shake. Had he seen them look a little too friendly from time to time? Had he seen Nathan's idle hand brush against Laura's hip once or twice? Had he come home from a trip to the store to find them in the house together, sweating a little more than would be explained by the temperature while sipping on some expensive wine he'd brought over?

No, that was just letting the power of suggestion get to him. If anything had happened, he'd have known it long before now. This was finding evidence to fit a conclusion rather than the other way around. He wasn't going to let some anonymous, nonsense text from someone who couldn't even take a minute to type out full words turn him into some paranoid, jealous husband. He didn't even need to ask her. All that'd do is start a fight. And based upon what? Just those texts? He was going to basically accuse his wife of cheating on him because of *that*? No, that'd be stupid. He'd delete them, block the number, and forget he ever saw them.

Who is this? Stephen typed, finally. *Why should I think you know anything about me and my wife?*

No response ever came.

Stephen came down the stairs and heard the front door open. He froze for a moment, then saw it was Laura. Normally, he'd be happy she cut her day short. That meant more time together as a family, and she could take on half of the load of keeping an eye on the two boys. But he'd only had twenty minutes or so to process the texts he'd received, while he fed Kevin a snack and tried to talk him into joining them outside. He insisted he'd rather rest in bed.

Now, Stephen was faced with the one person he wasn't ready to see, a person he expected to have at least several hours to sort out his feelings for, if not until the next day.

THE LITTLE TRAGEDY

"Hey. Rough morning," she said, closing the door and laying a pile of mail on the table. "Some bastards tore up the brewery."

Stephen stared, trying to work up words.

"Did you hear me?" Laura said, walking closer to him. "Are you okay?"

He shook his head, as if to rattle something loose.

"Oh. Yeah. Yeah, I'm fine. Tore up the brewery?"

"Broke glasses and bottles on the floor. Beer and paint everywhere. Broke windows. It's a mess."

"Um, wow. That's awful. Is everybody all right?"

"Yeah. Nobody was there when it happened. Must have been overnight. Some of the other brewery folks and regulars stopped by to help clean up. After a little bit, they said I looked like a wreck, and sent me home. My hair must be a nightmare."

"No, of course not. You've had a tough morning. You should probably get some rest."

"Yeah, I'm gonna need to work up some energy to deal with the insurance people. I'm gonna grab a glass of water and head up to bed. You mind?"

Stephen was trying to be comforting and sympathetic, but there was a tug of war inside him. He still knew it was probably unwise to bring the texts up at all, especially when she'd just been through so much that morning. When she was away, he knew he'd be able to push it down and hold it there. But with her right there in front of him, heading up to their bedroom where maybe she'd slipped out of her panties in front of Nathan, unbuckling his belt and sliding down his pants while falling to her knees by the bed, it was difficult for him to just forget.

He still knew there was a good chance the texts were nonsense, just trying to rile him up and divide their family. But there was a nagging feeling that maybe they weren't. That maybe there was some truth to it. Nathan had spent a good deal of time at their house, much of it alone with Laura. Their marriage hadn't been the most sexually adventurous in recent years, particularly since The Sleep took Kevin. Had she wanted more? Had she found it in another married man, maybe who also wasn't satisfied with his spouse? Of course he wanted not to believe. But he couldn't shake it.

He stood still as she got water from the dispenser on the fridge and headed toward the stairs. As she passed him, she paused a moment.

"Oh, I meant to tell you, Nathan said hi."

Bells rang in Stephen's head, as he slowly turned to her. "What?"

"Nathan. He stopped by the brewery to help. He wanted me to say hi to you and the boys for him."

Stephen licked his lips and lowered his head. He was trying to control his breath, in and out, in and out.

Of course Nathan came by the brewery. Good ol' Nathan. She probably called him the moment all this happened. But Stephen couldn't help but wonder where his call was. He was sure she'd say she knew he couldn't break away from the kids anyway, so she didn't want to bother him. And Nathan didn't have kids anymore, so he could get over there. But she didn't even call Stephen to tell him something terrible happened. She didn't want to commiserate with him, to cry on his proverbial shoulder, even over the phone. No, it was Nathan who showed up to be strong for her, to help her pick up the pieces.

The thought of seeing him strolling into the brewery, his blonde hair and tan skin smiling as he pulled her into a tight embrace, telling her it was going to be okay and that they'd all get it fixed up just like new, brought a scowl to Stephen's face. The man he had trusted with their children, to tease out their greatest fears and their worst nightmares, to help them deal with the stresses that inevitably came with being a child in this weird world they lived in. He suddenly wanted to strangle Nathan, to wrap his hands around the man's neck and squeeze until he apologized for trying to rip their family to shreds.

He couldn't stand it anymore. He couldn't look at Laura without thinking about it. He had to confront her. She was walking up the stairs, her back to him, when he looked up.

"Have you ever slept with Nathan?" He didn't have any interest in playing coy.

She stopped, and her water glass crashed down, tumbling between her legs and falling to the next step, water splashing around her. She turned around.

"What did you say?"

"You heard me."

She walked back down the stairs. "You're asking me if I've *slept* with Nathan?"

Stephen nodded, his lips pursed. She stared at him, her eyes narrowed, hands thrust forward.

"What are you talking about? Where'd that question come from?"

"Are you denying it?"

She ran a hand through her hair. He could see sweat beginning to bead on her forehead.

"Is *that* what you want? I come home from some bastards practically tearing my brewery to the ground, and *this* is what you want to talk about?"

"*You* brought up Nathan. Not me."

She shook her head. "I told you he fucking *said hi*. Not that he grabbed my ass. What is going on with you?"

Stephen tilted his head, putting one foot up on the bottom stair. "You still haven't said no."

"This is incredible." she rolled her eyes. "You really want to do this right now, huh? Sure, let's just make this day even shittier. Why not? So, okay. No. No, I didn't fucking *sleep* with Nathan. There's your answer. Happy?"

Her indignation surprised him. He wasn't sure what he'd expected—Contrition? Sadness? Fear? But she was just acting pissed. As usual, she was taking the upper hand. Confrontations weren't his specialty; he thought he'd be on solid ground in this situation, but it was like she was turning it all on *him*. Like *he'd* been the one who cheated.

Was it possible he'd been hasty to bring it up? He thought maybe he would have been better off obeying his initial instincts. And he probably would have if she hadn't mentioned Nathan's name. It just set him off. He was suddenly jealous, thinking about how she might be closer to Nathan than to him. He couldn't control it. He wasn't quite ready to walk it back, though.

"And is that it?" he said. "Nothing ever happened between you two? *Nothing*?"

Laura scowled and looked toward the kitchen, one hand on her hip, her head shaking slowly. She let out a loud sigh.

"Did someone say something to you?"

"Nope. Just something I've been wondering about for awhile."

"And you thought *this* was just a *peachy* time to bring it up?"

"Are you gonna keep not answering the question?"

Her eyes closed.

"We kissed. All right?" Her head dropped, and she ran her hand to the back of her neck. "One time. *Once*. I fucking swear. That was it."

Stephen's mind swam, and his body started to go numb. His head felt underwater, gasping for breath. It was true. Some of it, at least. And that was *if* she was telling the truth. The texts were true. What did this mean for their relationship, their family? If he'd found this out after both the boys were in a coma, maybe they'd figure out the best way to walk away from each other. But with the kids both awake and relatively healthy, it was impossible for Stephen to imagine a life without them all together. So fresh, though, the betrayal struck him deep.

He couldn't find any words. He stood still, then collapsed against the wall next to him, his feet planted on the floor. Laura put her hands out and grabbed his shoulders, trying to hold him up.

"Look, it was nothing. I'm sorry. Really," she said, her voice frantic now. "We were drinking. It was a weak moment I'm *really* not proud of. It never should have happened. And we both knew that. That's why it never happened again. It was five seconds of...*delirium*. You were at that conference in New Orleans. I was lonely. The kids were stressing me the fuck out. And he was just...*there*. I mean, I can't excuse it. It was wrong, and I take responsibility for it."

His eyes clicked back to focus, and he looked at her. "You're only taking responsibility because I found out."

"Well, what do you expect me to do? Tell you I kissed Nathan? Why? I'm not in love with him. I'm in love with *you*. All telling you would have done is upset you, and for good reason. It *should* upset you. I fucked up. But you popped into my mind *so quickly*. It was over in no time. I backed off, so did he, and he left. That was it. All I can do is apologize."

"How do I know that's all that happened?"

"I can't ask you to totally trust me, I guess. I probably don't deserve that. But it's all I've got. I told you about the kiss because I didn't want to lie. And I'm telling you, I swear, on our marriage, on our kids, on everything I love in this world, that was *it*. Be hurt if you need to. I totally understand. But we can get through this. Okay?"

He looked at his wife, trying to tell if she was being truthful. He tried to recall what he knew about body language. What suggested lying? Darting eyes? Too much gesturing? Hiding her face? He was far from an expert, though. He doubted he'd pick up on much of that, even if she was doing it.

Maybe it really did just come down to whether or not he could trust her. She was right that it would have been easier for her to lie about the kiss if she was going the denial route. On the other hand, he figured some people would cop to a lesser crime in the hopes that the contrition would get them off the hook for a bigger one.

Without any evidence, though, shouldn't he give her the benefit of the doubt? The texts hadn't even technically said she slept with Nathan. They just said to ask her about him. Well, he had, and now he knew about the kiss. He could let that ruin their marriage of fourteen years, he could hold it over her head in order to make her feel guilty, or he could show some faith.

Looking into Laura's eyes, he knew he still loved her. She still had that glow, that fire that attracted him to her in the first place. He loved her independence, her strength, intelligence, and vitality. He knew she'd challenge him, and be a better version of him in many ways. But he wasn't looking for some subservient woman to build him up. He wanted a partner who could be strong where he was weak, who could be beside him when he needed it, and vice versa. Maybe she'd earned his allegiance.

He nodded and leaned toward her. She kissed him, and wrapped one hand behind the back of his head to pull him closer.

"We can talk more later about this if you want, okay?" she said. "But I'm about to collapse on my feet here. I need to get some rest. You good for now?"

He nodded again. She kissed him once more, and he pressed harder back, his mouth opening against hers, anticipation welling up within him. She stumbled backward, hitting the wall next to the stairs, and he stepped in to fill the space. She put her hands on both sides of his head, holding him against her. His tongue danced, brushing against her upper lip, tracing a line around her mouth and then meeting her own. His hands slid down to her hips, then slipped underneath her dirty T-shirt and pulled it upward, the sight of the swell of her breasts making his throat catch slightly. She raised her arms, and he yanked it quickly over her head. Then he took his own off, and wrapped his arms around her, pulling her closer and swinging her around to the island.

Stephen leaned in and his lips touched her earlobe, his teeth gently playing with it as he unfastened her bra. When it fell loose, she threw it to the floor, a moan escaping her throat. He sucked on her neck, wanting to feel every inch of her. She put her hands on his hair, digging her nails into the tangles, teasing them with her fingers as he migrated down to her breasts and then her stomach. He grabbed the waistband of her sweatpants and yanked them off with her panties in one motion, then unbuttoned his pants and dropped them to the floor. He couldn't think of anything but being fully connected with her, two bodies as one. Kicking his pants out of the way, he reached his hands around Laura and grabbed her ass, lifting her into his arms. She shrieked and tossed her hair back, kissing him as he carried her toward the couch.

He dropped her there, and put a pillow down underneath her head. As sweat dripped from his forehead onto her stomach, she folded her knees to her chest, and he climbed onto the couch in front of her, leaning forward and entering her. His heart pounded, and he could see her draw a quick breath as she felt him slide inside. He pressed forward and back, trying to devour her, their mouths interlocking, straining for one another. She scraped her fingernails down his back, like she was trying to hold on to something that might fly away, wanting to feel flesh on flesh. Then he felt it coming, and arched his back, a yell escaping him at the same time he felt her muscles contract around him; he shuddered, slumping onto the couch, wedging in beside her, seeing her chest rise and fall rapidly.

Stephen lay there for a few moments thinking, his breaths ragged, his arm draped across Laura's chest. It had been months since they'd spontaneously made love in the middle of the day like that. He wasn't sure if it meant anything more than what it was. Did he forgive her? Was he ready to trust her? He wasn't sure. He thought they still had some work to do. But, in that moment, he loved her, and wanted to wrap himself around her. And he needed to feel wanted.

"I guess…" She smiled, in between breaths, "I wasn't…quite as tired as I thought."

Laura threw on her clothes and went upstairs; Stephen pulled his pants on and slumped back onto the couch. He laid back, resting his head on the pillow Laura had used minutes before, her scent still encased in the fabric. He hadn't been planning on it, but a nap might not be a bad idea. He felt exhausted. He rolled over to his side, and his eyes began to close.

"Stephen!" He heard Laura call from the stairway. "Stephen, where are you?"

He opened his eyes slightly. "Just lying on the couch."

"Where's Ryan?"

Stephen's eyes widened; he jumped up and pulled on his shirt.

"Shit. He must still be outside in the back. I was supposed to just be inside for a minute."

"You left him out there?"

"I just came in to check on Kevin and get some water, but I got…distracted."

They both started walking toward the back of the house.

"How long has it been?" she asked.

"I haven't exactly been watching the clock."

He opened the back door, and they both stepped onto the patio. The chair Ryan had been sitting in was toppled over on its side. They scanned the yard. It was quiet. There was no sign of Ryan.

Laura turned to Stephen. "Where is he?"

Stephen just stared.

34

Walking in his front door, Nathan wiped his work boots on the mat, scraping paint off the bottoms. It wasn't even noon on a Friday, and he already stunk of beer.

He saw Denise sitting on the couch, watching some home-hunting show on TV.

"Hey." He nodded, preparing for her to say nothing as he walked past.

"Where've you been all morning?" she asked, her eyes never leaving the TV. "I woke up, and you were gone. Have you been drinkin' already?

He lifted a bit of his shirt to his nose and sniffed. "You can smell that all the way over there?" he said. "Must be worse than I thought."

She snorted dismissively, but didn't say a word. The couple on the show was ogling a bathroom that connected two bedrooms.

"No, I wasn't drinking. Laura's brewery got vandalized badly overnight, apparently. Got a call from her brewmaster asking me if I had time to come help. There was beer everywhere, and it got hot in there with so many people working. I probably smell of sweat and booze."

She laughed. "No probably about it. Go take a shower."

Nathan lowered his head and started to walk toward the stairs, then stopped. He looked back, and she was still leaning back on the couch, her arm draped over the back of it, watching people complain about the brightly colored backsplash in the kitchen.

He wondered how he and Denise had gotten to this point as a couple. She barely seemed to acknowledge him anymore. Maybe he could trace it back to them giving up their son. But, sometimes, he wondered which came first—her losing interest in their marriage, or her desire to surrender their only child. It wasn't a matter of affording it. They could have handled the money to take care of him, and Nathan had told her that. She had insisted, though, that it would be too much of a burden. She didn't want them to be another one of those couples that poured everything they had into care for a comatose child only to see their own relationship dissolve while they weren't paying attention. The kid only had ten years, and they had the rest of their lives; they had a responsibility to be there for each other.

It had all sounded logical. Difficult, heart-wrenching, but imminently logical. So they'd signed up for the government program that signed over rights to the state, and left the decision up to them for what to do with Matthew. Once you signed the paperwork, you could never see the child again or have any knowledge of what happened to him. It would be as if the kid had never been born. Technically, they could find another family more prepared to take the child. There were no official records about how many they successfully homed. But there was little reason or evidence to suggest there were many cases like that. In all likelihood, handing your son over meant his death. The state just allowed you to think maybe it wasn't.

They signed the paperwork while sitting on that very couch, him watching her calmly go through the waves of her name, then dot the i at the end, just like she always did. It was all so formal, so sudden, so final. They handed the papers to a social worker in a charcoal suit and tie, then kissed their baby on the forehead one final time before placing him in the social worker's arms. He thanked them, told them they'd done the best thing for everyone involved, and took their only child out of their lives forever.

Had there been signs before that of her distance? Had she not wanted to keep the child because she didn't want that anchoring her down to the marriage any longer than she had to be?

If so, why didn't she just leave? Why drag this out? He needed to talk to her. He couldn't remember the last time they'd had a real conversation. It'd been far too long. He went back into the room and sat on the chair opposite her.

"We need to talk for a minute," he said. "Can you turn off the TV?"

Denise didn't turn her head, only her eyes to glare at him.

Nathan sat forward in the chair. "At least mute it. This is important."

She grabbed the remote and hit the Pause button. The wife on the show had her mouth stopped mid word, and her blue eyes reflected the light from the camera.

"Okay. What is it?"

"Do you hate me?" The question poured out of him far faster and easier than he expected it to.

Denise narrowed her eyes and shook her head. "Are you serious? What kind of question is that?"

"What?" He shrugged. "What do you want me to think? We never talk. We never go to bed at the same time. We never even eat together anymore. You act like you don't even want me around. What do you expect me to think?"

"Think whatever you want. But I don't *hate* you. You think I'd still be sitting here if I hated your ass?"

"So, tell me, Denise. What is it? Do you still love me? Why *are* you still here?"

She looked away and crossed her arms, then quickly uncrossed them, bringing her feet onto the couch beside her. "Shit, Nate. We've been through a lot, ya know? Do I still love you?" She paused, then sighed. "Love evolves. It changes. But…yeah. Deep down. Somewhere. Yeah. I do. But I don't know what to do with a lot of my feelings for you, ya know? Haven't for some time. So it's easier if I just sit here with 'em and let 'em lie."

"If you still love me, how are your feelings so complicated? I don't understand. Why is it so hard?"

She looked at the floor, her head shaking slowly back and forth. "Of course there was Matthew. I can't blame you. Not rationally, anyway. But the mind isn't always rational, ya know? Love isn't rational. I loved our son too, and you let me give him away. It's not fair, but there it is."

Nathan looked back at her, his temples starting to throb.

"And," she said, "Well…There's one more thing."

35

Her shoulders in knots and her stomach tightening like a fisherman's rope, Laura ran back into the house, looking for any hidden corner where Ryan might be hiding.

"He didn't come back in," Stephen said, stepping through the door. "We would have heard it. He has to be outside somewhere."

"Fucking *where*, then? Where?" She turned and held her arms out in an exaggerated shrug. "He's not fucking Houdini. He didn't just disappear. The gate's locked. He's four feet tall. He's not scaling the fence like a god damn spider monkey!"

"I…don't—"

"*Jesus*, Stephen. Where the hell could he be? Ryan! Ryan!" she began calling out his name as she walked through the kitchen.

Stephen headed to the living room to look through the window and see if he might have somehow gotten into the front yard. Laura heard him yell.

"Son of a bitch!" he said, turning and running for the front door.

"What? What is it?" she ran after him, the door nearly hitting her as he threw it open.

When she got to the opening, she saw what Stephen had seen—a maroon Ford Taurus screaming to a halt in front of their house, and a mask-wearing woman with strawberry curls opening the passenger door, carrying what looked like a ten-year-old boy. Reporters were starting to swarm toward the car.

Stephen started sprinting, faster than she'd ever seen him. Most physical therapists were in at least passable shape, and Stephen did have a reasonably hard body for a man in his later thirties. But he'd never been much of a runner. Colleagues had tried to convince him to train for a half marathon a handful of times, but he'd never been interested.

But, in front of her now, she saw a machine, arms thrusting back and forth at his sides, churning him toward the car that contained their son. As Stephen got within ten feet of the vehicle, the driver—wearing a mask of what looked like a goat with backward horns—gripped the wheel with both hands and slammed on the gas, the passenger door still swinging open, the woman's legs dangling outside the car. The tires squealed against the pavement, sending smoke and the smell of baking rubber wafting into the air. As the car peeled out down the street, toward the bottom of the hill, Laura saw the woman's legs slide into the car, and the door slammed shut. Stephen got to the curb and stopped. Laura ran up behind him, and reporters were scrambling into their vans.

"Let's go!" Stephen said, turning and running toward the driveway, where their navy Jeep Renegade sat.

"Shit."

They leapt into the vehicle. Laura handed him her keys, and he started up the engine, then threw it into reverse and pressed the gas to the floor. She was still trying to buckle her seat belt when the SUV lurched backward and braked hard. Stephen jerked the car into drive before it had a chance to stop, and it was quickly hurtling forward, two media vans turning the corner in front of it.

"Left! Left!" Laura was pointing to the bottom of the hill. "I saw them go that way."

Stephen kept his foot on the gas and took the turn without slowing, the force pressing Laura's right shoulder and side against the door. For a brief second, she thought the vehicle was going to flip and roll into the grass, but it held the road. After getting around the corner, they didn't see the Taurus; they only saw one media van cresting a small hill ahead. A thousand feet or so ahead was the neighborhood exit.

"Betting they headed toward the interstate," she said, her mind swimming and doubling over itself. "No reason for them to circle in here."

"This may be the first time having these reporters on our asses helps us. They want to catch up to those fuckers as much as we do."

"We need to call the cops."

"With what?" he said. "I don't have my phone. You got yours?"

She realized she'd set it down on the bedside table and plugged it in to charge when she went upstairs, before she peeked into Ryan's room and didn't see him there. She hadn't thought to go back for it. And Stephen's was apparently still somewhere in the house. It flashed into her mind that one of her handguns might come in handy, but she would also have worried about putting Ryan in the line of fire.

"Fuck," she said, the tires squealing as Stephen turned onto the road to the neighborhood exit. "But, damn. Surely one of the reporters will call. That might be what saves us."

"Yeah. Look, we're gonna find him and get him back, whatever it takes. Trust me."

She still worried, though. Were the reporters paying enough attention? It all happened so quickly. Maybe one of them jotted down a license plate, but they had no way of knowing. If one of them called the cops, they could issue an amber alert within minutes, and there was a good chance somebody would spot them before they could get wherever they were going. Still, she didn't want to bet Ryan's life on a bunch of reporters calling the cops or being able to keep up in a bulky van that probably had 150,000 miles on it.

But there was also something she appreciated about Stephen's determination. He knew he'd screwed up in leaving Ryan alone for that long, and she knew that was at least part of what was driving this. His eyes wild and on fire, knuckles white against the wheel. Even if she thought turning around was the absolute best plan—and it just might have been—she saw little chance of convincing him of that, and he was the one in the driver's seat, taking turns practically on two wheels. She'd always wanted him to take more control, to show more backbone in stressful situations. Well, this was his chance. And, so far, he was showing he could do it.

He stopped at the end of the street, where it intersected Ebenezer Road, a wide-open five-lane street running in both directions. Laura looked left and didn't see any cars headed away from them toward the turn about a quarter-mile away, then spun her head right, where she saw brake lights disappearing over a hill.

"There!" She pointed right. "That was one of the media vans."

Stephen looked right, then back to the left.

"Can we trust that they know what they're doing?"

"I don't think we have a lot of choice, unless we're gonna go back."

Stephen sighed, and punched the gas, swinging the wheel to the right.

Ebenezer took them around a soft curve, then down a short hill to another dead end at Northshore Drive by Fort Loudon Lake. They swerved into the left lane and sped past two cars, hitting nearly seventy miles per hour within a few seconds and bearing down on one of the white media vans. They could see the next one not too far ahead.

Once they got over the hill in front of them, they'd be able to at least see down to Northshore, and maybe catch enough of a glimpse to tell if they were on the right track. If not, it might be time to head back and take their chances with the cops. But they weren't going to give up until they'd given it every shot they could.

They just had to get over that next hill. It was maybe two hundred yards ahead, and the SUV was driving ahead at close to eighty; Stephen swung into the right lane to get around the second media van, which looked to be almost rattling at around sixty-five. Laura knew they were going to have to brake hard shortly after going over the hill to make sure they could make the turn in either direction without skidding into the lake that lay straight ahead.

The dotted lines in the middle of the road were passing by in a blur as their speed climbed—eighty, eighty-five, windows rattling, wind wheezing through them like air through the lips of a child just learning to whistle, all hissing and spittle. She peeked at the speedometer and saw it hit ninety before they hit the top of the hill and Stephen began laying on the brake.

Laura looked right and only saw a silver coupe making the turn, but visibility wasn't good in that direction. If they'd gone right, she wouldn't see much past the gas station, headed into a sharp S-curve. Then she heard Stephen.

"Look left," he pointed with one hand, as both of their bodies pressed hard against the seat belts trying to hold them in place while the vehicle's speed slowed below fifty and they got within two hundred yards of Northshore. "Is that them?"

She squinted to get a better look at the car that was accelerating away from them down the road. And, just like that, it was out of sight.

"That was them! Go left," she said, bouncing excitedly in her seat.

"Shit, really? How sure are you?"

"Hundred percent," she lied, knowing they couldn't afford indecisiveness. "Do it. Go."

Without checking his mirror, Stephen yanked the wheel left, turning the SUV into the other lane with little space remaining before they hit Northshore. When Laura looked up, she saw the light was turning from stale yellow to red. She guessed they still had about three seconds before they got it, which was enough time for the cars on Northshore to start moving into their path.

At this point, heading diagonally across the left lane and approaching the intersection at forty, they couldn't stop at the light even if they wanted to.

Stephen laid on the gas to get to the intersection faster and accelerate through the turn. Laura dug her fingers into the armrest and made a noise she didn't recognize, a squeal that emanated from deep in her throat, a sound of panic and excitement. To their left, a red convertible began inching its way toward them, and they were moving at close to fifty, ready to cut across them. Laura was bracing for impact, and she could picture a collision flipping them, sending them rolling into the water.

She could see the convertible moving faster into their path, and Stephen was trying to angle the SUV so it would skirt them; the closer they got, the less she thought it would work. There were just a few feet between them when their SUV's front tires crossed the white line onto Northshore and Stephen pushed the horn, sending a loud, bleating noise into the air. The convertible stopped at the sound, and so did a dark green Toyota coming from the right, which was also threatening to squeeze them out. She thought they either had *just* enough room to slide through, or they were going to end up in the lake.

As Laura ground her teeth, the front end of their SUV cleared the convertible by inches. She was on the wrong side of the car to tell for sure, and her eyes were squeezed shut hard anyway, but she was ready for impact and the squeal of tires scraping over to the gravel shoulder. Stephen turned the wheel sharply to straighten it into the right lane, and she felt a bump from behind. The back left quarter panel had caught the convertible, and the SUV began fishtailing behind them. They were losing control, the back of the car skidding near the edge of the road; they'd been so close to getting through the turn, but they'd clipped the other car at too high a rate of speed.

She opened her eyes and looked at Stephen, who turned the

wheel right, and the front end started coming back around, sending their back side sliding in the opposite direction. They weren't accelerating at the moment; he'd taken his foot off the gas. A little upslope was helping them slow the skid, and maybe regain control. Stephen steered back to the left and applied the brake, bringing the back part of the car into line, almost like it was clicking into place, then pressed the gas, and they were picking up speed again. Laura looked in the rear-view mirror and saw the man standing outside his convertible, walking in their direction and waving his arms, but there was no way they were slowing down.

"How…did you *do* that?" Laura said, her right hand still gripping the door handle.

"Instinct?" He shrugged. "That's my best guess."

"Let's keep going with that. Instinct. Holy shit, that was scary."

Now they were moving, crossing forty miles per hour, fifty, just hoping they weren't going to come across traffic between them and the Taurus. Unlike Ebenezer, this was a two-lane road without many good opportunities for passing. Lots of curves and double yellow lines. And, while they weren't too worried about breaking traffic laws at this point, they'd prefer not to die in a head-on crash.

Up and over a small slope and around a soft left curve. No sign of any cars ahead of them yet. This was the route Laura took to the brewery every day, so she knew it well. They were entering the best straight section of the road they were going to see. The only other straight area went through a small commercial district called Rocky Hill, and there were too many cars turning in and out of the road there during the middle of the day to go fast. If they were going to make up ground, this was the place to do it. She told Stephen to floor it.

Approaching seventy miles per hour, they saw a car ahead.

They must have been going almost double its speed, because they were closing on it like it was standing still. There were double yellow lines to their left, and a short blind hill in front of the car. There was little time to make a decision. If they were going to stay behind the car—even temporarily—they were going to have to brake hard. That not only meant the possibility of rear-ending them, but also slowing way down and waiting for a safer opportunity to pass. And they had to assume the kidnappers weren't petering along at twenty just waiting for them to catch up. There was also the possibility they could turn off on a side road or into a neighborhood at practically any moment. Every second they didn't have the Taurus in their sights was a second when they could lose Ryan forever.

Stephen glanced at Laura as if to ask permission, and she nodded. He pushed the gas down harder and steered into the left lane. They hit eighty, eighty-five, reaching the back bumper of the car in front of them when they saw another vehicle approaching them in the other lane. Laura held her breath as she tried to do the math in her head—how many seconds did they have to complete this pass before it all blew up? Two? Maybe? The car in front of them flashed its headlights and laid on the horn. There was no turning back. The SUV hit ninety as Laura crossed past the front bumper of the car beside them.

Just the back end to clear, she thought. *Please let us have enough room.*

It looked like the car in front of them was braking, which would buy them precious fractions of a second. Stephen would have to gauge the moment they were safely clear and yank the SUV back into the correct lane. It couldn't have been more than a quarter-second, but she swore it was more. One car heading toward them, and another beside them. How many lives potentially hung in the balance? Theirs, the people in the cars around them, Ryan, Kevin. The stakes on getting this right were higher than she was comfortable with. Stephen had to thread a needle she didn't know if he could thread. The SUV veered hard right just as the car in front of them swung to its right, nearly glancing them on the driver's side before slamming into a guardrail. The SUV cleared the other car, and straightened up in the right lane. Laura looked back again, hoping whoever was in the car they ran off the road would be okay.

"Hey," Stephen said. "Look."

She turned back around and looked in front of them; no more than a couple hundred yards ahead was a maroon sedan. She couldn't quite tell the make and model yet, but it seemed like it had the look and feel of the car they'd seen up close ten minutes earlier.

She smiled. "Told you they went this way."

"Never doubted you for a second."

They sped forward and were gaining on the Taurus, closing to within 100 yards before they realized they were being chased and began matching the SUV's speed. Laura wondered how well the driver knew this area, because there was a notoriously tight S curve at Tooles Bend not far ahead. And there was no way any of them were taking that at seventy or eighty. She hoped Ryan had his seatbelt on.

The hard turn wasn't the easiest obstacle to see coming. You'd come around one soft left turn, have a short straight stretch, and then there it would be. There were no warning signs, other than the brakes of the cars in front of you. If you didn't know the road well, and were going way faster than you should be, it was easy for it to sneak up on you.

They were through the soft turn, and neither car had to even slow down there. Still, no cars were in front of them, and they streaked along at over eighty. Laura reached over and put a hand on Stephen's shoulder; he pushed softly on the brake, carefully letting the SUV lose speed. The Taurus began pulling away from them. Laura wondered if they glanced in the rear-view mirror, and thought they were going to get away. Maybe they let out a little cheer. Maybe that distracted them from what was up ahead.

Stephen got them down to about forty as they watched the Taurus hurtle ahead. Laura was hoping to see brake lights. Surely they'd notice the hard turn. Surely they'd know they couldn't take it at close to ninety. She didn't want to see them navigate it flawlessly, but she also didn't want them to crash at too high a rate of speed with her son in the car.

But there were no brake lights. The car got closer to the turn. Too close now to save it, she was sure. A lump rose in her throat.

Then, finally, the brake lights came. Flashing first on, then off, then back on again, the car rocking, almost appearing to shrink before growing back to its original state as it struggled to maintain contact with the road. The front end started to go left into the turn at Tooles Bend, but the back end swung too far. They were skidding sideways, and the brakes locked, leaving black streaks on the pavement and flipping the car to the right. It rolled over and bounced on the street, smashing off the top of the guardrail and tumbling into the small field on the other side. Laura gasped as the vehicle rolled three more times before coming to a rest upside down in the grass, smoke billowing from under the hood.

Stephen hit the gas again, speeding up to Tooles Bend and pulling up by a stop sign near the guardrail. They flung their doors open and ran toward the car, the smell of burning tires and gas fumes filling the air. An arm hung out of he driver's side window, draped across the grass. Laura noticed that but headed straight for the back window; Stephen was right next to her when she got there.

She got on her knees and bent to see inside. Ryan was lying face down on the crumpled, upside-down roof, his hands tied behind his back with nylon string. The window was already damaged, and Stephen kicked it in the rest of the way, trying to knock away as much broken glass as he could. Laura stretched her arms inside but couldn't reach Ryan; she pulled back out and moved aside so Stephen could try. Media vans were arriving at the scene, and Laura could feel eyes on her as they worked.

"It might be easier to get him from the other side anyway," Laura said, scrambling to her feet to run around the car. "I can grab him by the legs."

When she got to the other side, she could see that Stephen was having trouble reaching Ryan too. His fingers were just brushing the wisps of his hair, but it wasn't enough to get any sort of grip. Kneeling on the passenger side of the car, Laura could see the roof was far more damaged there, and the window had already shattered. It seemed the car was resting with more weight on that side of the car, and she thought this was probably the part that crashed against the guardrail as it flipped off the road. That gave her less vertical space to work with, sliding her body inside the car, but Ryan was considerably closer. She wasn't sure if she could make it inside, but then the roof started lifting higher; she turned her head to see Elizabeth Cassels and Peter Leigh pulling up on the car to give her a bit more space. She gave a quick nod of acknowledgement, then turned her attention to Ryan.

She wedged her head and the top of her shoulders through the window, and her hands wrapped around Ryan's ankles. Stephen stood and hurried to her side of the car while she pulled Ryan toward her. Her arms scraped against broken glass, digging deep into her skin, but she didn't feel any of it in the moment. She was trying to keep Ryan off of it, but it was impossible for him to completely avoid it. As he got closer, she noticed his mouth was taped shut, and she could hear him mumbling.

Stephen watched her drag Ryan's legs across the mangled roof, drawing some glass cuts but shielding him where she could. She got his feet out of the car, then reached in and cradled his butt in her hands, lifting him up and through the open window before laying him in the grass. She tugged at the tape and gently pulled it off his mouth.

"Mom!" he immediately said, and she smiled at hearing his voice. As if he'd been encased in a bubble as the car tumbled into the field, he didn't seem to be hurt at all.

Laura pulled him close to her and remembered his hands were still tied. While she held him against her chest, Stephen pulled the string apart; Ryan climbed up to her neck and clung to her as she fell down to the ground. Stephen laid down beside them as sirens blared in the distance and cameras clicked.

36

All the doors locked, with bulky dressers, chairs, and tables pressed against them from the inside, windows with knotty wooden boards hammered across them, the house was as close to a fortress as they could make it. Stephen, eyes bloodshot and hair scattered in many directions, sat on the couch across from Amanda; Laura paced nearby, sipping on a gin and tonic, a half-full bottle of Hendricks sitting on the island. Sleep had come in fits the night after the kidnapping, with Laura waking up from the couch in sweats to run upstairs and check on Ryan and Kevin every few minutes.

Stephen fell asleep in the hall outside Ryan's room at one point, but that didn't last long before he got up and walked the floor, a zombie. Ryan was still asleep beside Kevin in his bed, with the door closed. The only positive to come out of the previous day was that, after the crash, the media vans didn't make it back to the house with them. Whether another story had gotten their attention, or the cops had scared them off now that two people had died, Laura wasn't sure—they weren't reading the news these days—but she was thankful either way. When the police called to again have an officer stationed in front of their house for protection, this time she accepted the offer. She was told they'd have someone over by the end of the day.

When Laura texted about what happened, Amanda got to the house in five minutes.

"You guys *have* to rest," she said. "You're not gonna be any help to them or yourselves if you're this tired. Look at this place. There's no way anyone's getting in here."

Laura's mind was racing; she walked to the kitchen and back, sometimes topping off her glass, trying to count the steps to give her something else to think about.

She stopped to face Amanda. "Do you realize we have the most valuable child in the world? If there were a value put on Ryan, he'd be worth more in money, and fame, and future power than possibly any person in existence—an awake, healthy, strong, smart ten-year-old boy. The only one in the world right now. That's why they want him. That's why we have to protect him. *Everyone* wants him."

Stephen looked on from his corner of the couch, his head resting in his hands.

"I understand that what happened yesterday was traumatic and awful," Amanda said. "But do you think all this is too much? What are you going to do? Wall yourselves off from the world?"

"If that's what it takes!" Laura began pacing again. "Ryan could be anything. So could Kevin, if he can continue gaining strength. They're the youngest people awake on Earth by twenty years, Amanda. We didn't know those people who took Ryan. They were probably just parents, desperate to replace their own child. Do you know how many parents like that are out there? Parents who feel jilted by reality, look at us with *two* awake children, and think it's understandable—justifiable, even—to take one of ours? If not both? This is gonna happen again. We're pinned down. Those boys are our responsibility."

"I get that," Amanda sighed. "There's just got to be another way. Do you have any idea why they woke up? Have you guys thought of *anything*?"

"That's what people keep asking us. Over and over. Why did it happen? What did you do? And we *don't fucking know*. If we knew, for fuck's sake, we'd share it. Tell the world. Shout it from the goddamn rooftops! Don't they think we want this nightmare to end as much as they do?"

"He wasn't hurt at all," they heard Stephen say in a muffled breath, his hands still covering his face. "Not even a scratch."

They both stopped and looked at him.

"What?" Laura said.

"Ryan." Stephen lifted his head and dropped his hands, his skin a near-powder white, sweat beading on top of his cheekbones. "He was fine. He should have been dead. Again. How did he survive the car flipping off the road? The couple was dead. Ryan was just lying there peacefully."

"I..." Laura looked at Amanda, who shook her head. "I don't know. Weird things can happen, I guess."

"And when he fell from his window?" He sat forward.

"Are we *sure* he fell? The doctors weren't."

"You were there the same as I was. The window was open. How? No clue. I *know* I locked it shut. The key's still right where I left it. Which only leaves a few possibilities—the door wasn't actually locked; he snuck the key away to Home Depot some other day and got a copy made; he's an expert lock picker and we didn't know it; he developed superhuman strength to break the lock with his bare hands; or he had an accomplice. The only one of those that makes *any* sense is that somehow the lock broke down in a few days. And that still doesn't explain how he survived the fall."

Laura sat beside Stephen on the couch, and laid her glass on the coffee table.

"O-Okay. All right. I admit it's weird. He also didn't fall into a coma, like billions of children before him had. Sure. But what are you saying?"

"I don't know what I'm saying. Maybe something. Maybe nothing." He looked at the ceiling, his eyes searching for answers. "There's just too much coincidence. Too much weirdness. Too much neither of us can explain. There's something going on, but I don't know what it is."

Laura took another sip, then sat back. "Do you think it was more than just weird dreams? Ryan seemed sincere, but what connects it all?"

Stephen rubbed his temple and closed his eyes, his breaths getting longer. "Something happened with Kevin."

"*Something?*" Laura said, her eyebrows raised.

"Something…I can't explain."

Laura glanced at Amanda, who opened her mouth and shrugged.

"Go on," Laura said, then heard her phone ring on the coffee table next to them. It was a number she didn't recognize. Everyone looked at the phone as it rang. Laura's heart beat faster, thumping against her ribcage. She reached over and hit the button to stop the ringing.

"Not important. I'm not dealing with that right now. Tell us about Kevin."

"It was the morning you two found Ryan outside. I went upstairs to see if Ryan was hiding up there. I searched through Kevin's room."

"And something happened there?" Laura said.

Stephen licked his lips. "Yeah."

The phone rang again. It was the same number.

"It could be the cops following up on yesterday," Amanda said. "Maybe you should just answer it."

"It could also be some crazy person. No. Not right now. They're gonna have to wait."

She stopped the ringing again, and turned back to Stephen.

"*What* happened with Kevin?"

Stephen sighed. "I didn't say anything then because we found Ryan, and that was all that mattered. I didn't want to throw a bunch of other stuff at you. *And* I didn't want to seem crazy. I wasn't even sure I *wasn't* crazy, to be honest. I—"

Ringing, again. The phone vibrated against the table, rattling the wood and demanding their attention. Laura grunted and picked up the phone, then tapped it to answer the call.

"Who is this?" she nearly yelled.

"This is Denise. Nathan's wife," she said, almost as more of a question than a statement. "I hate to bother you, but we need to talk. Right now. Your family's in danger."

37

Leaning over the kitchen sink, her elbows on the counter, Laura's muscles began to tense up again. She could feel balls forming in her shoulders.

"What do you mean, our lives are in danger? You better tell me what's going on, right the *fuck* now."

"People are saying a lot of bad things about you guys, Laura. It's getting bad out there. I'm not sure you guys know *how* bad."

"It all looks pretty goddamn bad from where I stand right here. If it's even worse than I think, I'm not sure I want to know, to be really fucking honest with you."

"Right. I get what you're sayin'. It's been stressful for you all, I'm sure. I can't imagine what it would have been like to deal with those kids like you are."

"The kids have been the least of our problems," Laura said, her fingers digging into the marble countertop. Stephen and Amanda watched from behind her, keeping a few feet of distance. "Why are our lives in danger?"

There was a long pause, quiet except for the clicking of a keyboard. Laura's heart raced faster, her back tightening up, beginning to shoot pain up her spine.

"I never liked you very much, Laura," Denise said, her lips smacking between words. "Oh, sure. I did my best to act nice and chummy, for Nate's sake, and because I really didn't want a confrontation with you. It was never easy. I wanted to tell you off, wanted you to know what I know about you. About who you really are, not this image of loving mother and super businesswoman. Ya know?"

Normally, the words would have cut deep, but Laura didn't have the luxury of having thin skin at the moment. She'd grow a firm lizard skin if that was what it took to protect her family.

"Anyway," Denise continued, after a few more seconds of typing, "some of what they're saying about you is probably…my fault, I guess. But it's hard to blame me, really. If you had been in my position, you'd've done the same thing. I swear, you would. It's just one of those things, ya know? And, so here we are."

Laura wanted to put her fist through the wall; she kept listening as splinters crawled up her back.

"Nate has helped me understand that maybe I *was*…a *little* harsh in some of my words about you. I had good reason to think they were right, but I'm now thinkin' you may not have *totally* deserved it all, ya know? So, I guess I'm sorry for that. If that, ya know, caused any problems or anything…yeah."

The words that popped into Laura's head were "I'm going to kill you," but she bit into her lip, nearly drawing blood. She couldn't say anything that would make Denise hang up. Once she figured out what Denise had been talking about with danger—whatever it was she was leading up to, in her meandering, condescending way—she could say anything that came to her head. But, until then, Laura knew she needed to keep Denise on the line. The pain in her back and her limbs, the prickling sensation in her hands, she had to push it all aside. Just *hear* this woman a little longer. Don't piss her off.

"Why are we in *danger*, Denise? I need to know. *Now*."

"I'm gettin' there. Just stay calm. It's gonna be fine, I'm sure. So, *anyway*, you know the Neighbors message board? Not sure if you're on there, but it's a great way to keep an eye on the people around you, and know what's goin' on, ya know? You should make an account. There are some interesting folks on there, and I've gotten to know several of them. I'll have you know, I've done everything I could to keep tabs on them after it looked like they were cookin' something up toward you guys. I couldn't have that on my conscience, ya know? What if they were to hurt your kids? No matter how I felt about you, I couldn't let that happen."

"Couldn't let *what* happen? What are they 'cooking up'?"

"Well, I don't know *exactly*. They sorta kicked me out of their group when they thought I was snoopin' around, and I think they were already talking about stuff behind my back, ya know? But from what I can tell, they got quite a group together. And they're gonna march on your house."

"March on our house? What do you mean? How many? When?"

Laura glanced behind her; Stephen and Amanda looked alarmed, and came closer to her.

"Not sure how many. Twenty? Thirty? Heck, could be fifty, for all I could tell. Like I said, I'm not in the loop as much now. But I do know one thing—Some random person from the board messaged me to say they're doing it *today*. Soon. They're pissed, Laura. They believe you're hoarding the secret to these kids waking up, and they're not messin' around at this point. Ryan staying awake clinched it in a lot of their minds. They're comin' for ya."

"Wha…What will they do when they get here?"

There was silence at the other end of the line. It was the loudest silence Laura had ever heard. The pain was climbing into her head now, lightning bolts clanking from one side of her skull to the other. She wasn't sure how much longer she could stay on the call.

"Denise?" Laura was frantic both to learn more, and to not know anything at all. "Are you there?"

"Yeah, yeah," she said, as if she'd just run back to the phone. "Um, I don't know, Laura. I don't know what they'll do. But you shouldn't be there to find out, ya know? Get out."

"Now?"

"Thirty minutes ago's prob'ly better. But now's the best you can do."

Laura tapped the "End Call" button and laid the phone down on the counter.

"Get the kids," she said to Stephen. "Wake them up. Grab whatever clothes you can stuff into a bag, and get them packed."

He ran upstairs, two steps at a time. She turned to Amanda.

"Shit, Laura. What can I do to help?"

"The suitcases are in our closet. Just throw in whatever you think we'll need. I'll be up there in a minute."

"Yeah. Sure.," Amanda said. She started heading up the stairs, then stopped and turned around. "Do you guys have somewhere you can go?"

"Yeah." Laura nodded. "Yeah, we'll be good. Make sure to pack some *warm* clothes, okay?"

The suitcase stuffed as tightly as she could get it, Amanda rocked it a couple of times and tossed it into the back of the SUV in the driveway. Laura came out the front door, and jogged over to her.

"I just now called the cops, and told them we've got a credible threat, though they're not sure how credible Denise is," Laura said. "Anyway, they said they'd dispatch someone, but I said we're getting the hell out. I'm not waiting here and hoping either Denise is wrong, or the police win the race."

Amanda nodded. "Is that everything?"

"I think it's all we can really fit," Laura panted, bent over with her hands on her knees. "This car's packed. Just enough room for us and the kids. Oh, where are my guns?"

"You and your guns. You expecting to need those today, Annie Oakley? The coast looks clear."

"Just wanna make sure they're there, and I know where I can get to them. You never know what sort of shit will go down, and

I'll have to shoot the apple off someone's head."

They laughed, and Amanda grabbed the gun case and handed it to Laura, who placed it on top of the pile of stuff so they'd be easy to reach.

"I hope you guys are gonna be all right," Amanda said. "This whole thing is just crazy. I can't believe how bad it's gotten."

"God, I know. But we'll be okay. And you should get the hell outta here. You've been a *massive* help today. I can't even tell you. You're the fucking best, you know that?"

Amanda smiled. "I like to think I am."

"But, seriously, get the fuck outta Dodge. You've done all you can do. Whatever's gonna happen, I don't want you getting caught up in it."

Amanda threw her arms around Laura, and they wrapped each other up, holding close. Laura couldn't think how many times they'd hugged in their decades knowing each other, but she was afraid this could be the last. After longer than usual, they pulled away, and Amanda headed to her car parked in the street.

"Call me so I know you got there all right, you hear me?" Amanda said. "Or at least a text. *Something.*"

"You got it, girl. Now, go."

Laura watched Amanda's car drive off down the street, out of sight. She hoped she'd see her again.

"Laura!" she heard Stephen call from the front door, and she turned in his direction. He was gesturing her to come. "I need your help. Fast!"

She jogged over, and saw him standing at the foot of the stairs; she followed him up. They went into Kevin's room, and Ryan was sitting on the bed; Kevin was in his wheelchair. Laura assumed he wanted help getting Kevin down the stairs, but Stephen went to the back of the room.

"Help me get this," he said.

She shook her head, trying to understand.

"Help you get *what*? That old chest?"

"Yeah. We need to take it."

"Wha-What for?" Her eyes narrowed.

"Don't have time to explain right now, and we don't have time to argue either. Just get one end."

"What are you talking about, Stephen? We barely have room for *us*. The vehicle's jammed. I like the chest too, but—"

"Then we'll have to leave something else behind, damn it, because we're not leaving *this*. Okay? Are we gonna do this, or are we gonna stand here and debate it?"

"I…" Laura had no idea why he wanted to take it. She'd never heard him express any particular affinity for it, but he clearly felt more strongly about taking it than she did about leaving it. And they needed to get on the road. "…Okay. Fine. We'll try to squeeze it in. Might just be tight for the boys in the back."

There were leather handles on either end of the chest; they lifted it and carried it toward the door.

"We'll be back up for you two," she said. "Mommy and Daddy are gonna get this big chest into the car, and we'll be right back.."

"Where are we going?" he asked.

"Just going on a little trip, honey. It's gonna be fun. When was the last time the four of us had an adventure together?"

"But I don't—"

"Honey, we can talk more once we're on the road. We've got to get moving. Mommy just needs you to wait here and keep an eye on your brother. Can you do that?"

He looked at his shoes and nodded. They lifted the chest and carried it out to the car. They set it down on the driveway to take a couple of breaths, then hoisted it up into the back, wedging it in against the door.

"See? Plenty of room still for the boys, and Kevin's wheelchair folds up in back," Stephen said.

Laura rolled her eyes and ran back to the house, with Stephen close behind. They went up the stairs and into Kevin's room. She bent over and put her hands beneath his feet, and Stephen got ready to lift from the back.

"Ready, Kev?" she said. "Just stay where we can see you, Ry. We're headed out."

They carried him down to the front door, with Ryan following tight on their heels. As she crossed the threshold onto the front porch, she caught motion to her right. At the bottom of the hill, there was a group of people walking around the corner, and her heart skipped.

"Shit," she said, taking a step down toward the walkway. "They're coming. Run to the car, Ryan! Now! We're right behind you."

They began moving faster, half-jogging to the car and practically tossing Kevin into the backseat next to Ryan, who had climbed in and was buckling his seatbelt. Stephen quickly folded up the wheelchair and shoved it on top of a suitcase. Laura looked behind her and saw the group was getting closer. There were at least thirty of them, some carrying baseball bats and other types of melee weapons.

"Buckle your brother's seatbelt, Ryan," she said as she slammed the door shut and jumped into the passenger seat, her heart pulsating madly. The driver's side door opened, and Stephen climbed inside.

"Let's get out of here," he said, turning the key in the ignition; the engine roared to life.

Laura glanced to her left and saw the group maybe seventy-five yards away, and some of them were starting to run. They'd seen them trying to get away, and they weren't going to let that happen easily.

Stephen mashed the gas, and the SUV jerked backward into the street, swinging around to face up the hill. Laura looked in the rearview mirror to her right and saw the crowd barreling in on them. Angry faces were starting to fill up the mirror, waving shovels and pitchforks and long wooden planks. As Stephen pushed the SUV into drive, it shook with the sound of something slamming into the back left quarter-panel. Laura then saw someone else wind up and take a swing with a shovel, connecting with the passenger's side behind the right wheel, and the SUV shuddered.

"Holy shit, these people are nuts!" Laura said. "Go go go go!"

He hit the gas, and nothing happened. The engine just made noise, and the SUV began drifting backward down the street.

"What?" she said, panic rising in her chest. "Why aren't we going?"

"I don't—" He looked around, his hands hovering above the wheel, his foot off the gas while the SUV slowly rolled backward. There was another metallic slam into the side of the car, this time on the back passenger-side door, right next to Kevin. Ryan was screaming, and saying some words Laura didn't have the wherewithal to pay attention to. She wanted to ask him to see if he could get to her guns, but it would expose him too much in case any of them had a firearm. She wished she'd have kept them up front with her, but it had looked like they were going to get out clear. That was a mistake she was regretting.

Laura could see the man in her mirror, but she didn't recognize him. Was he from Knoxville, or had he come from out of town just to terrorize her and her family? How could it possibly have come to this, being chased from their home by this group of crazy people?

She saw the man try to open the door, and her chest tightened. *Wait...is it locked?* He pulled at it, but nothing happened; it was sealed shut. Oddly, she was fairly sure she didn't lock it herself, and she didn't see Stephen do it after he got inside. She also knew the SUV didn't lock its doors automatically. Had

Ryan reached over Kevin to lock his door? Kevin didn't have the motor skills to lift his arm that high yet. Regardless, she was thankful.

But now the man was wrapping both hands around his shovel again; they felt more bangs from the back part of the SUV, rocking the car on its shocks, a rapid-fire cacophony of dings and crashes. She heard the back left window crush on contact with a man's baseball bat, and she was suddenly glad the chest was there. If not, glass would have been raining down on Ryan; instead, it landed on top of the chest and scattered mostly onto the floorboard. The window's tempered glass was holding some of its form, but just barely.

Now she saw the guy on her side wind up, the shovel back in a position like he was waiting for a fastball. She unbuckled her seatbelt and turned around. She pushed Kevin's head down toward his lap and got her arms on top of him as best as she could, bracing for the shower of glass. She wasn't going to be able to completely shield him from it, but she could at least take the brunt of it. Her arms were still covered in cuts from the previous day—some small and shallow, others long, meandering and deep.

Suddenly, the SUV raced to life, the wheels churning it forward, and the man's shovel connected a few inches behind the window, one more metallic thud as they pulled away, up the hill. Laura looked in the mirror and saw some of the men running after them, but most were behind them, either standing in the yard or walking through their front door. In the panic to escape, they hadn't had time to lock the door, and now they were flooding inside. She wondered what they thought they'd find. And was anybody calling the police, or were their neighbors participants in this?

They took the corner to the right without slowing down, and the mob faded behind them. They'd made it. After everything Denise had said to her, Laura hated to admit it, but she'd saved them. Amanda too, in fact. Without Denise's warning, they'd have been sitting there without any plan when the mob charged onto their property and rushed their house. It didn't look like it was a crowd they'd have been able to reason with. What would they have done? Would they have beaten Laura and her family? Killed them? Taken everything they owned? Clearly, they didn't seem concerned with breaking the law. Had people's desperation turned so intense that the rule of law didn't apply anymore? These were questions she didn't know the answer to. But, as they drove away, maybe she didn't have to. At least they were safe, together. Whatever happened from there, they at least had that.

She let her mind fall away for a moment and turned to Stephen. "Man, that was close. How'd you finally get the car going?"

He shrugged and wrinkled his nose. "I, um, I guess I accidentally threw it into neutral rather than drive."

She tried to stifle a laugh, but it slipped out, and then it burst loudly, her chest heaving, hands slapping her legs. Stephen laughed more hesitantly, first just through his nose, then more heartily and full. It felt like the first time they'd laughed like that in forever. So much stress was falling off of them in that moment. For Laura, it seemed like they were finally reclaiming their lives. That house had been a sort of prison since Kevin woke up. They'd walled themselves off from the world, turning it into their fortress. Now, they were escaping it, off into the world, with a chance to start something new. She hoped they'd be back one day soon. Knoxville had a lot of memories for them, and it was home. It'd be there waiting for them when the time came.

Then the first bullet hit the SUV, and Stephen slammed on the brakes.

38

Two cars honked and swerved as Stephen mashed the gas to the floor, sending the SUV hurtling backward into traffic, running a silver Pontiac over a curb into a stop sign and a purple Nissan Leaf skidding across gravel, sliding into a flowerbed.

He heard three more punctures into the back half of the SUV, bullets thunking through the metal into the interior of the car. He didn't think they'd hit a tire yet, which would have meant the end for them. If they hit the gas tank, it would eventually take them out, but he figured he could still drive for a little bit.

The men were leaning out of a large, dark green truck, sparkling in the afternoon sun as they fired quick shots toward Stephen and his family. It was incredible how quickly they'd gone from merely concerned about Ryan, sitting at the house chatting with Amanda, to dodging bullets and trying to stay alive. The instinct to survive was a strong one, and his muscles seemed to be running on autopilot. He wasn't thinking about the next move; his body was moving in harmony, whipping the wheel around to spin the SUV into the right position to speed away from the shooters.

He pressed the gas, and they were moving again, this time headed in the opposite direction of the interstate, back toward Fort Loudon Lake and Northshore, just where they'd been the previous day.

"Son of a bitch," Laura said, her fingers threading gripping at her hair. "What the hell was *that* about?"

"Is everybody all right?" Stephen said, the SUV's speed climbing. He glanced back and saw Ryan huddled into a ball, his seatbelt still strapped. Kevin sat still, but his eyes met Stephen's.

He didn't look scared. Stephen couldn't tell if none of this bothered him, or if he just wasn't processing it all. It was disconcerting either way.

In the rearview mirror, he didn't see the truck coming after them.

"It doesn't look like they're following us," Stephen said, as they passed their neighborhood entrance again. "We'll turn right at Northshore and hit Pellissippi Parkway to get to the interstate."

"Fine. Shit," Laura said. "Let's just get the hell out of here."

They passed the second neighborhood entrance, hitting sixty miles per hour. Stephen was having a weird sense of deja vu, remembering the stress of chasing Ryan down, worrying they'd never see him again if they didn't find that car. At this spot the previous day, they knew there were no givens. Ryan could have been gone forever. Now he sat just a couple of feet away from Stephen. Scared as he might have been, Stephen liked that he could reach out and touch both his sons at that moment, and they'd react. They were awake. Alive. Together. His family, intact.

They came over the crest of the hill, and Stephen moved into the right lane in order to make the turn ahead, and another truck pulled out in front of them. It looked nearly identical to the first one. *That can't be the same truck*, he thought. *It never passed us. I would have seen it.* It sat still on the side of the road as they approached fast, closing ground, the road lines zipping by them on both sides.

Maybe it's just another truck. A coincidence. There's probably nothing to be worried about. You're understandably paranoid, after people have tried to murder you and your family multiple times in the past twenty minutes. Don't let that mess with you. Keep going. You're almost there.

About 100 yards away from the truck, he saw its wheels turn toward the road, and it was pulling in front of them. Same truck or not, it was going to crash into them. Stephen laid on the horn as he applied the brake and turned the wheel left. Then he saw it—a head was poking out of the back left window, followed by the long barrel of a gun.

"Stephen!" Laura cried, seeing the same thing. "Hit the gas! We can't go right."

He sped up again and veered left, approaching Northshore at the same angle as he did the previous day, cutting diagonally toward the intersection, speed picking up as he rambled down the hill. In the rearview mirror, he could see the man pointing the gun at them, and it looked like it fired. He didn't hear or feel a shot, but the truck was moving in their direction, gaining speed of its own. It was filling up his rearview mirror by the time he prepared for another tight left turn onto Northshore.

Laura was loading her guns in her lap, getting both ready in case they needed them. Nobody was saying a word. There wasn't much to say at the moment. They were on the only path available to them, and they didn't know where it was headed. The truck was no more than fifty yards behind them, and they knew Tooles Bend was getting closer with every tree they passed, every dashed line on the road.

They owed it to Ryan and Kevin to do whatever they could to find a way out of this. If there had been a time for diplomacy, it seemed that time had ended. They were animals being hunted. Stephen knew he'd gladly give up his life to secure the safe release of the rest of his family, but he also knew that wasn't an offer that was going to be on the table. Although every instinct within him wanted him to give in to his fear, to shut down; he was doing everything he had to suppress that. Driving helped. It gave him something to focus on, something that required all of his attention. He didn't have time to go still, for his mind to throw up a wall between him and reality. That reality was whizzing by him at more than eighty miles per hour, as the wind whistled through the window next to him.

They came around a soft curve, and he could see Tooles Bend

up ahead, just a couple of hundred yards. The truck couldn't have been more than twenty-five yards behind them at this point, and gaining steadily. He didn't want to brake, but he had no choice. It was just a matter of when, and how much. What could he get away with? What could the SUV handle? He wished they had a vehicle with a lower center of gravity,. The risk of rolling in the SUV was far higher than he'd have liked.

Now just 100 yards from the curve, Stephen pressed on the brake, hesitantly at first, then hard with the hairpin turn lurking. The brakes squealed, the tires screeching as tread scraped away against the asphalt, trying to keep some grip with the road. He turned the wheel left, trying to take the turn at a softer angle, but he could tell he'd never make it; he pressed the brake harder, feeling like he might lose control of the vehicle.

"Hang on, guys," he said. "Just grab ahold of something."

Laura stiffened beside him, her right hand digging into the passenger door handle. Stephen saw the SUV's speed fall from nearly eighty-five to thirty in a matter of a few seconds, and his back pressed against the seat as if a wrecking ball was slammed into his chest. The SUV skidded right, and he felt the back right tire slide just off the road. The momentum of the SUV shifted, the top beginning to lurch right, and the left tires wanted to leave the ground. But then he felt grip with the road surface. Not perfect, but something. Enough. Maybe.

He switched to the gas and carefully accelerated, trying to move deeper into the turn. The SUV was upright, and he got into the first part of the S, then he swung the wheel right, taking it through the last part of the turn. They were through it; he glanced into the rearview mirror, and he didn't see anything. No truck. Had they slid off the road? Did they give up? Whatever it was, the truck wasn't there anymore.

Relief started to wash over him. He felt like he hadn't breathed in half an hour. He needed oxygen, and the breaths came quick; he bit his lip and raised his head, thinking the end of this nightmare finally looked like it might be over.

Then he caught some motion from his left. It was the truck, bearing down on them on the driver's side, going at least fifty, maybe sixty. The diagonal cut he hadn't been able to make across the turn, it seemed they'd made it. And now the two vehicles were side by side. The truck's passenger-side window slid down, and a man holding a handgun leaned out, firing several rounds toward them, at close range. Stephen hit the brakes, and the truck went a little ahead, at least making it a little harder to fire straight into the SUV. He couldn't tell where the bullets had gone, but his tires seemed to be okay, and Laura said nobody was hit.

The truck braked too, pulling back to them. It swerved toward the SUV, and the crash shook it, sending it rocking to the right, shocks depressing, driver's-side doors crumpling under the pressure. Stephen tried to keep the road, the back wheels trying to slide out from under him. Then another slam, this time forcing them onto the gravel shoulder and then crashing into a field, mud and dirt flying up as he laid into the brakes to stop them before they ran into the copse of trees just ahead.

They came to a rest ten yards short of the trees, muddy tracks marking their trail. He looked into the mirror and saw the truck driving slowly into the field, then coming to a stop. He turned to Laura; her eyes were cold but resolute. He saw the men exit their truck maybe 100 yards away. Stephen knew there was no easy way out. Running was no longer an option, especially with a kid who couldn't even walk. For now, they had to fight.

"We have to get out of the car." Laura's mouth dried up as she looked out the window at three men walking through the grass toward them. "This thing's a death trap. Car doors are about as useful against automatic weapons as tissue paper. Get out. Now!"

The SUV had slid sideways, with the driver's side facing away from the men. Stephen climbed out, and Laura went around the center console to go out on his side. Stephen opened the back door, where the large chest was sitting between him and the kids. He reached over it and got ahold of Kevin. Fortunately, he was still light, and Stephen had little problem lifting him over the chest and onto the ground beside the SUV. Ryan began climbing on top of it himself, and Stephen carried him the rest of the way.

"Set them against the front tire," Laura said. "We need the full tire and engine compartment between them and the shooters. That's the safest place they can be if shots start firing."

Stephen took Ryan, and Laura carried Kevin. They set them down next to each other, sitting in the patchy grass, their backs against the SUV's front tire.

"Stay with them for right now, okay?" Laura said, crouching next to Stephen. "I'm gonna go see what the situation is. And take this."

She held out her Smith & Wesson M&P. Stephen hesitated, but she pulled his arm toward her and wrapped his fingers around the grip, then looked him in the eyes.

"Look, I know you're not in love with these things, and I hope like hell you don't have to use it. But they've got three men, and I see at least one large automatic weapon. So we're already outnumbered. I just need you to be my backup, not a sharp shooter. This thing's pretty user friendly, very little recoil. Okay? For the boys? You remember that one time you shot at the range? What I told you about how to stand and hold it?"

He bit his lip and nodded. She took another glance over the SUV, and saw they were slowly advancing across the field, within fifty yards now.

"Good." She leaned over and kissed him, putting one hand behind his neck to pull him a little closer. She knew they didn't have much time, but she also knew this could be the last kiss they ever had. She wasn't going to waste it. After several seconds, she pulled back. "Just keep ready."

Staying crouched, Laura ran to the other wheel and pressed her back against the SUV. Slowly, she slid up and leaned over to look into the field. She could see all three men. They were close enough that she could start to guess at their weapons. Two were carrying handguns, which made her feel better. Looked like maybe Glocks, but she couldn't be certain. The other man had what looked from this distance like an AK-47. It had the signature curved handle, and front sight housing being close to the tip of the barrel meant it would be a 47 rather than a 74. The bad news was that meant it had more power and fired larger rounds. That gun could rip their SUV practically to shreds if given the chance. The good news was that it was also heavier than the 74, and much more difficult to control. Laura knew she might not be able to get off nearly as many shots with her CZ-85, but she could be far more precise with the rounds she fired.

She guessed the men were at about forty yards, definitely within the range of her CZ-85, one of the most accurate pistols she'd ever fired. At that distance, she was confident she could more or less hit what she wanted to. She was fairly confident with a gun in her hands, but it was the last situation she wanted to be in—maybe the last line of defense between her family and three mysterious killers strolling menacingly across a field toward them. She'd have preferred to run into the nearby trees, put as much distance as possible between them and these men. With the kids, though, there was little choice. Even as light as Kevin was, he was still over sixty pounds, with long, bony arms and legs that made him unwieldy to carry very far. Ryan was over eighty pounds, and wouldn't be able to keep up with them on foot. She knew they wouldn't get far with the boys in tow. They were stuck.

She focused on the man carrying the AK-47. If she took him out, that'd potentially eliminate their most powerful weapon too.

Sure, one of the other men could risk running over to grab it, but they'd know they were exposed to gunfire in the open field. And, if that man was carrying the AK, there was a decent chance he was the one who was the best at handling it. Those handguns were far simpler machines.

She laid on her back, her feet pressed against the wheel, and looked under the vehicle. She thought this would be her best position for shielding herself against any return fire. From there, she wouldn't be able to hit them center mass while they were walking, but she could also get off more rounds while still essentially under cover.

Seeing his legs walking in their direction, the SUV blocking her vision at about his waist, she sighted in the man with the AK. Lying on her back with her feet propped against the wheel gave her a surprisingly stable shooting position; she thought she could be as accurate there as she would be standing straight up. Her heart began to race, and stiffness was cascading into her shoulders as she braced herself for the shot. Once she fired, there was no telling what would come next. Would the men panic and begin madly firing rounds toward them? Were they on a suicide mission, so they'd come charging harder? Would they turn tail and run? She had no idea who these men were or how well they were trained, but she was about to find out.

She closed one eye as she looked straight down the sight, pushing that pain in her neck into the distance, trying to pretend it wasn't there. Her finger rattled against the trigger, her right hand shaking just a bit. She thought of her dad, his arms encircling her from behind, showing her the proper form, how to wrap both hands around the grip and how to gently pull the trigger.

"You don't want to jerk it, sweetie," he'd say. "That'll mess with your aim, and you only aim at something you intend to hit."

She closed both eyes for just a moment, then opened her right one again. The men were within thirty yards; it was time. She glanced at the boys, and saw Ryan covering his ears; Stephen had his hands pressed to Kevin's. She took a deep breath, lined her right eye down her sight, and pressed on the trigger.

The recoil jerked her back, but it wasn't too bad. And her shot had the effect she'd hoped. The man had dropped the AK on the ground, and was rolling in the grass, in apparent agony, his leg bent and his knee blown open inside his rapidly darkening green pants. The sounds he was making were terrible, a high-pitched wailing that she'd never heard a human produce before. It seemed unnatural, a guttural moan that she instinctually wanted to stop. This was the first time she'd shot another person, and she couldn't help a wave of guilt from rising within her, watching him writhe on the ground and hearing him suffer. She couldn't imagine the pain.

Laura knew, though, that she had to put it out of her mind. The most pressing issue was where the other two men were. She'd evened the odds a little bit, but she was still outnumbered, assuming Stephen wasn't going to be quick to take anybody out with the other gun. She had to assume this job was on her,.

Still lying down, she leaned to her left and right, trying to see the other two men. It didn't take her long to find one. It seemed he had immediately fallen to the ground and was lying on his stomach, still for the moment. That was smart. He'd be difficult to hit in that position; he basically reduced the amount of his body he exposed to a shooter. In an open field, that was probably the best option he had. He was off to her right a little bit, just a little clear of the SUV and thirty yards away. She swung back to the left and scanned the ground, but didn't see anything. There was no sign of the third man. The wounded man's screams continued, the only sound in an empty field, the road still quiet.

She rolled to her left and climbed into a crouched position, then crab walked over to Stephen, keeping her eyes behind her.

"Did you see where the third man went?" she whispered.

He shook his head. "Never saw him. Maybe he ran back to their truck when you shot?"

She hated not knowing. There was a big open field in front of them; if he was there, they'd be able to see him. So where was he? He hadn't had much time to run.

"Just keep an eye out, okay? If you see him anywhere, signal to me. Point or something."

He nodded, and she crawled to the back end of the SUV, getting into her prone position against the wheel. She looked right, and the man lying down was still there, but he was starting to move, doing a military crawl toward her. He got several yards closer fairly quickly, then stopped, held his handgun in front of him, and began firing.

Laura turned left, curling her body away from where the bullets were coming from, trying to put as much of the wheel as possible between her and the shots. If that was a Glock, she couldn't remember how big a magazine it would probably have. Ten? Fifteen? The bullets came fast, clanging off the wheel well, tearing holes in the side of the SUV, others embedding in the ground or piercing the air as they whizzed by her into the trees.

She was trying to count the shots, but she lost track after six or seven. She couldn't get a good look at him, because she was afraid he'd hit her if she exposed her face. Laura had spent plenty of rounds over the years firing at paper targets, silhouettes of men with concentric circles around their chest and head. But, real combat was a whole new situation she wasn't entirely prepared for. Even as someone who knew a bit about guns, and was a solid shot, knowing those shots were meant to kill her and her family changed everything about what she was doing. This wasn't a target hanging on a range in a controlled environment. This was life or death.

The shots finally seemed to have stopped; Laura uncoiled and turned to her right. She saw the man pulling a fresh magazine out of a pack hanging off his belt. He fumbled with it and dropped it on the ground; Laura thought she had an opportunity. She held her CZ-85 in front of her and fired, his head her only target.

She saw him flinch, hold still for a second, then continue bringing the magazine up to the gun. She knew she'd missed, so she fired again. Still nothing. It was frustrating. He was out there in the middle of a field, thirty yards away, and she couldn't hit him. Between him lying down to shrink the amount she could target, and her nervously shaking hands, it was too tough a shot for her to manage. Maybe on a range, in ideal conditions. But in that moment, she thought she'd be lucky to hit one out of ten.

He pointed the gun in her direction again and fired, the sound reverberating in the silence around her, shot after shot, her body turned away, bracing to feel one embed itself inside her. She wondered what being shot would feel like. Would it burn? Would you feel the pain right away, or would it be something you wouldn't notice at first? Does your body go into a sort of fight-or-flight mode, knowing it could be near death? The man she shot came to mind in that moment. His screams had stopped. Could you die from a bullet to the knee? Maybe he was just passed out, in shock. She didn't know enough to say. But if he was any indication, it seemed like getting shot was a pretty horrible experience. If this man was going to hit her, she kind of hoped it would go straight into her brain. Just turn the lights off, and she wouldn't have to feel the pain. Wouldn't have to watch them execute her husband and sons. With every shot, her body jerked.

When she thought the shots had stopped firing, she tentatively turned right and didn't see the man anymore. He wasn't where he'd been lying. Her throat constricted, nearly choking her, and her mouth went dry. Where had he gone? What if he'd picked up the AK? She was confident the wheel rim would stop a nine-millimeter bullet, but an AK was a different story. Keeping that man pinned down had been essential, and she'd let him move because she didn't know how to face someone who was firing at her. She wasn't trained in combat, and she knew that may have cost her—and her family.

Still using the wheel for cover and the car for concealment, she writhed on the ground, left, right, trying to spot someone. She could see that the AK was still lying next to the motionless man in the middle of the field. At that, at least, she breathed a quick sigh of relief. She looked at Stephen and shrugged, but he only shook his head and frowned. Ryan's face was buried in Kevin's sweatshirt. Kevin stared ahead, his face a blank page.

She kept scanning the ground, not wanting to be coaxed out of her position, which she felt was the best place she could be other than where the kids were. It made her tougher to spot, but it might not do much to keep her alive if the shooter guessed right.

Then she heard a noise, the sound of a foot scraping against the dry ground. It was close. But where, exactly? She kept her feet pressed against the wheel, and bent her body right, trying to see what the back wheels were blocking from her view. She stretched almost as far as she could go, and then she saw it—a black shoe behind the wheel opposite her. The man had used the distraction of his shots to scamper up to the SUV, and now he was no more than five feet away. She got into a crouching position and leaned in tight to the wheel. Her heart thumped, back clenched. If he stood up and fired, could he take her out from there? Was he hoping she'd eventually come out of concealment and give him a clean shot? Was this a game of chicken?

Laura spun and looked at Stephen, waving to get his attention. When he looked, she pointed at him, then made a gun shape with her fingers and pointed it over the car and out toward the field, jerking her hand for emphasis. He picked up the gun lying at his feet and held it up as if he was asking a question. She nodded, gesturing again toward the field beyond the SUV, interlocking the fingers of both hands to remind him how to hold the gun.

He lifted the gun and pointed the barrel over the hood of the SUV. She didn't care where the bullet went, as long as it didn't ricochet back at one of them. She watched him press his eyes shut, his arms tightening as he braced for the recoil. She turned back to her right, thinking this would be her chance. She needed to be quick. The split second that gun fired, she needed to move.

She waited, in a sort of modified sprinter's-block position, listening for the sound. She wanted to get him to hurry, but she thought any gestures she made now would distract him. She had to trust that he'd fire it when he was ready; she just didn't know how long they had before the man would fire shots of his own.

Stephen's gun fired, and she sprung out of her spot, pulling herself around the back of the SUV as quickly but quietly as possible, sliding low to the ground and holding the CZ-85 up in front of her. As her head cleared the other side, she saw the shot had the desired effect—the man was turned away from her, toward where the gun had fired. Looking down the sights, she fired into his back left side just below his arm and he yelled, crumpling toward the ground. The gun in his right hand, he brought that arm around as he fell, and Laura could see the barrel swinging in her direction. He fired, the shot ringing in her ears, and she pulled the trigger at nearly the same time. She heard his bullet go into the side of the SUV above her, then his body hit the ground with a heavy thud. She got onto her knees and took one more shot, this time into his chest from a couple of feet away. His mouth in a coarse curl, eyes still open, he was still.

Laura's head fell into her hands, and she dropped the gun. Tears started to form in her eyes. They'd survived. Her family was intact. Somehow. Through everything. She'd found a way to protect them. She'd never doubted that she'd kill in order to protect her sons, but no one ever thinks it'll come to that. For her, it just had. And it was overwhelming. Sobs rose in her throat, and she wiped her nose against her sleeve, trying to pull herself together before she went back to her boys.

Then she heard a sound. Footsteps. Fast. Followed by gunshots.

39

Relieved, Stephen wrapped Ryan and Kevin in his arms. He hadn't known what Laura's plan had been when she'd insisted he fire toward the field, but he started to get it when he saw her setting up to run. Then he saw her leap, graceful, lithe, then swing around the back of the SUV before he heard the gun fire. He'd had a moment of near-panic then. Had one of them hit her? When they stopped, he slowly stood and, through the windows, could see the man laid out motionless, and Laura sitting on the grass, her head bowed, alive.

"She's okay," he said to Ryan and Kevin, as he pulled them close. "*We're* okay. We're gonna make it, guys. I don't know how, but we did it."

After a few seconds of embracing, he heard a sound from the trees to his left. Something was moving back there, pushing leaves and limbs around. Then a man holding a gun came running at full speed, directly toward him and the boys, his face a twisted grimace. Stephen froze.

When Kevin heard the man running out of the trees, he knew that was his cue. It was what he'd been waiting for. Everything had been leading to this moment.

He threw his body onto Ryan, pinning his brother to the ground. He looked into Ryan's eyes, which were wide, darting left and right, then fixed onto Kevin's. Time seemed to stop around them, the world slowing to a crawl.

"You need to listen to me," Kevin said, in a voice perfect, not a trace of scratch. "It's time for you to stop this. There's no In

Between for you. This is your world. I've done everything I could to shield you, but you've got to stand on your own two feet. This is your family. It's time you committed to *them*. They need you. Lots of people do. You represent life. Hope. A future. There's more for you to do. Do it for me. Okay?"

Ryan trembled underneath his brother, struggling at first, then listening. He nodded, then swallowed hard. He barely blinked, looking deeply into Kevin's eyes, searching for something beyond the surface, the answer to questions unknown.

Waving the gun as he ran, the man coming from the trees began firing shots wildly. It didn't look like he had any particular place he was aiming; he just wanted to create chaos and pin them down. It was working. Stephen held in place, not knowing what to do. He couldn't run. The kids were there with him. He had to think of them first. But what did that even mean? What could he do in such a short period of time? The man would be on top of them in seconds, and his wild shots would get more accurate the closer he got. And Stephen had no confidence he could hit a still target, much less a moving one.

As a fourth shot came from the man's gun and he got within ten yards, Stephen finally decided. Holding the Smith & Wesson in his right hand, Stephen got to his feet, lowered his head and ran toward the man. They were bucks charging for a head-on collision. With both of them running at full speed, the distance closed quickly. The man never diverted from his path, and neither did Stephen. It was no more than two seconds before they slammed into each other, Stephen's right shoulder burying into the man's midsection as two more shots fired over top of Stephen.

He drove the man back hard, both of them tumbling into the grass, rolling several times, Stephen hanging onto the man's shirt and pulling him away from the SUV. When they stopped rolling,

Stephen was on top of the man, looking down at him. He glanced at the man's hands, and there was no gun. He figured it must have shaken loose at some point. The thought of shooting someone nauseated Stephen but, straddling this man, he didn't think he had a choice. There was no way to trust him.

The man was awake, staring up at Stephen, not moving. No struggling. Just lying there. He was wearing a sleeveless camouflage shirt with green cargo pants and burgundy hiking boots. He was white, of nondescript ethnicity. Just a guy. Could easily have been a neighbor of theirs. Nothing special, different, or out of the ordinary about him. Why was this happening? What could possibly have prompted him to do something like this? Who *were* these people?

Stephen closed his eyes and turned his head. He pointed the gun at the man's chest and pulled the trigger, the body jerking beneath him. He shook his head and turned his eyes to the sky.

"Stephen!" he heard Laura yell, then started to hear Ryan shrieking. "Holy shit, Stephen! Come over here!"

"Shit! The line's still busy? What the *fuck*? Jesus!" Laura said, after dialing 9-1-1 for the fourth time. "What's going on?"

She kneeled next to Stephen, who was performing CPR on Kevin, lying still on his back. Ryan was sitting against the SUV's front wheel, his arms wrapped around his knees pulled up to his chest, his body shaking.

Laura crawled over to Ryan and put her arm around him. He laid his head on her shoulder.

"It's gonna be okay, sweetie," she kissed the top of his head. "Your dad's doing everything he can. The bad man who shot your brother can't hurt us anymore, okay? We love you very much, and we'll protect you."

She could hear him choking against his tears, his chest heaving as she pulled him closer to her, watching Stephen perform chest compressions. She kept watching Kevin's eyes and fingers, looking for any movement, any sign of life. But there was nothing. It took her back to when he was in thrall to The Sleep. Just a lifeless husk lying in front of her, for more than a year. He'd only been a shell of himself for the previous week or so, but it'd been so nice to be a full family again, even if it hadn't been quite the same as before. She'd looked forward to seeing Kevin improve, physically and mentally, to watching him slowly become his old self again. She knew it'd take a long time, but it was a journey they'd been ready to follow alongside him. They were going to watch this cocoon blossom into a butterfly, be the first parents in a very long time to see their oldest child become a man.

Stephen raised up from Kevin and placed two fingers on the boy's neck. Laura waited. He was still, feeling for a pulse. It had been several minutes. How many, she'd lost count. But she knew the clock was ticking, especially if she couldn't get through to 9-1-1. How could they be so busy that they couldn't take a call? She tried once more, and it finally rang. Quickly, she heard a voice on the other end of the line.

"Nine-one-one, what's your emergency?"

"Yes! I've been trying for forever to get someone! My son has been shot!"

"What's your location?"

Laura looked up and saw Stephen's head drop. He shifted his body weight around to fully face her. He looked her in the eye and sucked in a large breath, then shook his head and frowned.

"We're…um…in a field along Ebenezer Road near Tooles Bend."

"Okay. I'm sending an ambulance. Can you answer a few questions for me?"

Tears were filling Stephen's eyes, and Laura furrowed her brow. He mouthed the words "He's gone," and threw his arms around her. Ryan crawled over and slumped in between them both. The phone fell to the ground as they lay there, tangled together under the midday sun.

40

Ryan didn't fully understand what happened in his recent life, or in that field when gunshots stole Kevin from him for the final time. It had been like he was in a fog, being pushed and pulled between two worlds, unsure of where he was going to end up.

He knew Kevin had somehow protected him, somehow known what was going to happen, though none of that made sense. And he suspected it'd make even less sense to his parents if he tried to tell them what Kevin had said. They'd tell him he dreamt it. That Kevin couldn't talk. That Kevin couldn't heal Ryan after he fell from the window, couldn't cocoon him within a flipping car, couldn't shield him from bullets he somehow knew were coming or pause the very world around them. That Kevin couldn't make Ryan fly.

But there were things his parents didn't know. Couldn't ever know.

What he kept going back to was that morning when he heard them talking about the dilemma they faced with two comatose children, and then wandered into Kevin's room. That was the moment everything changed. The moment he split time, connecting the two worlds and disconnecting his own life in the process.

He'd stashed the knife in the old chest, knowing his parents would never have any reason to check there. This had all been planned. He wasn't sure if he had the guts to follow through with it, but he was as determined as ever that morning.

He couldn't be the reason his parents had to make that impossible choice, and maybe cost Kevin his life. He couldn't stand the idea of being the reason it all fell apart. That knife was his way of solving the problem before it became one.

Ryan took a look at Kevin, then walked calmly over to the chest. He felt at ease, like this was exactly the right decision. No hesitation. He unlatched the chest and pushed it open, seeing the chef's knife lying neatly on top of a blue blanket. He picked it up and laid it on the floor next to him while he cradled the chest's lid in both hands so he could lower it softly. This wasn't the time to get his parents' attention.

Picking the knife up, Ryan walked to the bed and laid down to Kevin's left, mimicking his position—flat on his back, arms neatly at his sides. Holding the knife in his left hand, he grabbed Kevin's hand with his right and took a deep breath.

"None of this can happen this way," he whispered, his eyes clear. "It's not the way it's supposed to be. I'm not waiting for The Sleep to take me, Kevin. By then, it's too late. This'll be better for everybody. Thanks for being a good brother. Maybe I'll see you when I get there. I love you."

Still gripping Kevin's hand, Ryan picked the knife up with his left hand. He'd read several articles online about where to cut on your neck so that you died as quickly as possible. You wanted to hit something called the "carotid artery." He thought he knew enough to hit it on the first try. Then he'd be gone within minutes, if not seconds. It would all be over. He'd be out of the way.

As he lifted the knife toward his neck, his heart began to pound. The closer to it becoming a reality, the more his mind and body would rebel against it, fighting against himself for survival. He needed to push through. He was so close. He couldn't chicken out.

He brought the knife closer to his neck, but thought he felt the bed move. Just a slight shift, but it was noticeable. He didn't think he'd caused it; he was still, except for his arm. He paused for a moment, his eyes looking around, trying to figure out if he'd imagined it.

Then there was a twitch. Almost imperceptible, but unmistakable all the same. Kevin's finger, wrapped in Ryan's hand, moved. Slightly, but still. It was movement. He was sure of it. Were little muscle spasms like that common? Maybe that happened all the time, and he only picked up on it because he happened to be holding Kevin's hand at the time.

Ryan's left hand began to shake. The time was now. He needed to do it.

He laid back and gritted his teeth, shutting his eyes as tight as he could, trying to block out the world around him, turn it all into black. He lifted the knife to his neck and rested it there, moving it around, trying to find the exact right spot he'd read you needed to hit. He was trying to keep his hand steady, but it was impossible. The knife's edge danced on his skin, and he pressed his grip more firmly into the handle.

Suddenly, pain shot from his right hand, up his arm, his fingers being squeezed into knots, Kevin's hand enveloping them. Kevin's head rose from the bed, and he stared at Ryan. The knife slipped out of his grip and tumbled onto the bed, then to the floor. Ryan couldn't pull his hand free; Kevin's eyes were deeper than any he'd ever seen, like they could go on forever, deeper than any ocean, down into some sort of abyss. This couldn't be happening. He knew he had to be imagining it. But his hand and those eyes told him a different story.

Ryan screamed.

Climbing aboard her dad's boat, Laura watched Stephen take the last suitcase downstairs to the sleeping quarters. She didn't know how long this was going to be their home, but they were going to make the best of it while they had to. She got her phone out of her pocket and tapped Haley's name.

"Laura?" Haley said as she answered. "Oh, thank god. I've been trying to get ahold of you to talk about the brewery, but I hadn't heard anything, and nobody—"

"It's okay, Haley. Just listen for a minute."

"All right." She sounded tentative.

"You know my life's a little crazy right now. And, well, it's gotten crazier. I'm gonna need to step back from Palmyra for a little while. I want you to run it for me."

"What? What do you mean? How long?"

"I really don't know. A month. Maybe longer. Maybe *much* longer. I'm just not sure. But will you run it for me? I'll owe you big time."

"But I don't—"

"I've emailed you all the information, bank logins, everything you'll need. It's all there. You can do this, Haley. You're one of the most capable, professional women I know. There's nobody else I'd trust to do this more than you."

"I just…Thank you. It's just so *sudden*."

"I know. And I wish I could have given you more notice. It's not fair to you, and I know that. Hopefully, one day, I'll be able to tell you all about what happened over a beer or two, and we can laugh. But right now, I want to know you'll do this for me."

"I…Yeah. Of course. As long as you need me to. Just tell me you'll be all right, and that you'll be back."

Laura smiled. "I'll be all right, and I'll be back. Before you even know I'm gone. Thank you so much. You're the best. I'll see ya soon."

She ended the call not knowing if that was true. Her dad was standing at the wheel of the boat, and her mom was next to him. They were looking out at the lake. Ryan was downstairs, asleep.

Losing Kevin was hard. Maybe harder than losing him the first time. They placed him in the large trunk and closed the lid so they could take his body with them. When they did, they noticed three bullet holes in the side of the chest that had been closest to the door, which had three matching holes. The bullets laid inside the chest. If it hadn't been there, those bullets would likely have been inside Ryan.

As they buried Kevin behind her parents' house, Laura held Stephen close, thinking they at least had one of their sons left, and that was more than most anyone else in the world could say about their ten-year-old. They were ready to get away.

Her dad had made this offer earlier, and they were going to take him up on it. He knew the trip from Knoxville to the Gulf like he was driving along the interstate. They'd made it so many times with friends that he'd have no problem getting them out to the ocean. Along the way, he could teach them about how to handle the boat, and make sure they were ready to take it out to sea. He and Paula would take a one-way flight back from New Orleans after seeing them off.

It was going to be a strange life for a while, Laura knew. It wasn't what they'd envisioned. She didn't know how long they'd have to be gone, and she didn't know what would be left for her when they got back, or even whether returning to Knoxville would be at all possible. Maybe if kids started waking up all over the world, if The Sleep was finally eradicated, they could go back without any issues. Or maybe it would eventually blow over. They weren't going to have much news to trouble them while they were on the boat, but her dad knew how to reach them to let them know when it was safe.

You could be anonymous out on the ocean. The sea knew no animosity toward any of them. It was as uncaring as the world around them, oblivious to their presence, content to let them survive as long as they could. They had enough food for six months, and money to procure more as needed. Her dad knew some ports where they'd charge just a few dollars and ask even fewer questions. For a while, that'd be their life. Just living. Day to day. Nothing more. But doing it together. Family was what would ultimately prevail. There was work ahead, but they'd survive. It was all that was left. The ocean was vast and lacked a memory. It was the perfect companion for the next chapter in their lives.

ACKNOWLEDGMENTS

I knew there was going to be a next novel for me, but I wasn't exactly sure what the story was going to be as I was wrapping up my last book, *The Solitary Apocalypse*, for an October release. Right around that time, my favorite band, The National, released the album "Sleep Well Beast." The more I listened to it, the more the dark mood of it wrapped itself around me in a sort of melancholy embrace. I loved it. And, seeking out more information on it, I read an interview with lead singer Matt Berninger talked about how the album's title was a reference to Uppgivenhetssyndrom, a mysterious phenomenon unique to Sweden wherein the children of refugee families fall into a catatonic state upon learning they were being sent back to whatever war-torn country they fled. It was fascinating to me, and my mind almost immediately began imagining a world where that happened not to a small subset of children in one country, but to all children in the world, writ large.

And that's how a great album by my favorite band became the inspiration for this novel. I even listened to the album through much of the writing, and it fueled me, keeping my mind in a place of anticipating and dread even on the brightest of mornings, as the sun slowly brightened the window next to my writing desk. The National carried me through this one, dragging me into the story from the beginning, and lifting me into the place I needed to be in order to stick with it. So, even though the likelihood is high Matt and his bandmates never see this, I wanted to acknowledge them and their brilliant music, music which has become a veritable soundtrack for my thirties, and which I feel I understand more with each passing year, first.

Of course, the publication of this story took much more than just my wallowing in moody rock music. My wife, Jamie, is always the most important person for helping me get these projects done. She supports this crazy work of mine, accepts that I'll spend time alone in my little upstairs room, and lets herself be the only person I truly trust to work with me through the early story itself, as it's just becoming real in my head. None of these stories would be remotely as good without her. So, if you like anything I write, feel free to send her a note of thanks as well.

I also couldn't do this without the selfless, time-consuming work of my beta readers, not merely reading a hairy, very early version of the story, but then offering extremely valuable feedback that helps me start to see it through a reader's eyes other than my own. I can't thank Oliver Boudreaux, Emily Connor, Bryan Nale, and my PA Evelyn Summers enough for their help and support. I feel fortunate to have the sorts of friends who know they can rip my work apart, and I'll turn right around and thank them profusely for it.

Finally, I need to acknowledge the professionals who helped me create the final product you see. My designer, Monica Haynes, from The Thatchery, has been with me for two books now, and it's hard to imagine what I did without her. She's not only an amazing cover designer, but she's also shown so much passion, enthusiasm, and support for my work. I found my editor, Julie Tibbott, through a site called Reedsy, and she did a tremendous job of tightening the story while offering insightful, precise feedback that helped me intensify the focus of the story and make it a better reader experience. She was exactly what I needed. And, as always, any mistakes that still linger are mine.

Finally, thanks to you for reading. You are why I do this. Hope you enjoyed it. I've got plenty more where this came from.

MORE BOOKS BY JEFF HAWS

Novels

The Solitary Apocalypse — Surrounded by people, Michael is alone. Along with the rest of a North Georgia town that survived a deadly worldwide plague, Michael's forced to wear a steel ring around his waist wherever he goes. He's seen cohabitation banned. Marriages dissolved. Families torn apart. Now, Michael must enlist help to confront the awful truth about the town of Alessandra, and the fate of what may be the last human colony on Earth.

Killing the Immortals — Would you murder for god? Would you stand in the way of those who would? Cain and Hannah have to decide what side they're on in this fast-paced thriller about the dangers of fanaticism in a world where people are living indefinitely.

Novellas and Short Stories

Tomorrow's News Today — When Walt suddenly discovers that anything he writes at his small newspaper job will come true, he believes he has the power to reshape his crumbling marriage and career. But he also has the tools for his own destruction. Which path will he choose?

The Slingshot — Taylor's a typical geeky teenager who just wants to fit in with the cool kids for once. But soon, events spiral out of his control, and his moment of mischief threatens to tear apart his life, and his family's along with it. His older brother is the only one he can trust to save him.

FREE WITH NEWSLETTER SIGNUP

The Trolley Problem — Andrea will do anything for her son. She wants what's best for him, so she's doing her best to work a custody arrangement with her husband, and juggle a relationship with her new boyfriend. But now her ex wants to cut her out of her son's life, and she has to decide how far she's willing to go to keep her boy in her life.

REVIEW AND RATE *THE LITTLE TRAGEDY*

Now that you've finished *The Little Tragedy*, please consider posting a review and rating on Amazon and Goodreads. This serves both as invaluable feedback for the author, and as social proof to other readers that this book is worth their valuable investment of time to read. Also, if you liked what you read, follow Jeff on Amazon and Goodreads to interact, and be among the first to know when he writes something new.

ABOUT THE AUTHOR

Jeff Haws is a long-time journalist who has turned his writing eye to fiction. This is his third published novel and fifth published book. With a mind that likes to ask "What if …?" and tends toward the dystopian, his first two novels *Killing the Immortals* and *The Solitary Apocalypse* are also available. Over the past 20 years, his writing has appeared in the *Washington Post, Atlanta Journal-Constitution, Miami Herald, Arizona Republic, New Orleans Times-Picayune*, and many other publications. He lives with his wife in Atlanta, Georgia.

SIGN UP FOR NEWSLETTER FOR UPDATES: jeffhaws.com/newslettersignup
TWITTER/FACEBOOK/INSTAGRAM: @ByJeffHaws

Made in the USA
Columbia, SC
15 November 2018